Her blood r_____

Spinning light_____ night.

Fear clamped_____ that
erupted came_____ arcing
through her as if she'd stuck _____ cket.
Not that way. Not that...

Irrational terror shot through her. She spun around,
ready to dart across the road, race away in the
opposite direction. The sound of squealing brakes, the
flash of bright white paint and blinding headlights had
her shielding her eyes. The truck skidded to a halt,
veering slightly, but not enough. The front bumper
grazed her thighs and she jumped back, frozen as she
stared through the windshield. The shocked gaze of
a teenager stared back at her. Breathing ragged, she
backed away.

He shoved his door open, jumped out of the truck.
"Are you all right? I'm so sorry. I didn't see... Hey!
Where are you going? I think you might be hurt!"

She ran. She ran as fast as she could. Ran away from
the truck. Ran across the road and scrambled into the
protection of the trees.

Away from the spinning, colored lights she feared
more than the night.

* * *

**The Coltons of Roaring Springs: Family and true
love are under siege**

* * *

**If you're on Twitter, tell us what you
think of Harlequin Romantic Suspense!
#harlequinromsuspense**

Dear Reader,

Long before I became a Harlequin author, I was a voracious reader of nearly every line, but especially the Romantic Suspense line. A few years ago, the impossible dream of writing for them became a reality. This past year, another came true when I was asked to write for the Colton series.

The unexpected is a pretty big theme in Skye Colton's story. But if there's one thing we know about all the Coltons, it's that they've never met a challenge they didn't conquer. Despite her situation, Skye is plowing ahead...just uncertain of whether she wants the life she left behind, or a new one with Leo Slattery.

Local rancher and down-to-the-bones good guy Leo might be the first person to see Skye for who she really is. Their meeting becomes a crossroads—do they forge ahead together or return to the very different worlds they're each from? Well, it is a romance novel, so I bet you can guess how it ends. But how they get there? That's the fun part. I hope you enjoy Leo and Skye's journey as much as I loved writing it.

Happy reading,

Anna J

COLTON ON
THE RUN

Anna J. Stewart

HARLEQUIN® ROMANTIC SUSPENSE

Special thanks and acknowledgment are given to
Anna J. Stewart for her contribution to
The Coltons of Roaring Springs miniseries.

ISBN-13: 978-1-335-66213-2

Colton on the Run

Copyright © 2019 by Harlequin Books S.A.

PLEASE RECYCLE

THIS PRODUCT IS RECYCLABLE

Recycling programs
for this product may
not exist in your area.

Printed in U.S.A.

Bestselling author **Anna J. Stewart** was the girl on the playground spinning in circles waiting for her Wonder Woman costume to appear or knotting her hair like Princess Leia. A Stephen King fan from early on, she can't remember a time she wasn't making up stories or had her nose stuck in a book. She currently writes sweet and spicy romances for Harlequin, spends her free time at the movies, at fan conventions or cooking and baking, and spends most every night wrangling her two kittens, Rosie and Sherlock, who love dive-bombing each other from the bed...and other places. Her house may never be the same.

Visit the Author Profile page at
Harlequin.com for more titles.

For Kathryn Lye.

For the vote of confidence and the many laughs.

Chapter 1

A thin beam of sunlight streamed against her aching, heavy lids.

She blinked. The simple, ordinary action sent blades of pain slicing through her head. Her stomach churned as bile rose in her throat. She cried out, but the sound barely reached her own ears, caught behind the taut tape stretched across her mouth. Her eyes widened before blurring against the dim light. She tried to tug her arms forward, but they wouldn't move. Her wrists strained against the rough rope wrapped so tight she couldn't feel her fingers.

Her mind cleared, but in stages, slowed by the pain and confusion coursing through her. Her ears buzzed. Her head throbbed. Gray tinged the edge of her vision as she tried to hold on to consciousness.

Something harsh and scratchy scraped against the side of her face as she rolled from her side onto her back. The smell of rotting, moldy hay and old dirt made her choke and lose her breath. Above the ringing in her ears, she heard the chill-inducing scrapings of tiny paws and claws skittering as creatures darted back to their hiding places.

Other than that… She took a deep breath and held it. The world pounded in silence.

Her heart vibrated like a jackhammer against her chest, competing with the earsplitting thudding in her head. Long tendrils of hair caught across her sweaty face and obscured her vision as she winced up at the gaping, worn holes of what must have once been a shed.

She turned her head, scanning the room in the dimming light. Old, warped slats of wood sagged against one another as if about to surrender. Rough, uneven, knotted planks gouged splinters into the sides of her hands, through the fabric of her shirt and deep into the skin on her back as she shifted position. The more she moved, the more every inch of her body ached and burned. Angry, frightened tears she couldn't hold back trailed down her cheeks. She closed her eyes, desperately searching her memory for how she'd gotten here. What had happened? Where was she? Who had done this to her?

A new tendril of fear curled up from her toes, twining through her body, choking the air from her lungs.

She didn't know. She had no answers for any of those questions. She had…nothing. A sob escaped her control. Her mind was empty.

Don't cry. She squeezed her eyes tighter until all she could feel was the pain in her head. *Can't cry. Crying won't help.* Nothing would help except getting out of wherever she was and maybe, hopefully, finding someone to help her.

Help. There was no help to be found here. She had only herself to rely on.

Stop panicking! Giving in to hysteria would only muddle her brain and make it even more difficult to breathe. Breathe. In. Out. In…out.

It took minutes, each passing second echoing in her skull like a sledgehammer against her brain, but she was able to force herself to relax. Muscle by muscle, extremity by extremity. She took a long, shaky breath and turned her head one way, then the other, attempting to get her bearings. A small, square, grime-covered window was situated above a forlorn rider mower with a deflated tire. A table saw, tools and equipment that looked to have been stashed there back at the turn of the century sat against the wall. Ropes, twine and tools hung suspended from rotting cords and blackened or rusted nails. She pushed herself up, dragged her sore legs under her, her bare feet scraping against the raw wood.

Bare feet. She didn't even have on shoes. She squeezed her eyes shut. She didn't want to think where they might be.

Breath heavy in her chest, she pushed forward onto her knees. Her legs trembled as she stood, pulling first one foot, then the other, under her. She swayed. Her head spun and her stomach churned as nausea rolled deep and strong. She braced her feet apart, took long, deliberate breaths. She couldn't afford to vomit. She'd suffocate for sure.

Turning in slow, determined circles, she squinted into the growing darkness to scope out her surroundings. To memorize every detail.

The sun was dipping fast, taking with it her only chance at visibility. She needed to escape before whoever had left her here came back. And they *were* coming back. They knew she was still alive; why else would they have tied her up and gagged her? They didn't want her making noise, didn't want her bringing attention to herself. Which meant she couldn't be too far from civilization. Right?

Curling her bare, polish-chipped toes into the dirt-caked floorboards, she took a step forward and focused on walking. One step, two. Her legs burned. Another step and then another. The thin thread of light caught against a metal circle with rusted, razor-sharp edges. A quick survey of the shovels, spades and trowels gave her little hope by comparison. She tugged at her arms again, hoping the rope digging into her wrists had given way, but they remained as tight as before.

She arched her back, shook her head to whip her hair behind her shoulders and took a cautious step, angling her bound hands toward the exposed blade of the table saw. Slowly, even as her fear screamed at her to hurry, she attempted to stretch out her numb fingers until she felt the blade against her skin. Her shoulders strained and her thighs burned as she stooped to press the rope solidly against the jagged edges of the saw blade.

Forward, back, up, down. She kept a steady rhythm, increasing her speed when she heard the rope begin to rip. Her hands slipped and the blade sliced against the newly exposed skin. Ouch! She sucked in a breath, choked, but kept cutting. The dizziness was getting worse. Her stomach hurt as it clenched around the rising nausea and panicked pressure.

When her hands finally broke free, she nearly face-planted on the floor. She caught herself on the wall with one hand, digging her broken nails into the soft wood, then tugged at the corner of the tape across her mouth.

She whimpered as the adhesive clung to her cheeks and lips, then, irritated with herself, she ripped it off in one violent yank. This time she surrendered to the urge to bend over, retching even as she gripped the splintering stud of the wall and dragged in lung-expanding air.

Pushing her hair out of her face, she looked down and then caught her shirt between blood-caked fingers. The white silk shirt and linen pants were covered in dirt, grime and now her blood. Her left pant leg was shredded, as if she'd encountered a wild animal at some point. A circular bruise around one ankle began to throb.

Darkness wouldn't be her friend. She needed to get out, away from here, and put as much distance as she could between herself and this place. She spun back to the stash of tools that would have been of benefit to a gardener or farmer, but certainly not a woman in need of aid and defense.

Although…

She bit her lip and lifted a pair of shears free of their hook. After a few attempts, she managed to get the

rusted blades open, then headed for the rickety door
across the room. She pressed down on the latch and
pulled.

Nothing happened. The wood creaked. She tried
again, more forcefully. Her entire body shook as she
desperately willed the latch to yield. The metal hinges
strained, but the door didn't budge. Anger swamped
the frustration mounting inside her, and she pounded
a fist against the door before turning to brace her back
against it. She hit it again, this time with two fists, as
she turned her attention to the shadowy window above
the forgotten equipment.

Ignoring the pain in her feet and pushing the garden
shears into the back waistband of her pants, she darted
across the room again and grabbed hold of the table
saw and pulled it out of the way so she could get to the
mower. She could feel the rough metal of the shears
pressing against her lower spine and shivered. Pulling a
long-handled shovel free of its fellow tools, she plowed
it through the window and shattered most of the glass.
Then she circled the shovel around to clear the opening before tossing it aside and brushing shards of glass
off the ripped seat of the mower. A second later, she
stepped onto the cushion. Cooler air burst through the
window like a slap, a slap she welcomed as it cleared
her head. She pulled the shears free and threw them
outside before pushing herself through and dropping
to the ground.

She hit harder than expected, hard enough to make
her head spin, but she didn't stop. She *couldn't* stop. She
rolled and shoved herself to her feet, grabbed the shears

and, after taking a moment to get her bearings, dived into the shrubs. Trees lurched up and around, shielding her both from the elements but also the dwindling light. Branches and overgrown shrubs obscured just how dense and deep the wooded area around the shed was. Heart pounding, she circled to the front of the cabin, where she found fresh tire tracks heading down the unpaved, dirt road.

There, in the distance, a dilapidated cabin erupted from the tree line, made of the same rotting wood as the shed. The out-of-control flora told her the land was uninhabited. Or at least appeared to be. She couldn't take a chance. Whoever had left her in that shed might be inside. She needed to move!

She was already shivering as the temperature seemed to drop by the second. Her feet and toes had gone numb, either from cold or from pain. There had to be some kind of road that would lead her to civilization or at the very least help. Her head aching, her wrists still burning, she quickly tied her hair in a knot at the base of her neck and headed into the woods beside the road. She'd follow it. And hope she'd find safety at the end.

Minutes, hours, or had it been days already? The nausea had returned, the physical manifestation of panic and fear, churning in her empty stomach. Sweat, blood and anxiety mingled on her skin.

Whatever adrenaline boosted her through the window faded fast. Her headache was getting worse, but at least her hands and wrists had stopped bleeding. She found herself wondering about a tetanus shot, but that thought passed through her mind as quickly as the sun dipped out of sight and the air grew cooler, leaving the humidity behind.

Her vision was blurring, and she could hear herself breathing as if she'd been sucking on a scuba tank's regulator. The bottoms of her feet had gone numb as she crunched her way through the woods and whatever else in the direction she'd chosen. Because her arms and legs were getting heavy, she'd stuck the shears back into the waistband of her pants so she could grab hold of the trees as she passed.

She licked her desert-dry mouth. Whatever her life had been before the shed, obviously she'd never taken any survival training, otherwise she wouldn't feel so completely lost and inept. Even without a memory, life-saving techniques would have stuck…wouldn't they? What she wouldn't give to sleep. Just for a few minutes. Just to reboot and regain her energy. Of course, she'd take some water as a second choice. Water. She stumbled, tripping over a thick vine. She landed hard on her chest, the shears pinching into her back, the breath driven out of her.

She braced her hands. Her fingers squished in the mud. For a moment, she thought about staying here. Just…surrendering. But a voice, hers, but not hers, echoed in the back of her mind. *Get up! Keep moving! You aren't dying here. You're not giving up!*

There! Ever so faint, she heard it. The distant echo of an engine. Of a car passing by. And another car. Traffic! She squinted into the distance. Was she imagining the flash of headlights? Was she seeing only what she wanted? Had she finally lost her mind? Or had she somehow found exactly what she needed?

She couldn't stop now. Not when she might be so close. She shoved herself up and staggered forward, pushing herself from tree to tree. The two-lane road opened up in front of her like an oasis in the desert, but there were no headlights to be found. She stood on the side of the road, her breathing ragged, and, shielding her eyes to narrow her vision, peered into the distance. First one direction. Then the other.

Her blood ran cold.

Spinning lights—red and blue—cut through the night.

Fear clamped hard around her throat. The sob that erupted came up from her toes—a chill of terror arcing through her as if she'd stuck her finger in a socket. *Not that way. Not that...*

Irrational terror shot through her. She spun, ready to dart across the road, race away in the opposite direction. The sound of squealing brakes, the flash of bright white paint and blinding headlights had her shielding her eyes. The truck skidded to a halt, veering slightly, but not enough. The front bumper grazed her thighs and she jumped back, frozen as she stared through the windshield. The shocked gaze of a teenager stared back at her. Her breathing ragged, she backed away.

He shoved his door open, jumped out of the car. "Are you all right? I'm so sorry, I didn't see... Hey! Where are you going? I think you might be hurt!"

She ran. She ran as fast as she could. Ran away from

the truck. Ran across the road and scrambled into the protection of the trees.

Away from the spinning, colored lights she feared more than the night.

It had been three months since Leo Slattery had returned to Roaring Springs, Colorado. Three months since he'd dropped his duffel containing everything he owned onto the front porch of his grandparents' farmhouse. Three months and he was still getting used to the quiet.

Ollie, his grandfather's German shepherd, returned to his side after having finished his breakfast and plopped his behind on the linoleum floor. Leo smiled down at his only companion these days, a zing of energy coursing through him.

After growing up off and on at this ranch, he'd spent the majority of his post-high-school years working oil rigs and pipelines up in Alaska. The absence of whining, grinding machinery, workmen's yells, and the clangs and bangs of metal against metal took getting used to. He wouldn't have thought it would be difficult to acclimate to the quiet of his grandparents' ranch.

The morning began as it always did, with Leo standing at Grandma Essie's favorite spot—the kitchen window—sipping fresh-brewed coffee as he stared out at the sun peeking up over the glorious mountains on a late-July morning. A sad smile curved his lips as he could hear Essie's soft, commanding voice echoing through the house she had run with a general's attention to detail and a gentle, guiding hand. A former army nurse who had left the service after falling hard for navy man Isaac Slattery, this house had been Essie's pride and joy, while the ranch and the land had been his grandfather's.

Now the ranch—all of it—was Leo's.

Unease and grief percolated low and deep in his belly. Some days he still couldn't believe they were gone. His grandfather had passed of a stroke while out tending the herd late last year, his grandmother only four months later, in her sleep. Their longtime foreman had found her lying in bed, on her side, her hand placed over the spot where Isaac had slept beside her for more than fifty years.

Tethered, Leo had thought when he'd received the news. His grandfather had always declared he and Essie were tethered at the heart; they weren't meant to be here without one another. And so they'd gone on. Leaving their legacy and all their hard work to their only surviving grandchild. A grandchild who, once his contract expired up north, headed back to the only place he'd ever called home.

"Time to get a start on the day." Leo's declaration had Ollie whining in anticipation, and the dog trotted over to the back door to wait. He filled a thermos with the last of the coffee, grabbed a stale bagel left from the grocery run he'd made early last week and shrugged into his grandfather's old, long suede riding jacket. Isaac's hat was an afterthought as Leo inhaled the aroma of his grandfather's cigars—the only thing Isaac and Essie had ever argued about.

Leo took a deep breath of cool morning air once outside. What he wouldn't give to hear their teasing bickering again. Or to see his grandfather's dark, obsidian eyes glimmer with love as he gazed upon the woman he'd fallen for at first sight.

He closed the back door behind him and headed for the stable to saddle Duke while Ollie raced to the barn several yards away, no doubt to hunt down that pesky cat that had been lurking around the smaller structure a few days before. The dog was still excited to be back home after being boarded with a foster family after Essie's death. One of Leo's many regrets was that he hadn't been able to claim the dog sooner so they could grieve their loss together.

There were days he wished he had someone to share this life with, someone besides his canine companion, but who had the time to go through all that when there was work to be done. Work that at times took him from sunrise to sunset.

"You'll do for now, won't you, Duke?" Rotating among the four horses his grandfather had kept when he'd downsized a few years back seemed the appropriate way for Leo to go about things, but there was something about the chestnut gelding that always called to Leo. Maybe it was that he'd been Essie's favorite, too. Maybe it was that he could feel the horse grieving his grandparents' loss as much as he did. Or maybe he had been spending far too much time alone out here on the seemingly endless two thousand acres.

"Won't be alone for long, though." Leo grunted as he saddled up Duke, then gave the other horses a good-morning pat. He had his eye on a truckload of new cattle by the end of the year, and he'd need additional help to keep the ranch running smoothly. His grandfather's foreman had stayed long enough to get Leo acclimated, help with the season's hay cutting and storage, then retired to spend the rest of his days in New Mexico. The other ranch hands had moved on, as well.

Which just left Leo and Gwen, his grandfather's right-hand woman for the past four years. Part horse whisperer, Gwen had put herself through school as a large-animal veterinary assistant. The thirty-two-year-old was currently on safari in Africa, an extended honeymoon with her bride, Lacey.

Only problem with taking care of fifty head of cattle on his own was that by the time he got back from ranch duties, all he wanted to do was curl up with dinner and a book.

His hope that by the time Gwen and Lacey returned he'd have at least one of the outbuildings ready for them to move into was a fading hope, despite it being the perfect enticement for Gwen to accept the promotion. Until then…

With such a small herd, Leo didn't need to be spending the extra money on help when he could handle things himself. But once that count quadrupled and grew, well, Gwen was going to be thrilled she'd had a vacation.

"You up for a morning run, Duke?" Leo ran his hand down the gelding's nose. "I know I am."

A sharp bark exploded from the direction of the barn. Duke neighed and stomped back. "That's just Ollie," Leo reminded the horse even as his own curiosity

piqued. The German shepherd wasn't normally quick
to bark and certainly wasn't easily spooked. "I bet he's
gotten himself tangled up again." The still-young pup
had a tendency of playing with ropes left lying around.
On the bright side, Leo would bet the dog could win his
share of knot-tying contests.

"I'd best go see what's going on. You wait for me
here, okay?" As if the horse was going to go anywhere.
Other than to the feed bag Leo had filled the second he
came into the stable. Chuckling to himself, he looped
the reins around the hitching post and headed to the
barn.

Ollie's barking was getting louder. Leo found him
just inside the door of the barn, at attention, nose
pointed to the back corner where the hay was piled as
high as the second story. "What's going on, boy?" He
bent down to scrub the dog's undercoat. "Something
got you spooked? You find that mean old cat you were
chasing the other day?"

Leo froze at the rustling in the corner. That wasn't
any cat. And that barely there whimper set his ears on
alert.

"Whoever you are—" Leo rose to his feet "—I don't
mean any harm, but you need to be moving on."

More rustling. More scrambling. Metal scraping
against the plank siding.

"I mean it." He moved forward, Ollie close beside
him growling low in the back of his throat. "I know it
was cold out last night and you probably needed a place
to—" he rounded the back of the hay bales "—sleep."
Whatever else he was planning to say evaporated from

his mind. The woman crouching in the corner of the barn stared back at him with wide-eyed fear. "Hello."

Was it possible to be perfectly coherent and still think he was imagining things? The woman huddled before him had hair the color of a summer bonfire, bright red with copper-and-gold highlights. Hair that was tangled around her shoulders and her face. A beautiful face that reminded him of his grandmother's bisque china collection. Delicate but sturdy enough to withstand the trembling coursing through her. Dark blood had trickled down the side of her face to soak the once-white silk blouse. Silk? Out here on the outskirts of town? Her equally bright slacks were torn and muddy, and her filthy bare feet were covered with cuts and scrapes.

The dazed expression in her eyes triggered every protective instinct within Leo. He crouched, trying to make himself appear as small as possible as he continued his assessment. Beneath and around the grime on her face, he could see the distinct impression of a large hand—a welt that had bled, but not as profusely as the gash on her head. The way her shirt was ripped told him it hadn't been the result of errant branches or trees but by angry, determined hands.

Had she been raped?

Leo swallowed his fury. Whatever had happened, she didn't need anger or outrage. She needed calm understanding. She needed his help…and his protection. He forced himself to relax, to act as if they were doing nothing more than meeting over coffee at the diner in town. Ollie finally relaxed and sat down, then looked from Leo to the woman.

She shifted, only slightly, and the rusted garden shears in her hands glinted in the morning sunlight streaming through the upper opening of the barn. He remained still, his hand deep in Ollie's fur.

"You're hurt." He kept his voice low. Soft. Gentle.

She flinched. And nodded once.

"Was there an accident? Were you in a car?" He resisted the urge to look behind him to scan outside, but he would have noticed a vehicle in the vicinity.

Her fingers went white around the shears.

"Were you alone?" He tried again. "Is someone else hurt? I should go call—" He shifted back, turned as if about to stand and felt her hand grip his arm. Leo tried to ignore the instant jolt that shot straight through him as if she'd dived at him, as if she'd jump-started his dormant heart.

Ollie growled, moved in, sniffed the woman's hand and, after a moment, pushed his nose solidly against her arm as if demanding a pet. Given Ollie was a pretty good judge of character, Leo relaxed.

"Please." Her voice was barely a whisper before she cleared it. "Please don't call anyone. I just need—" She frowned as if uncertain of what she needed, but then she released his arm. However, instead of regripping the shears, she placed her trembling hand on Ollie's determined head. Tears glimmered in her eyes. "Pretty dog."

Ollie blinked over at Leo as if to verify his master had heard the compliment.

"Best dog around." The only dog at the moment, Leo added silently. At least with Ollie his unexpected visitor seemed a bit more at ease. "Can you tell me what happened to you?" He reached a hand out to her face, determined to check how badly she'd been struck, but she flinched. "I won't hurt you…" He waited for her to tell him her name.

Instead, all he got was a blank, brown, doe-eyed stare.

"All right…you can tell me later," he murmured. "I'm Leo. Leo Slattery. You're on my ranch." He considered offering his hand, but didn't want to pressure her. She wasn't in any condition to be on her own, and one wrong move on his part would have her scurrying away. "Would you like to come inside? You can get cleaned up and something to eat. Something to drink. Coffee? Water?" Maybe once she was over the shock of whatever had happened to her, she'd be ready for him to call for help.

Leo glanced around for a bag, a cell phone, anything she might have that would help tell him who she was without him having to push for her to trust him. He didn't see anything.

"W-water," she choked out. "Water would be nice."

Polite. Polished. Beautiful. Leo shook the last thought loose before it could grab hold. "Water I can do." He inclined his head toward the door. "House is close by. Would you like me to show you?" Now he did reach out his hand. She stared at his hand for a long moment before slowly taking hold. He rose to his feet. She glanced down at the dog before rising. "Ollie can come, too. And you can bring those. If you want."

She looked down at the shears still clutched in her other hand. An odd sound erupted from the back of her throat as she dropped them, covered her mouth and stared as if she didn't understand why she had them.

It was all Leo could do not to sweep her into his arms, carry her inside and tend to her wounds. But he'd have to be blind not to see the physical signs of trauma were nothing compared to what was going on inside her head. What she needed most right now was to feel safe, to feel comfortable. To feel in control. Only then would he be able to help her.

He expected her to move away from him once they were outside, perhaps even race off and disappear into the sunrise. Instead, she curled her hand tighter around his and walked—or rather limped—beside him back to the house.

"I need to go get my horse back in his stall," Leo told her as she sat at the kitchen table. In his grandmother's chair. The thought brought a smile to his lips even as he wished Essie was here to help him. Help *her*. He poured the woman a glass of water and set it on the table. "I'll be back in just a few minutes, all right? Ollie, stay." He didn't often command the dog, but Ollie moved in closer to the woman and bumped his nose against her leg.

The ghost of a smile played across her full lips as she returned to petting the dog.

"Okay. Just a few minutes." Leo hurried back to the barn, found Duke exactly where he expected and led the now cranky horse back to his stall. "Gonna be a bit of a delay, I'm afraid." Not to mention he'd have to head out later than he wanted to fix that downed fence on the eastern pasture. But he wasn't about to leave the woman alone for long. At least not until he knew more about her. He certainly wasn't going to just abandon her. His grandmother would have had a fit. "We'll get you out and running later, Duke. Promise."

The horse neighed.

Leo returned to the house and found his visitor sitting where he'd left her, her hand gently stroking Ollie's back, her brown-eyed stare vacant and confused. But she'd drunk the water. That was good. "Okay, then." He glanced at the phone on the wall. "I think maybe I should call the sheriff—"

"No!" She all but catapulted off the chair, stumbling forward to stop him from lifting the receiver. "No, please. No police. No hospital. I don't want to see anyone. I'll go. I'll leave if you want. But I…" She pushed her hair away from her face and exposed the determination hovering behind the fear in her eyes. "Please. I don't want anyone to know where I am."

"All right." Leo hadn't been sure in the barn, but now he was. He recognized that barely restrained panic, that fright and flight response he'd grown up with. His father's bouts of PTSD after returning home from Iraq had taught Leo early on that the mind was something that shouldn't be played with. At least not before a modicum of trust had been established. "But I want you to tell me something. And I need you to tell me the truth. Can you do that?"

She nodded.

"Have you been raped?"

She blinked. "No." She winced, inclined her head

as if giving the question more thought. "No. Nothing hurts or feels odd there."

"Okay, that's good." A breath he hadn't realized he'd been holding released. "If that's the case, we'll hold off on calling the authorities. For now. But how about your name?" He couldn't stop himself. He reached out and caught her hair between his fingers, tucked it behind her ear so he could get a better look at the gash on her head. It had stopped bleeding at least. But it needed tending to. "Can you tell me who you are?"

"No." There was that whisper again. Not quite as desperate, however. This time, tinged with a bit of anger. "I've been trying and trying, but I don't know. I'm sorry." She winced, then pressed a hand against the bridge of her nose. "All I have is this headache that won't go away. There's nothing else. Not in here." She poked a not so gentle finger against her temple. "Why can't I remember?"

"Okay, let's not add to the damage." He caught her hand and pressed it gently back to her side. "We'll come back to that later. Sit back down. Let's get you some more water." He poured another glass and watched as she finished it. Ollie followed him to the sink and back, as if verifying what he was doing was for the best. Leo pulled a chair over so they were knee to knee. "Do you remember my name?"

"Leo. Your name is Leo. That's Ollie." She pointed to the dog.

"Nice that you didn't get us confused."

She smiled a little. "How can I not know who I am? It doesn't make any sense. I don't know…anything."

Shock. Trauma. And that bang on the head couldn't have done much to help. "You will. You've had a shock. Something you aren't able to process right now." He held his hands out palm up, and after a moment she dropped hers into them. "How about for now I call you Jane?"

"Like Jane Doe?" She let out the most unladylike snort he'd ever heard. A sound that lightened his heart more than anything had in a long time. "That's original."

"My grandmother was the writer, not me." Essie's letters had been a continuous gift while he'd been working in Alaska. He still had them all bundled, no longer in his duffel, but on his dresser. "I didn't get one ounce of her creativity. Is Jane okay?"

She shrugged. "It's better than nothing."

"A rave review indeed," Leo joked. "Are you hungry? I've got some eggs I can cook. And, um, some steaks. I bet you don't eat steak much." Given her slight figure, he'd bet she didn't eat much of anything. A good summer breeze would probably blow her off the property.

"Eggs sound good. I can help."

Leo glanced down at her ragged and broken nails, but given the high shine on that coral polish, he'd bet she'd had her share of manicures. "I'd prefer you didn't. Not until we know what's going on with that knock on your head. How about I run upstairs and see about finding you some clothes? Then you can take a shower and we'll tend to that gash on your head. And your wrists." He turned her hands over and tried not to wince at the angry welts, scrapes and cuts marring her skin. "I'm betting those feet of yours hurt a bit, too."

"Not really." She scrunched her toes into the wood floor. "They're numb."

He was afraid of that, but toward the end of summer she was less likely to end up with frostbite, something he'd become more than acquainted with up north. "All the more reason to get you into the shower. Sound okay?"

She chewed on her bottom lip and nodded. "Yes. Okay. Thank you, Leo."

He led her to the bedroom closest to the kitchen, the small guest room his grandmother had always kept made up. It had its own small bathroom with an old-fashioned, claw-foot tub, pedestal sink and a corner shower stall he could never fit into. The bed was old, nothing fancy other than the simple wooden headboard, but serviceable and comfortable with its thick handmade quilt thrown over the double mattress. The added photographs of Leo and his family from various stages of the last twenty-seven years added to the homey feel. "Are you okay by yourself?"

"Yes." Ah, now there was a genuine smile. One that sparked her previously dormant eyes as she looked up at him. "I'll call if I need help." She looked down at her ripped shirt. The frown was back. "Why can't I remember what happened to me?"

"You will. Don't push it," Leo urged as he backed out of the room. "It'll come, Jane. Whoever you are, whatever happened, you'll remember. And we'll deal with it together. Give me a few minutes to find you some clothes."

He nearly stepped on Ollie when he turned to head upstairs. "Well, boy. Looks like we have company for a little bit. Hope that's okay with you."

Ollie chuffed as he circled Leo and sank to the floor, stretching across the doorway into Jane's room.

"You let me know if she needs anything."

Ollie blinked up at him and Leo sighed, rubbing a hand across his forehead.

Today was definitely going to be one for the books.

Chapter 2

If only the water could wash away the fear.

Jane—she didn't *feel* like a Jane—scooped warm water into her hands and pushed it over her tangled hair. She turned one side of her face into the spray of the shower, then the other, grimacing as the gash on her head protested. Looking down, she saw the water turn dark, tinged with blood as it cascaded off her body, swirling into the drain as if taking what had happened to her with it.

But something had happened. Something she couldn't remember. She tucked her arms tight around her waist. Whatever did happen had robbed her of her memory, and now she had no inkling of who or what she was.

It crossed her mind to bang her skull against the

white tile wall in the hopes of jarring something loose, but she didn't want to alarm Leo or Ollie.

Leo.

Jane moved deeper into the spray and let the water pound over her ears. Finding the barn last night had seemed like heaven on earth. A solitary floodlight had blinked on as she'd approached from the cover of the trees and she'd stopped, frozen as if caught in a spotlight. But the flash of light had given her enough to see by so she could squeeze through the open door. The night hadn't cooled off much, but she couldn't stop shivering as she'd made her way into the back corner, digging and pushing her way through the hay until she'd collapsed.

Jane had lost track of the miles she'd walked. And had no clue of the direction she'd come from. If anyone were to ask her where she'd been held, she'd never be able to tell them, other than that it was near a road that led…somewhere.

When she fell asleep, she'd fallen hard and deep, and hadn't awakened until she'd heard Ollie's bark cutting through the peaceful silence.

"Jane." A gentle knock sounded on the bathroom door. She jumped and nearly slipped. "I've left some clothes for you to wear on the bed, okay?"

"Yes." She gripped her fingers against the tiles. Leo. It was just Leo. Leo Slattery, who, for whatever reason, didn't evoke that sense of unrestrained fear she'd been harboring since she awoke in that shed.

Leo with the kind, dark, soulful eyes. The slightly unkempt, slightly curly hair that tempted her to reach out and brush her fingers through it. He was a beautiful man, probably more beautiful that he'd ever be comfortable with her thinking. But it was that gentle, understanding smile he'd offered upon seeing her that had soothed the bruises around her heart. That and the way he'd held her hand.

As if he'd protect her from whatever was out there. Whatever was to come.

And something *was* out there. Something was coming. She could…feel it.

Dark. Dangerous. Almost as if she were prey in a hunter's sights. She shuddered. A hunter with an agenda she couldn't begin to fathom. Why her? Why had this happened to *her*?

And what was she going to do about it? She couldn't explain the abject terror that struck at the thought of calling the police, and going to the hospital would only result in the same. She didn't know much at the moment, but she knew enough to trust her instincts and right now her instinct told her the only person she was safe with was Leo.

Beneath the warmth of the water, she shivered and focused on ridding herself of the last of the mud, dirt and blood. The soap and shampoo smelled of wildflowers and honeysuckle. For an instant, she flashed on the image of a luxurious spa reminiscent of… Jane frowned. France? Why on earth would she be reminded of France out here in the middle of—

She hadn't even asked Leo where she was. Other than the obvious—that she was on a ranch in the rural countryside—she had no notion of her actual whereabouts. She turned her hands over, watched the water cascade over broken nails and scraped skin. Leo had looked at her hands. Had he seen what she saw? She chipped at the polish that remained before dragging her fingers through her hair.

A few minutes later, she stood in front of the small mirror above the sink, wrapped in a buttercup-yellow towel and dragging a fine-tooth comb through the knots and snarls in her hair. Staring at herself, tears blurred her eyes. The face was unknown. It was her, but not. She traced gentle fingers over the welt on her face. The ghostly image of a handprint marring her cheek had broken through; the raw scrape might very well scar. Taking a shuddering breath, she popped open the door a bit to let some air in to defog the mirror and found herself smiling when Ollie poked his nose inside.

"Are you watching out for me, boy?" The very sight of the canine made her feel better. As did the comforting cooking sounds emanating from the kitchen.

Ollie plopped his butt on the floor, wagged his tail and inclined his head.

"You and your master have the same intent, I see." She peeked out into the bedroom and noticed the door was closed. "A gentleman, too."

She'd washed her underwear and bra in the sink, left them to dry over the shower door. She wadded up what was left of her clothes to throw away in the trash. The soles of her feet felt more tender now that feeling had returned, and she found herself walking on the sides of her feet as the pain began to set in.

The sweatpants and button-down shirt would do for

now. The garments were large and comfortable. She rolled up the cuffs on both the legs and sleeves before braiding her hair down her back. She held the tail of her hair in one hand and carried her ruined clothes and the clean socks back into the kitchen, where she found Leo standing in front of the stove stirring a mound of eggs.

"Two would have been enough," Jane told him, and earned a sheepish smile tossed over one strong, firm shoulder.

"I thought I'd join you. I'll get the toast going in a minute. Here." He pulled the cast-iron pan off the stove and put a plate on top of it to keep the eggs warm. "Let's get those cuts of yours tended to."

"Do you have somewhere I can throw these?" She held out the silk top and linen pants. Regret she couldn't quite relate to swept over her. "They must have been expensive."

"They're designer," Leo said as he took them and glanced at the labels. "Which is why we're going to keep them. When you're ready to remember who you are, the labels might come in handy."

When she was *ready*? "You make it sound like it's my choice." She watched him put the clothes in a paper bag and place it on a shelf on the back porch above the washing machine. A stack of rubber bands nearly obscured the doorknob of the pantry, and she snapped one off to secure her braid.

"Maybe it is." Leo's casual tone made it sound as if they were discussing the weather rather than her obviously severe case of...

Amnesia.

Jane groaned and dropped back into the chair she'd occupied earlier. "How can I know what amnesia is but not remember who I am? That doesn't make any sense."

"It does if your amnesia is somehow connected to who you are." Leo retrieved a bright white metal box from the back porch and set it on the table. Before he returned, he poured them each a cup of coffee. "The brain is a complicated thing. I told you, don't push it. You'll remember what you're meant to remember when you're ready."

"That sentence alone gives me a headache." The pounding in her head wasn't getting any better, but at least it wasn't getting any worse. "I don't even know where we are."

"Colorado," Leo told her. "Roaring Springs. Well, the farthest edge of it." He arched a brow as if expecting the information to open a floodgate of memories. "Nothing?"

"Zippo." The frustration began to eat at her. She just felt so…stupid! And it was not a feeling she liked. At all.

"How do you take your coffee?" He set a flowered mug in front of her.

"Cream. No sugar." Her laugh sounded strained even to her own ears. "Would have probably taken a complete lobotomy to forget that."

"Everyone knows how they take their coffee," Leo teased. "Ollie, you're becoming a pest. Go get in your bed."

"He's fine." Jane pressed her hand into the dog's neck. "I'm fine with him around."

"Good to hear it. Now, drink some caffeine and brace

yourself. This is probably going to sting." He swabbed a large cotton ball with rubbing alcohol and pressed in against the long gash in her hairline.

She sucked in a breath, gritting her teeth as her eyes watered against the pain. "Oh, wow. Yeah." But she didn't pull away. It was something that had to be done. Besides, the comfort she felt with Ollie so close was nothing compared to how she felt around Leo Slattery. The man was…smoking hot. In more ways than one. She found herself transfixed by the muscles in his arm as he tended to her. He smelled amazing, too, like soap and wood with a hint of citrus that set her nose to tingling. She took a deep breath to steady herself, but that only set her head to spinning in a completely different way.

"Why don't you scare me?" Given what must have happened to her, she should be terrified of everyone and yet…

He stopped, pulled his hand away and sat back in his chair. "What?"

Jane's cheeks flamed. "Did I say that out loud? Oh, wow." She pressed a hand against her face. "My brain must have been seriously bashed. That was—"

"Honest." The smile that broke across his handsome face could have healed a thousand wounds. "I don't have an answer for you other than I think it means you know I don't mean you any harm." It was the way he said it, not as a question exactly, but the inquiry was there nonetheless. Her mind raced for a response as Leo turned his attention to the welt on her upper cheek.

"But someone did. Mean me harm," she added as if needed. "Who?"

"Again, I don't have an answer." He tossed the soiled cotton ball onto a napkin and retrieved three butterfly bandages from the kit. "I'm not sure we'll know until you remember who you are. And it's doubtful we'll find that out without help."

"No police." The protest was out of her mouth before she even thought the words. The very idea of talking with the police was enough to turn the coffee in her empty stomach to bile.

"They might recognize you."

"Why?"

Leo smiled, but for the first time, there didn't seem to be any humor behind it. "You're not from around here, Jane. Your clothes, your hands. Your hair. You. You don't live a rancher's life. And around this part of Roaring Springs, that would make you stand out. I hate to disappoint you, but I don't think you're a country girl. There." He pressed his fingers against the bandages. "Now, let's see your feet." He scooted his chair back and patted his thighs. "Up."

"Um. Okay." She drew her feet up and did as he requested. The second his hands landed on her feet, she shivered. Strong, determined fingers examined the soles, pressing and checking for open wounds. "How bad?"

"Not as bad as I thought. You're going to want to stay off them for a day or so. Let them heal a bit." He repeated the process he had with her head, cleaning the scrapes with alcohol before applying ointment and covering them with gauze that he secured with tape. "What's this?" He angled her left foot to the side, narrowed his eyes as his fingers gently grazed her skin.

She shook her head, that sick fear clogging her throat.

"They look like finger marks."

Jane squeezed her eyes shut and tried not to shake. "I know," she whispered. But that was all she could manage. Watching him, she took comfort in the shift of expressions over his face. Concern gave way to curiosity, which sharpened to anger at her words. But his touch didn't change. The featherlight pressure of his fingers danced along her skin like a healing balm.

"Those socks should help." He picked up the pair of thick, white socks from the table. "Besides, you shouldn't be moving around with a head injury. We'll give it a day or so, see how you're feeling, then discuss what comes next."

"What comes next?" Panic dropped over her again like a blanket.

"People are bound to be missing you, Jane. They're bound to be worried. If you aren't going to let me go to the police or take you to the hospital, then we'll have to find those people ourselves."

"Or I could just stay here." Here, in this pretty little country kitchen with sunflower curtains over the windows and a collection of teapots behind one of the glass-door cabinets.

"You mean hide," Leo corrected. He slipped the socks on her feet, gave her ankles a quick pat, then placed her feet back on the floor. "Wrist, please."

"Lord, I'm such a mess." She winced, remembering

the feel of that saw blade scraping against her skin. "He was going to come back."

Leo's hand stilled for a moment before carefully dabbing at the scratches. "Who was?"

"He. They. Whoever left me in that shed." And just like that, the anxiety and terror she felt when she'd first come to overtook the panic at the thought of leaving. "As soon as I woke up, as soon as I realized what was happening, I knew whoever took me was coming back."

"Tell me what you remember about where you were."

"Mmm." Jane frowned and wished she'd get used to that stinging sensation coating her skin, but the pain was offset by Leo's tender touch. "It was an old shed. One window. One door. I'd been tied up. Obviously." She lifted her hand as proof.

"Rope." He traced a finger over the burns among the cuts. "Not duct tape. Interesting."

"Why? Duct tape might have been easier to cut through."

"Maybe. What was in the shed?"

"Garden tools. A lawn mower, shovels. That kind of thing." Her mind raced back there. "And old woodworking tools, too. The door wouldn't open."

"So you broke through the window." He reached behind himself for a pair of tweezers.

"How did you— Ow!"

He plucked a tiny shard of glass out of the side of her wrist and held it up for her to see. "Glad there weren't any in your feet."

"Me, too." She watched him examine every inch of her hands and wrists and forearms. "You sure you aren't a doctor?" She felt her face warm again, and wished she didn't sound like a teenager with a crush.

"I did some emergency first aid up in Alaska over the years. Nothing major, but what you learn sticks. Most of the time."

"So you aren't a rancher? But I thought—"

"I am now." He rubbed a soothing salve into her skin before wrapping her wrists in gauze. "This was my grandparents' place. They passed last year, so now it's mine."

"The pictures in the bedroom." Jane looked behind her toward the photographs she could see perched on the dresser. She'd glanced at them earlier. An older, laughing couple. A young woman holding a grinning baby she assumed was Leo. A man, a more intense version of Leo, standing in full military uniform. "Your family."

"Yes. My grandmother Essie showed us off at every opportunity. One thing that isn't lacking in this house is photographs." Even the smallest smile lit up Leo's face. "Every celebration, every get-together, we had to take photos."

"What about your parents? Did they not want to take over the ranch?"

"My mother died when I was little. My father was in the army for most of my childhood, so I lived here when he was deployed." He cleaned up the kit, threw away the garbage, washed his hands and dropped a few slices of toast into the toaster. "He served three tours in the first Gulf War. I was supposed to go live with him when he was discharged, but he came back...different. So he moved in here with us. Until he died."

The thought that Leo Slattery was alone in the world, that he'd lost all his family, pierced something inside her. "I'm so sorry, Leo."

"It's life." He didn't shrug, didn't try to make light of it, but what he said rang true. "Bad things happen, Jane. To all of us. It's how we deal with it that matters."

She resisted the urge to squirm in her chair. "It's a bit early in our friendship for you to be sending subliminal messages. I'm not going to the police." The very idea still made her shudder.

"It wasn't subliminal if you got it." The grin he tossed her eased the uncertainty that continued to course through her. "Maybe you didn't take such a big whack on the head after all."

"Oh, I think I did." In fact, the headache was coming back full force. "What painkillers do you have in that magic box of yours?"

"Let's get some food into you first. Don't want an upset stomach on top of everything else." He set a plate of eggs in front of her and retrieved her toast. "Wait." He opened a cabinet near the refrigerator and pulled out a jar. "It isn't toast without my grandmother's blackberry jam. Trust me." He opened it and set it on the table.

"I do." The fact that she did still didn't make sense. But it did bring her the only semblance of peace she could find at the moment.

"Jane." He caught her hand as she stabbed her fork into her breakfast. "We're going to find out who you are and who hurt you. I promise."

"You do?"

"I do. And I don't make promises I can't keep." The determined glint in his eye convinced her. Settled her. Warmed her. "I'll get you home, Jane. You have my word."

Chapter 3

Since coming back to the ranch, Leo had grudgingly adjusted to the poor internet connection and cell service. One of the reasons his plans for the ranch were on hold. Difficult to run a business these days without being online. But for now, a landline was all he had.

The absence of anything other than local channel television hadn't been a disappointment as he much preferred books or music to wind down his day, and he had his grandfather's vinyl record collection on permanent rotation. But as he stood in the doorway to the living room, where Jane had curled up on the sofa, tucked in under his great-grandmother's hand-stitched quilt, he realized how many problems technology could solve for his current predicament.

Predicament.

Odd choice of words for a beautiful interloper.

"You sure you'll be okay?" He set a glass of water and new cup of java on the coasters on the coffee table. "I can postpone the repairs until—"

"Unless you plan to stand there and watch me sleep, there's nothing more you can do for me, Leo." She snuggled down on her side, her eyes already drooping. "I'm just going to sleep for a while."

"Yeah. Well, since I'm not going to be here to check on you, I set the kitchen timer for an hour."

She flicked her gaze to his.

"If you won't go to the clinic in town to have your head checked, that's the trade-off. When you get up to turn it off, set it again. I mean it, Jane."

Her nose scrunched. "That's such a silly name. And I don't need a babysitter."

Leo wasn't so sure. "Hey." He crouched so they'd be eye to eye. "It's either the timer or I pack you into the truck and take you to the clinic."

Shuddering, she ducked her chin and curled into herself. "They'll call the police."

Which was what Leo's gut was telling him he should have already done. Someone had attacked her. Kidnapped her. Stashed her in some secluded shed so he could come back and do whatever he'd planned to do with her. "Then I think dealing with a kitchen timer should be an easy enough compromise."

"Logical. That's irritating."

She might have meant it to be teasing, but he saw the flash of fear in her lovely brown eyes at the mere idea of calling the authorities. "I shouldn't be gone more than a few hours. TV remote is by the chair over there. Some movies are on the shelf. Help yourself to whatever you need."

"I just want to sleep," she murmured even as her eyes drifted closed.

"Yeah. Sleep." Leo knew he should leave. But he found himself positively transfixed by the vision of this beautiful, strong-willed, mystifying woman on his sofa. He didn't want to leave her. But he couldn't stay, either. Not when there were chores to be done and questions to answer.

The sooner he got to both the better. He stood up and patted his leg, quietly calling Ollie. The dog obeyed, looking up at him with expectant eyes. "You stay with her, boy. Okay?"

Ollie whined, no doubt realizing he wouldn't be venturing outdoors much today.

"How about we go with steak for dinner," Leo offered with a gentle, encouraging pet.

A quiet bark of approval set his mind at ease. "Then you keep an eye on Jane. I'll be back soon."

Leo retrieved his jacket and hat and headed outside, his boots hitting the ground with purpose as he walked to the barn. The morning breeze had obscured most of the barefoot tracks Jane had left on her arrival, but an occasional drop of dark blood gave him a good enough trail to follow, which he did, into the tree line on the far end of the property.

Admiration and anger mingled inside Leo as he realized just how far and how difficult her walk had been.

She had to have been disorientated. Dizzy. Confused. And yet somehow, she'd found her way here.

Broken branches and disturbed shrubs gave him a general idea as to the direction she'd come. It was a good two, three miles in before he'd hit anything resembling a road, but that road would circle back and outline a good portion of Roaring Springs. Not that he'd had much time to explore as of yet. But maybe this was the excuse he'd been looking for.

"First things first." He needed to get that line of fence repaired before the cattle decided to test its strength. Leo returned to the barn and house, circled around to the front porch and climbed into his truck.

He made the drive up and around to the far end of the property in silence with the windows open and the Colorado summer breeze his chosen companion. Not quite as entertaining or comforting as Ollie, but he felt better about leaving Jane knowing his dog was with her.

It wasn't long before he'd loaded up the feed trailer at the silo, and made a more efficient trip up to the herd. Normally he let them graze the pasture, but he needed them away from the fence line, so he deposited the feed well away from the sagging sections of fence. Tomorrow he'd move them to the northern pasture, which should give him a breather for a couple of days.

They thought he'd killed her.

He'd have found the idea of murdering Skye Colton amusing if it didn't irritate him. Why hadn't he thought of that himself? He could have. There had been plenty of opportunity, given his proximity to the friendliest and most outgoing of the Colton offspring.

Reason overruled him. Killing Sabrina Gilford had brought enough attention. Attention that included the FBI, and they were nobody's fool. Better to play it safe. Stick to the plan. Remain where he was, in plain sight, watching every move the Coltons and Gilfords made.

Every day he listened to the worry, felt the barely retrained fear over Skye's disappearance, the dead women he'd all but laid at their door. It fed him. Nourished him. Emboldened him. The tension gave him a particular kind of jolt, and wasn't nearly as satisfying as squeezing the life out of those women. One after another after another.

Maybe…maybe he was wrong. Maybe it was time to strike harder, deeper, rip their hearts right out of their chests by eliminating their precious Skye. Maybe…

Tight lips stretched into a thin smile as he allowed himself to daydream watching the life drain out of those lively brown eyes. Pleasure shot through him like an intoxicant as his mind raced, settled. Planned.

Perhaps, he told himself as he offered a pleasant smile to the group of guests who passed by him on their way to The Chateau. Perhaps it was time he joined in the search for Skye Colton.

It was after noon before Leo wrapped the last coil of barbed wire hard and tight around the metal post. Wiping the sweat off his forehead with his sleeve, he tipped his hat back and surveyed the cattle in the distance. He hadn't been far off base thinking they'd be up for testing the fence line, but for now, all was secure on the Slattery Ranch. As far as he knew, anyway.

He gathered his tools and the last of the wire, slung it all into the bed of his truck before drinking the last of the water in the cooler he kept. Even as he considered what should be done next, he rethought his to-do list. It had been a few days since he'd done a fence check on the west end of the property, but he had something more important in mind.

Which was why, after dropping off the feed trailer, he didn't stop at the house. He kept driving. Right out the gate, off the property and onto the fifty mile road that would take him into town.

By the time the kitchen timer beeped for the fourth time, Jane gave up any hope of sleep.

"Probably part of his evil plan from the start." She tossed off the quilt with a growl loud enough to startle Ollie, who did a quick spin and check to see if he'd missed an intruder.

"Just me, boy. Ready to strangle your owner."

The German shepherd made an odd noise in the back of his throat. Jane froze halfway off the sofa, wondering just how much the dog actually understood. "What got your attention? My growl or the word *owner*?"

Ollie barked. Jane swore the animal grinned.

"At least one of us is having a good day." She climbed off the sofa and trudged into the kitchen, pushing the button to silence the DEFCON 1 blaring that cut through her head like a knife. Maybe Leo was right. Maybe she should have her head checked out.

Or maybe she should just take another painkiller. She shook out a pill and downed it with a full glass of water. The view out the kitchen window was enough to take her breath away. The distant mountains provided the perfect country backdrop to the lush acreage and land stretching before her. With the barn and stable on the other side of the house, she could see far and wide, and memorized every curve, every hill, every…shadow.

Jane gasped and dropped to the floor. Ollie came over immediately and pushed his head against her chest as her heart pounded. She squeezed her eyes shut as fear roiled through her. The buzzing in her ears returned, blocking out rational thought as she tried to filter through what she'd seen in a glimpse. A man on horseback, along the top ridge of the property. Leo had taken his truck, hadn't he? He hadn't come back without telling her, right? Was she wrong? Was she imagining things?

Skin clammy, hands shaking, she gripped the edge of the sink and pulled herself up, peeking over the edge of the window ledge. Her gaze froze on the solitary figure on horseback turning one way, then the other. He was so far away that logically she knew he couldn't see her. But she could see him. Who was it? Did Leo have someone on the ranch he hadn't told her about?

She should have asked him. Stupid, stupid! She should have gotten all the information she could before urging him to leave. Not that she couldn't protect herself.

Heart hammering in her throat, she pushed herself

up, watching the figure as she blindly reached for the knife block on the counter.

She wrapped her hand around the thickest handle and pulled the carving knife free before ripping the curtain closed. She crouched on the floor again, knife clutched in her hands, close to her chest.

"You're being ridiculous," Jane whispered to herself, but the fear wouldn't dissipate. Behind closed eyes, the flashing lights returned. Red. Blue. Bright. Blinding. The ghostly sound of heavy boots approaching had her crying out and darting to the other side of the kitchen, still crouched into as tight a ball as she could manage. She took long, deep breaths, coaxing herself to pry her eyes open, and when she finally did, she found she was alone. Other than Ollie, there was no one in the kitchen—just shadows and her own terror.

"No one knows you're here. No one could." But even as the words seeped out of her mouth, she knew she couldn't believe it. She didn't even know her own name let alone what anyone outside this house would or wouldn't do.

She couldn't take any chances. Here, alone, with no one to trust, she needed to feel safe. She kept low, moving along the edge of the cabinets until she reached the living room. Before she could talk herself out of it, she darted to the windows and pulled the drapes shut. Then she raced through the house and did the same in every room.

The Slattery house went dark and dormant. Ollie abandoned his stance by the door and followed her from room to room, a low concerned whine issuing from his throat. If dogs could speak, she had no doubt he was telling her to calm down. To try to relax and not worry that every person outside the house was the one responsible for hurting her and stashing her in that shed.

But she couldn't stop. Not until she found the darkness again. The last room had no curtains. The bookshelf-lined study was both practical and elegant, with a heavy desk and an outdated desktop computer situated on top. She bypassed the array of files and papers, the opened mail and the stack of unattended envelopes in favor of the corner, where she dropped down and huddled. She struggled to breathe around the feeling that her lungs were going to explode, all the while hearing the intermittent pounding of footsteps and wailing sirens. Dim sunlight streamed in through the western-facing window.

Ollie inched toward her, lifting his paws onto her updrawn knees.

Her arms ached. Her fingers had gone numb around the hilt of the knife. But she wasn't letting go. Not now. Maybe not ever.

Ollie blinked big, concerned eyes at her.

"It's okay, boy," Jane lied. "It'll be okay. I'll be okay." But she couldn't do anything more than close her eyes and rest the back of her head against the array of books behind her. "He'll be back soon. Leo will be back." *Leo.* She forced the image of the ruggedly handsome cowboy into her mind, shoving away the darkness, the fear, and focused only on him. "Leo will be back."

She wasn't safe. Not here. Not inside. Not outside.

Whoever had locked her up in that shed was still out there. Looking for her.

But why? Who was she? What had she done that could have made anyone do what they had?

More importantly, when was she ever going to feel safe again?

Leo grabbed the first parking spot he found near M&P Grocery, the small mom-and-pop store located in the blink-and-miss-it town of Juniper Grove. It wasn't that he didn't like the hustle and bustle of Roaring Springs with its restaurants, shops, businesses and nightclubs, but Leo was the kind of man who preferred simpler offerings. Juniper Grove, less than an hour's drive from the ranch, was perfect for those looking for a more sedate side excursion with its kitschy antiques stores, gift shops and down-home atmosphere. But today? Today he was keeping his ears open. Small towns absorbed information like industrial sponges. And even smaller businesses like M&P Grocery? It was the perfect place to start.

He grabbed his hat before climbing out of his truck. His trips into town weren't infrequent, but this time of day put him in the middle of what would be considered the lunch rush and the lively energy of workday frenzy. The plate-glass windows of the diner across the street were filled with customers sipping on milkshakes and gobbling down burgers. The solitary gift shop had their OPEN signs ablaze to welcome the trickle of customers. He'd forgo the bookshop this time around, and he didn't need to stop at the hardware or the feed and supply store located a few doors down. Instead, he focused his attention on the grocery and stocking up on supplies.

Leo tipped his hat in greeting to the elderly pair of women hurrying out of the store, each with a reusable bag curved over one arm, and a drippy, strawberry ice-cream cone clutched in the other hand.

"Afternoon, Leo." Clarice Summers called from behind the front register. She tucked the too-tight blouse down over her obviously pregnant stomach with a grimace of frustration. "What brings you out and about today?"

"Just stocking up. Weekend's gonna be full." He pulled out a cart and made quick work of the meat section. One thing about living in cattle country—there was always plenty of selection. He looked at the plastic-wrapped packages of chickens and cringed. Did Jane like beef? Should he get some chicken just in case?

His culinary skills were passable; not that his grandmother would have agreed. But he'd pulled his own weight up on the pipeline and filled in a time or two for the kitchen help. Up there, you did what needed doing whether you were capable or not. You just dived in and hoped for the best.

While he'd certainly had his share of female companionship in his twenty-seven years, he'd never lived with a woman long-term. Would Jane prefer salad? Seafood? Or would her memory loss work in his favor? Maybe he should have thought this out a bit more.

By the time he loaded his items onto the conveyer belt, he felt better about his selections. Pasta, fresh vegetables. And dog treats for Ollie. Not too much he could screw up. One thing he did know how to make was his grandmother's buttermilk biscuits. Add a pile of strawberries and they make for perfect shortcakes.

"Branching out, I see." Clarice grinned at his larger than usual grocery haul. "One would think you were stocking up for the winter."

"Just being prepared," Leo said, smiling back. "You ready for the little one?"

"I was ready a month ago," Clarice groaned, and pressed a hand against the base of her spine. "I swear this kid swims laps. What am I going to do when he comes out? Not like we have a lot of pools around Juniper Grove."

"There's always The Chateau in Roaring Springs," one of her coworkers teased.

Clarice snorted. "Sure, if I turned over half my paycheck. You been up there yet, Leo?"

"To The Chateau? Ah, no." Fancy spas and resorts weren't part of his lifestyle. Not that he knew much about it. Growing up, he'd spent all his time out on the ranch being homeschooled by his grandmother. He'd never been concerned with the Coltons and the goings-on in downtown Roaring Springs. Now that he was back, nothing had changed. They lived in their world; he lived in his. He probably wouldn't even recognize a Colton if he saw one.

"Well, who knows what's going on up there these days what with that Avalanche Killer and all," Clarice's friend, whose name badge identified her as Betsy, declared in a singsong voice. "Not sure if that's going to bring more people in or frighten them away."

"The Avalanche Killer?" Leo did his best to sound casual.

"Honey, you've been spending too much time out on that ranch alone. Haven't you heard? They've found bodies up there on the mountain near The Lodge. Bodies of young women. Buried in the snow." Clarice shuddered. "Word is some go back years. They found another one just a while ago. Crazy times we're living in. I'm locking my doors for sure."

"Crazy times indeed," Leo murmured even as his mind raced. He wasn't a man who believed in coincidences. Knowing what he did about Jane and what had happened to her, now hearing about this crazy serial killer? Suddenly, all he wanted was to get back to the ranch and make sure she was okay.

"Thanks, Clarice. So who's in charge of the case? Have they brought in the Feds? I saw on one of those reality shows they bring in the FBI for cases like this."

Betsy shook her overdyed blond hair. "Last I heard Deputy Daria Bloom's overseeing things. Been working like a fiend trying to tie all the threads together." Her mascara-thick blue eyes went wide. "I bet this would make an amazing book or TV movie. You know, for that women in crime network they have. Oh, wow! I wonder if they'd film here."

Leo forced a laugh and accepted the bags Clarice finished packing. "I wouldn't put it past anyone not to have thought of that already. Thanks, ladies. You have a nice day. Clarice, you take it easy."

"You, too, Leo." Clarice beamed at him.

Leo loaded his bags into the truck, hesitating. Questions flooded his mind, as well as doubts. As much as he wanted to inquire further about the supposed serial killer and ferret out information that could, possibly, connect to Jane, he'd given her his word he wouldn't go to the authorities. Besides, going in and asking questions of the police would more likely result in him being put on a suspect list rather than being considered a curious resident.

No. Now wasn't the time. He couldn't break the promise he'd made to Jane, not when trust was the most important thing he could build right now. It didn't matter that she might never know. He would. *A man might not have much,* his grandfather often told him, *but he has his word and once he gives that, there's no going back.*

Which meant Leo would give the sheriff's station and Deputy Bloom a wide berth. For now.

Chapter 4

"Jane!" Leo dropped the overflowing bags onto the washing machine on the back porch. He'd stopped to get her some clothes and necessities at a convenience store just outside town, a store he'd only ever driven past previously. No one would recognize him as far as he knew; thus no one would question his purchases. He shrugged out of his coat and hung it and his hat on their respective hooks. "Sorry I took so long." He glanced at the unusually dark kitchen. Frowning, he headed to the stove and noted the timer was off.

Well, she'd turned it off at least once. All the while he was gone, he was making bets with himself as to whether she'd actually done as he'd asked. His smile dipped as he realized the curtain over the window had been drawn. And not neatly. The tension bar had slipped and the curtain hung at an odd angle.

Unease dripped through him. "Jane? Ollie?"

That not even the dog responded to his call had him racing into the living room. The quilt was wadded up on the sofa, but no sign of Jane. He checked her bedroom, the bathroom, even her closet before hurrying back to search the other bedrooms. In every room the curtains had been drawn, the light doused. Finally, he spotted her in his grandfather's study. "Jane." Leo sagged against the door frame and tried to steady his racing heart. "Didn't you hear me? What are you doing in here? Ollie?"

The dog whimpered but didn't move from his space beside Jane.

Jane. She'd curled herself tight into the back corner of the room, bookcases on either side of her, arms locked tight around her knees. With one of the kitchen knives gripped in her hand, she was rocking back and forth, that same vacant stare he'd seen in the barn.

No. Not the same stare, he realized as his throat tightened. This one was worse. This expression scared him.

"It's okay, Ollie." Leo approached slowly, keeping his eyes on the dog until he lowered himself beside Jane. As if dealing with a spooked filly, he didn't attempt to take the knife away from her. Nor did he push for a verbal response. Ollie got up and walked around to his side and pushed his cold nose against Leo's hand.

"Jane?" Leo kept his voice low. "What happened?"

"I saw someone. Outside." Her glassy brown gaze blinked quickly to the window before settling again.

"Just someone on a horse, but I thought… I was afraid." Tears gleamed in her eyes. "I'm sorry. I shouldn't be hiding. I shouldn't be here."

Where else should she be? "You've nothing to apologize for." Leo had been careful about touching her. While she'd been firm in her declaration she hadn't been sexually assaulted, with her memory the way it was, every gesture he made had to be thought out. He held up his arm, as if asking permission to hold her. Comfort her. Bring her some kind of solace. "No one is going to hurt you here, Jane. Not here. I promise."

"You can't promise that," she whispered before she leaned into him. Leo dropped his arm around her and held her close, hugging her against him so that he could press his nose into the floral fragrance of her hair. He took a deep breath and imagined an open field where a smiling Jane opened her arms and twirled in the Colorado sunshine.

It was his dream, he thought. To see her laughing, and smiling, and without the hint of terror clouding her beautiful brown eyes.

"I can promise anything I want," Leo whispered back. "I'm sorry I left you alone. I shouldn't have. I won't again."

"You can't babysit me every hour." And yet she didn't give any indication she planned to move. "I just need a little time to stop being scared."

"You need as much time as you need. How's your head?" He reached down and caught her face in his hand, tilting it so he could look into her eyes. "Truth."

"It hurts. But not as bad as before." She blinked at Leo, as if seeing him clearly for the first time.

"Have you changed your mind about talking to the police?" He'd planned on discussing what he'd heard in town, to try to press her on the memories she was missing in order to determine if she'd been the latest target of this Avalanche Killer. But given the traumatized state she was in at the moment, letting her know a serial killer might be after her could tip her further away from him. Far enough away he'd never get her back.

"No." The way she said it, with renewed anger in her voice, told him there was something else going on inside. "No police. You didn't talk to them, did you?"

As she looked at him, the pleading in her eyes piercing him to the core, he was relieved he didn't have to lie to her. "No, I didn't. I thought about it, but I promised. And I don't break my promises, remember?"

"I remember."

He tugged her back against him and covered her hand that held the knife with his much larger one. "I'm going to need that later. For dinner."

"Okay." She nodded, her cheek sliding up and down against his chest. "Just tell me when."

Leo couldn't help it. He laughed.

"What's so funny?" Her brow furrowed as she sat up and glared at him. But then, as his laughter continued, a smile tugged at the corners of her mouth. "I guess it is pretty ridiculous. Me sitting here with this."

"Not ridiculous." Leo caught the back of her head in his hand and pulled her close, pressed his lips against her forehead. It was, he realized, not meant to comfort her, but to bring him a bit of solace. He couldn't remember the last time he'd laughed. The last time he'd done anything other than go about his daily routine, the same routine his grandfather had perfected more than fifty years ago. "It is what it is. If that knife makes you feel more safe, I can make do with another."

"I don't need it now." He could almost hear her fingers creak as she released the blade and set it on the floor beside her. "You're here. I'm not as scared when you're here."

She lifted her hand and pressed her palm against his chest. Right over his suddenly stuttering heart. The heat of her touch zoomed through him, from head right down to his toes, hovering slightly around his core before settling. He squeezed his eyes shut and willed the flame of attraction away. Wanting her wasn't an option. Not now. Not when she didn't know who she was. Not when she had no control over any aspect of her life.

Other than choosing to stay with him.

"We're going to get you through this, Jane." If her hand remained on his chest, he knew she'd brand him for life. He lifted her fingers lightly in his and pressed his lips to the back of her knuckles. "We're going to find out who you are and what happened. But we'll do it when you're ready. When you feel strong enough. Does that sound like a deal you can make?"

She nodded, tilting her head far enough back that he could see the confusion in her eyes. Confusion he was willing to embrace far more easily than the fear that had hovered moments before.

"What if you're right?" she whispered.

"About what?"

"What if you're right that whoever attacked me did so because of who I am. Maybe I shouldn't try to find out. Maybe not getting my memory back is the only way to stop it from happening again."

Leo's chest constricted. He wasn't sure he'd ever seen anyone look so lost before.

"I think letting fear rule your life is never a good way to live. It's not living, Jane. It's surrendering. And from what I've seen of you, I don't think surrender is part of who you are. You're a fighter." He caught her chin in his fingers. "You fought your way out of that shed. You fought your way through the woods. You fought your way here. And now—"

"And now I have you to help me fight."

And then it happened. The fear, that despair and terror that radiated through the room vanished.

"And now you have me." He clicked his tongue for Ollie to move, and Leo got to his feet. He stretched out his hand and waited for her to take it. "We're in this together, Jane. Until you get your life back, I'll be right by your side."

Until you get your life back.

Almost a week later, Leo's words still echoed in her mind.

The ancient mattress creaked as Jane rolled onto her side. The days were folding in on themselves. She was so bored. Every day that passed, it seemed as if she moved from her bedroom to the kitchen to the living room, then back to the bedroom. The same routine, the same TV shows. The same books staring back at her from the bookcases in the living room. Even Ollie was getting restless, casting forlorn looks at the doors as if hoping for escape.

Escape. She plucked at the blanket. Her headaches had eased. For the most part. The bruises, which were still visible and angry looking, had stopped aching. She could almost forget they were there unless she looked. But it was the fear that was hardest to shake. The overwhelming sensation that something horrible was going to happen the second she stepped foot outside this house. Of course, maybe that feeling would go away if she could just remember something, anything, about her life before she'd come to in that shed.

And then there was Leo. Poor, handsome, concerned Leo was running himself ragged between all the ranch chores and coming back to check on her. If she had to guess, he barely had the energy to push her toward going to the police, but in that she was adamant. She knew, somehow she *knew*, going anywhere near the cops was only going to make things worse. Which meant something had to change.

The warm Colorado morning stole the air from the room, but she'd refrained from opening the window. Much as she longed for a breeze, tempering her fear had gone only so far. A ceiling fan whirred, attempting to keep the air moving at least, but the T-shirt she wore was sticking to her and the blankets had long been discarded.

She wasn't sure of the time. The utter darkness of the night had passed, so she assumed it was nearing dawn.

Jane curled her fingers into the pillow under her head and reminded herself of what she did every morning: she was alive.

That was all that mattered.

Until you get your life back, I'll be right by your side.

Jane's lips curved into a secret smile. Even if her memory had been intact she'd wonder if she'd ever heard anything more…perfect. She needed something to be perfect. Everything else was just a total blank.

Beyond the closed door of her room, she heard Leo in the kitchen, puttering around. Speaking to Ollie in a low voice. Jane's smile widened. The dog had spent a good long time deciding where he preferred to spend his nights. At times she woke up and found the dog stretched out in her doorway, his attention rapt when she looked at him. Her heart had claimed the German shepherd for good at that concerned look in his eyes. He was as good and kind as his master.

Good and kind. She let out a breath she felt like she'd been holding since Leo had found her huddling in his grandfather's study. The way he held her, comforted her. Protected her. Even as she thought about it, a shiver of irritation slid over her as she questioned her independence, that she was so willing to rely on someone, a man, to take care of her. But that wasn't what he was doing.

Well. She rolled onto her back. It wasn't *all* he was doing. Every word he spoke, every action he took, it was clear he was giving her the choice as to what came next. From how he touched her to how far she was willing to go to discover who she really was.

This morning, the pain in her head was back. Sharp, pounding away at her like a pesky gremlin rattling around in her skull. She knew the headaches and pain concerned Leo. She saw it on his face at dinnertime while they ate overcooked pasta or burnt chicken. He'd actually laughed last night—that amazing, eye-lighting laugh of his—when she'd declared his attempt at pot roast the best meal she'd ever eaten.

"Of course it is," he teased. "It's one of the few you remember."

Her stomach growled now, triggered no doubt by the aroma of fresh-brewed coffee filtering through the air. No need lazing around in bed when she couldn't sleep. She'd only drive herself more crazy than she already felt. She got up, pulled open the door and stepped into the dimly lit kitchen.

"I'm sorry if I woke you." Leo looked up from the bowl of food he was fixing for Ollie.

"I was already awake. Couldn't sleep. Too hot." She fanned herself and tried to ignore the flare of desire that exploded in his eyes before he refocused on his dog. Interesting. So she hadn't imagined that spark of attraction she'd caught on occasion. A tiny thrill surged through her only to be doused by Leo turning his back on her. "You're up early." Now that she was near a clock she could see it was barely four thirty in the morning. Normally she didn't get up until after seven, by which time Leo was back from his first round of chores.

"Always am." He tossed her a grin before ducking into the open refrigerator. "Ranch work starts before sunup and I want to make sure... Oh." He turned and found her right behind him. He blinked. "Good morning." Just seeing her startled him out of his morning routine.

"Hi." She clasped her hands behind her back. "Can I help?"

"Pretty straightforward, actually. But, yeah, sure. Bagels okay for breakfast?"

"Sounds good to me." She retrieved two from the hand-carved bread box, sliced them and stuck them in the toaster. "But I wasn't just talking about breakfast." If she was going to face her fear of going outside, might as well go all in. "I meant with the ranch."

"You want to help me around the ranch?"

Jane couldn't imagine being more entertained than she was by Leo's nervous discomfort. "Sure. It has to be a time suck, coming back here to check on me, and you need to get a lot of stuff done. So unless there's someone else out there to help you…" She trailed off, remembering the man she'd seen on horseback. "There isn't anyone else around, is there?" she choked out.

"Not for another few weeks." As if understanding what she meant, he stopped cutting up Ollie's chicken and looked at her. "You're still thinking about whoever you saw that first day."

"On horseback. On the far hill." She'd have pointed, but the darkness obscured the view. "No details, but seeing him was enough to… Well, you saw what seeing him did to me." The memory alone made her stomach clench.

"Neighbors pass through all the time. Might have been Trapper." At her blank expression, he continued.

"Trapper's been living in this area going on about thirty years now. He used to take on odd jobs around the place for my grandfather. We've always just let him wander through when he wants. He usually turns up around this time of year."

"Where does he live?" Jane searched the refrigerator, came up with cream cheese, but chose butter and his grandmother's jam for herself.

"Oh, out and about. He doesn't have a home per se. Just moves around from site to site. Sometimes down by the river. Other times out by the highway. Never gets too close to civilization. Grandma and Grandpa always kept him stocked with food, as do others in the area. He's good people, Jane. You don't have to be scared of him."

She gnawed on her lip. These days she was scared even of the idea of anyone other than Leo.

"I was actually thinking about asking him to stay close to the place for the next few weeks," Leo continued. "You know. An extra pair of eyes couldn't hurt. Even now."

Jane's hand froze before she could pluck the crispy bagels free of the toaster. So she wasn't the only one worried. "You mean in case whoever took me shows up."

"Yes." That he didn't hesitate told her a lot about the kind of man he was. Honest. Reliable. Protective. "Plus I'm going to need some extra help with the herd now that you're here. There's always something that needs fixing on a ranch, but the herd also needs tending and I've got horses to care for, too."

"What, no chickens?" Jane teased. "I thought all ranches had chickens."

"We did have some. Neighbors took them after my grandmother passed. Which was okay since I couldn't get back here right away. Getting new ones is on my list of things to do."

Intrigued, Jane got plates and watched as Leo set Ollie's bowl of chicken and rice in a designated spot at the end of the counter. The dog sat there, patiently, waiting for Leo to give the okay. In the blink of an eye Ollie's face was in the bowl, gobbling up every morsel.

"What else is on your list?" Jane joined him at the table, wincing as she curled her leg under her. It really was going to be a while before she could move without hurting again.

"You don't even want to know." Leo poured a cup of coffee for both of them and even remembered how she took it. "I'm in a bit of a wait and see mode right now. Trying to decide how to move the ranch forward."

"Is that what your grandfather would have wanted?"

"Absolutely. You make a good bagel." There was that smile again. Jane's heart softened in her chest. "He had dreams of expanding the herd to one of the largest in the area. Of course he was thinking of taking them to market, but I'd suggested looking at other options."

"Which are?"

"You don't really care, do you? This can't be interesting at all to you."

"Why not?" Jane frowned. She had been interested. She wanted to know all about Leo and his family and his business. Not only because she cared but because, honestly, what else did she have to think about other than being kidnapped and tied up in a shed?

Leo shrugged. "You just don't strike me as the rancher type. Remember?"

"Because my nails were polished and my clothes were designer?" Something similar to offense coiled through her. "That's a bit rude and more than a bit condescending. Why can't I be interested in your life when you saved mine?"

"You saved yourself," Leo argued good-naturedly. Was there anything that ticked him off? "But if you really do want to know." He polished off his bagel and wiped his mouth. "Sure. Why don't you come with me today? I'll show you the ins and outs. I won't be moving the herd again until tomorrow, so it's a good day."

"And you can also keep an eye on me, right?"

Another shrug. "Not going to lie. It'll be easier than coming back here every few hours. I'll get my work done faster and when I am done, I can introduce you to the stars of the ranch."

"What stars would those be?"

"If I told you that, it wouldn't be a surprise. Finish up. I'll give you twenty minutes to get dressed. If you're up to it, that is."

"I might not know my name, but I do know one thing. I'm always up for a challenge."

As his truck rumbled over the rocky and pitted road of his ranch, Leo glanced over at Jane. He'd done pretty well choosing the right-size jeans for her. Maybe too well given the way they hugged her curves like well-worn leather. The lightweight yellow plaid button-down shirt strained ever so slightly in that special area right between her full breasts. That spot that acted as a bull's-eye for most straight, red-blooded males. Brand-new white sneakers covered her feet—feet she'd insisted on tending to herself this morning. Those shoes wouldn't be white for long, not with the way she was hopping out to open and close gates for him during the pasture check.

He'd been right about one thing. Having her with him did mean the morning went quicker, or at least the chores did.

"You're staring again." Jane didn't even look at him as she spoke, instead keeping her eyes pinned to the expansive land stretching out around them. "I'm not going to break, Leo. I can handle getting in and out of a truck."

"I know you can. How's your head?" It hadn't escaped his notice this morning that she'd never mentioned headaches or how she'd slept. He should have asked, but he didn't want to intrude too much into her personal space. After their close encounter in his grandfather's study, he'd come to the conclusion that distance, emotional and physical, was probably his best course of action.

Life was complicated enough without getting involved with a woman without a past. A woman who could, at the very most, be married with children and at the very least, be in a relationship. A woman like her didn't live a solitary life. It couldn't matter that she'd taken up permanent residence in his thoughts. Or that he wondered what it would be like to kiss her. Really kiss her.

Kiss her until neither of them could stop.

Kiss her until he'd explored every perfect inch of her.

His hands tightened on the steering wheel. Except he had to stop. He had to stop thinking about Jane in any way other than a woman who needed his help. Not only because it was the right thing to do, but any intimacy between them would be based on a lie.

"Jane?" he asked when she didn't answer his question the first time. "Your head?"

"It's on my shoulders where it belongs." She pushed the sunglasses higher up on her nose as if in defiance. "You didn't finish telling me what other plans you have for the herd. What else can you do with cattle other than sell them off for food?"

Boy, she was willing to talk about anything other than her headache, which he knew she had because she kept pulling the brim of his grandmother's old hat lower over her eyes. Well, she asked for it.

"Depends on what you want to do. There's breeding or milk production. Or there's the option of selling them to other ranches for their own purposes."

"What have you been doing?"

"Raising them for market." Leo set his jaw. "Beef prices aren't what they used to be. Dealing with ranching or farming these days is a risky business. I need to keep looking ahead if I'm going to keep this place going. Which is why I'm considering adding stud services. If that were to take off, I could change over completely. Would mean a different type of overhead, but I think it's doable."

"Can you? Keep the ranch going?"

"Is that your way of asking how much money I have?"

Ah, that did the trick. Leo grinned as Jane snapped her head around to glare at him. "It most certainly is not."

There was something in her voice, not haughty exactly, but definitely upper class. "I'm teasing you, Jane." And confirming something he'd suspected from the first time he saw her in the barn. She was *not* a country girl.

"My grandparents made a very good living off this place. It's been successful for a number of years and in no danger of going under even with the fluctuating market. Aside from annual taxes, I own it free and clear. As for myself…" He shrugged. "Most of the money I earned working up north is invested. I don't need a lot to live on. Don't have a lot of expenses. What I do have, I plan to use with this place. Make it even more than it is. Not a lot more. Just…"

"Just filling in your grandparents' dreams?" Jane shifted and leaned back against the door. Now she was the one who was staring. "That's quite lovely, Leo."

"Why, thank you, Jane." He was about to go on, but something caught his eye. He stopped the truck and climbed out. "Stay here."

"What? Why?" She was flipping her head back and forth as if to look in every direction at once. "Do you see something?"

"Runaway calf." Leo laid his hand on her arm for a brief moment. "I'm sorry. I should have said. It's nothing to worry about. Just a lost baby. Odd. I can't remember the last time that happened."

"I thought you counted the herd back at the feeding?" As if she hadn't heard his order to stay in the truck, she hopped out.

"Doesn't mean I was right." Whether he wanted to admit it or not, Jane was a distraction. Bringing her with him might have been a mistake. But leaving her behind…

He didn't relish the idea of walking in and finding her in the throes of another panic attack.

"Where…? Oh, there she is! I see her."

"Wait, Jane! Don't—" Leo found he couldn't move as he watched Jane dart away from the truck and head straight for the runaway calf. "She has no idea what she's doing, does she, Ollie?" The dog barked and rolled his eyes. "You want to go help her?"

Ollie sighed and dropped out of the truck beside Leo.

"One little calf isn't going to hurt her." At least, Leo hoped that was the case. Still, there was a sight to behold—Jane, in her brand-spanking new jeans and shirt, her glowing white feet darting across the field, holding on to her hat as her long red braid swung almost all the way down her spine. "Beautiful," Leo whispered, then whistled for Ollie to follow.

"You could have told me about the mud puddles," Jane grumbled when they were on their way back to the house. "I look like I've been wrestling with pigs." All she wanted was a shower and a change of clothes. And maybe for Leo to stop laughing at her.

"Pigs. Now, there's something the ranch might need."

"I was doing okay before you tried to help." At least, she thought she had. It might have been better if she'd had a rope with which to guide the animal back. How hard could it be to wrangle a solitary calf that was simply looking for its mother? A lot more difficult than she'd ever anticipated, that was for sure.

It was now an hour later, and after returning the calf to the herd, Leo had declared the day a success.

Jane was just glad to declare it *over*. She scrubbed a hand over her face. Leo sputtered with laughter again. "What?"

"Nothing. You look…as you would say, lovely." He chucked a finger under her chin and motioned toward the visor mirror.

Jane stared back at her mud-caked face and groaned. "You were right." She sagged back in her seat. "I'm not a country girl."

"Darlin', you've never looked more country in all the time I've known you."

Darlin'. My, how she liked the sound of that. She hid her smile as she hugged Ollie, but even the dog seemed put off by her extra coating of sludge. "Does this mean I get the surprise?"

"I'm saving that for tomorrow. You've had a big day. Don't want you passing out on me in this heat."

"What heat?" Jane asked with an innocent blink of her eyes. It was just noon, and the sun was pounding down on them with all the strength of a supernova.

Glancing at Leo, she bit her lip. Did he have any idea how handsome he looked, the sun reflecting off that face of his, droplets of sweat glistening. Not for the first time she had to stop herself from taking her thoughts too far. Attraction was one thing. Following through with it, that was going to take some planning on her part.

She'd learned enough about Leo to know an honorable man like him wouldn't make the first move. Not with a woman who didn't have a clue of who she was. That he wouldn't made him all the more appealing to her.

Jane fanned herself, the very mention of the temperature making her hot. What was it? Early August? Being baked by the sun certainly made her long for a snow-kissed Colorado winter. She'd bet this place was glorious coated in snow that sparkled beneath the sunshine. A longing pinged deep inside her. Christmas on the ranch. Christmas with Leo. Didn't that just sound... perfect.

Her sigh was cut off by a glint of light in the distance. There, by the house. Or were her eyes playing tricks on her? She became muzzy-headed, and she closed her eyes as the red and blue lights took over again. The footsteps pounded in her head. Coming closer. Reflections exploded, glass in the sunlight. No. Not glass. A window. Her window. A window she couldn't get closed...

"Jane?" Leo's hand landed on her arm and she jumped.

"What?" Bile rose in her throat, but she swallowed hard, determined not to lose control again. She wouldn't cower. She wouldn't surrender. She would fight. And keep fighting until whatever life she'd left behind was clear again.

"It's okay. It's Trapper. That's his horse, Spectacle. All those mirrors are part of Trap's warning system."

"Warning who?" Jane tried to joke. She must have been too out of it yesterday to notice them. "Him or us?"

"Yes." Leo's response didn't make her feel any better. "You want to stay in the truck?" He pulled to a stop between the house and the stable.

Yes! She didn't want to see anyone. Meet anyone. She didn't want to leave the protective bubble she'd found with Leo, but as he reminded her yesterday, life wasn't going to stop. Not for any of them. "No."

She might have imagined the approving glance he shot her. "Afternoon, Trap." Leo's door creaked as he slammed it shut. "Passing through?"

Jane dropped cautiously to the ground, gently pushing the door closed after Ollie followed her out. It was difficult to tell who was older—Trapper or his horse. Both displayed that weathered, bedraggled look she supposed one got when living in the elements, but she also noticed a resilience and sheer inner strength, too. Trapper turned cautious and stunning blue eyes on her. Eyes that crinkled with decades along the edges as he straightened and brushed off the front of the button-down shirt he wore beneath a midlength jacket. Jane began to sweat again just looking at him.

"Hoping you can help." Trapper gestured to his horse. "Something odd's going on with her front hoof.

Thought I'd stop in and use the stable for a bit. Is Gwen around?"

"Afraid not." Leo patted the old man on the arm as he passed before approaching Spectacle with an affectionate stroke. "Hey, girl. You feeling poorly?"

Jane stood away from them, arms crossed over her chest, fascinated, but not surprised at Leo's reaction to an unexpected visitor. After all, he'd taken her in, hadn't he?

"Afternoon, ma'am." Trapper tipped his gray, beat-up Stetson and cleared his throat. "John McHugh Trapper. Pleasure to meet you."

"Hello." Jane couldn't help but smile back at the twinkle in the old man's eyes. Most of his face was obscured by facial hair. Not quite a beard, but he was trying. He didn't stand as tall as Leo; she often had to tilt her chin up to meet his eyes. Where Leo was muscular and toned, Trapper was on the thin side. Scrappy. The word almost made her giggle. "I'm Jane. It's nice to meet you."

"You, um, visiting?" Trapper's eyes skimmed her up and down, and when his lips twitched she realized why. She was caked, head to toe, in mud.

"For a while, yes. Leo's been, um, showing me the land." She could all but hear the dried mud crunch under her folded arms.

"You need good shoes for that. Boots. Not those things on your feet." Trapper's brows knit. "What kind of idjit—"

"The selection wasn't vast," Leo said. "Looks like Spectacle here's got a sticker caught under her shoe.

Got an infection running. Not too bad, but needs to be treated." Leo glanced at Trapper and tilted up his hat. "I've got some antibiotics from Duke's last go-around. Can replace this shoe and keep her comfortable. If you're good with staying a few days." His gaze shifted to Jane, who nodded without hesitation.

Maybe Leo's land was her safety zone, or maybe it was the fact that Ollie was as excited to see Trapper as he welcomed his breakfast. Either way, she didn't find herself concerned about the old codger.

"Hmm." Trapper looked between the two of them before going over to his horse and running a hand down the side of her neck. "Wouldn't want to intrude."

"You wouldn't be intruding," Jane said before Leo could explain.

"Truth be told—" Trapper ran a hand across his beard hard enough for Jane to hear the whiskers scrape against his palm "—would be nice to hunker down in that bunkhouse of yours."

"Might need a bit of tidying up, but it's yours for as long as you'd like." Leo didn't have to explain the relief Jane heard in his voice.

"I won't be a lollygagging layabout," Trapper insisted. "I'll do my part around here. You just point and I'll get to hopping."

"I'll come up with a list," Leo assured him. "How about I help you unload and get settled. Jane, did you want to go take that shower?"

She might be clueless about some things, but not about the subtle hint he wanted to talk to Trapper alone.

"I do indeed. I can toss together some lunch after. About an hour?"

"Perfect." Leo's smile didn't quite reach his eyes. "Thank you."

"Okay. Come on, Ollie. Keep me company." She patted her leg as had become second nature, and stopped outside the back door long enough to toe off her shoes. Shoes she suspected were done for after one day. Only when she was in the kitchen and glancing out the window did she wonder, and worry about, what Leo and Trapper were about to discuss.

"Bet she's a pretty thing. Under all that mud." Trapper turned his fuzzy grin on Leo, who found himself chuckling. "She, ah, a new friend?"

"Something like that." Leo motioned for the other man to start unloading Spectacle, beginning with the various mirrors and reflective objects looped onto the saddle. He accepted pile after pile of items—saddlebag, tote, reusable grocery bags—and was topped off with a makeshift fishing line and reel, and a rusted metal toolbox filled, Leo recalled, with intricate lures and tackles. "Bunkhouse hasn't been touched since Buck retired. Hate to admit it, but I don't think I've been in there since he left."

"Doesn't matter to me as long as it has a bed and a roof. Gettin' a bit on in years to be crawling around on the ground."

Trapper had his own armload of…stuff as they wound their way around the back of the stable to the structure beyond. Almost as large as the farmhouse, the single-story building had gone up more than twenty years ago, when the ranch was running at peak capacity. Built to house up to twenty ranch hands, the structure was simply organized with a galley-style kitchen near the front, a long table with benches and generous sleeping partitions.

After choosing the room closest to the kitchen, Trapper deposited his stuff and came out to retrieve the items Leo set on the table. "You going to tell me why you lied about Spectacle back there? I saw you pop those pebbles out from under her shoe and readjust it."

Leo cringed. "Yeah, thanks for not letting on. Were you by any chance up on the ridgeline earlier this week?"

"Me? Nah. Was still on the other side of that monstrosity they call a town." Trapper's aversion to the downtown area was a local inside joke. One of the longest residents of these parts, Trapper went out of his way to avoid most anything to do with, well, people and their commercializing ways. "Why? You got rustlers?"

"No." Leo took a seat while Trapper finished putting his belongings away. One thing he'd learned a long time ago was the old man liked to be his own man. Agreeing to the offer of a room was about as far as he'd go when it came to accepting help. "No rustlers. Jane said she saw someone riding around. Spooked her a bit."

Trapper stopped inside the door to his room and narrowed his eyes. "Your girl in there looks spooked now. You want to tell me who she is?"

If only I could. "I thought maybe you might know." Short of gossip central in town, Trapper was as good as it got when it came to information about Roaring Springs.

"Hard to tell under all that mud. You know me, Leo. I don't pay no one no mind, and they don't pay me. That's the way I like it."

"I do know that. So that wasn't you she saw." So not the answer he'd been wanting. He hadn't been lying this morning when he said sometimes neighbors just cut through, but the truth was, it didn't happen that often.

"That why you want me to stick around?" Trapper wandered back into the kitchen. "You worried about your girl?"

"Stop calling her my girl. She's just staying here for a while. She had an accident. Hit her head. She's... scared." Leo struggled against the truth. He'd only promised Jane he wouldn't go to the police. He hadn't said anything about not confiding in a friend about her situation. Besides, Trapper was gold with confidences. "She's all alone and doesn't remember who she is."

"You mean she's got amnesia?" Trapper's eyes went wide as he dropped onto the bench across from Leo. "I thought that only happened in books. It's a real thing?"

"Apparently so."

"You don't think she's faking?"

"No, I don't think she's..." The very idea was offensive. "She's been traumatized. Believe me. There's no faking how she was when I found her. Someone abducted her and left her tied up in some abandoned shed somewhere."

"That's just plain evil. You call the sheriff?"

"No." And that decision weighed more heavily on

him every day. Was Jane in the right frame of mind to know what was best? He wasn't convinced. Especially now that he knew a killer was on the loose. What if she had been one of the lucky ones to get away? "Jane doesn't want me to." Honestly, if he didn't think she'd bolt, he'd reconsider his promise.

But what if she was right? What if whoever took her was looking to reclaim her? He'd do whatever he could to protect her, but if she could help the authorities catch the man responsible for the killings…

"You have any idea where she was before?" Trapper asked.

"Not really. I thought about maybe getting out a map and having her look at it with me, just to see if anything seemed familiar. It could just take one thing to snap everything into place."

"Could."

"You don't sound convinced."

"Leo." Trapper removed his hat and ran gnarled fingers through his too-long hair. "I've been on this earth a long time. Nothing one human being can do to another that would surprise me. No map is going to give you the answers you're looking for." He pinned him with a hard stare. "What's really going on here? I can understand why your Jane might be spooked, but why are you?"

"Who said I am? And stop calling her *my* Jane." He liked the sound of that far too much.

"I've known you since you were stumbling around here in your diaper, Leo Isaac Slattery. I know when you've got something on your mind. Same look as your daddy and your grandfather had. It's there." He circled a finger in front of Leo's face even as a pang of longing and grief swept over Leo. As much as he liked having Trapper around, he still missed his grandfather. And his father. Sometimes so much he ached. It wasn't easy going through the world alone. But he hadn't been. Not for a few weeks. Not since Jane had arrived. "So spit it out already before your girl sees it."

At this point he really didn't have a choice, did he? "Protestations about not knowing what's going on around town aside," Leo began and ignored the flash of irritation in Trap's ever-searching eyes, "what have you heard about this Avalanche Killer? About the victims up on the mountain?"

"Up near The Lodge, you mean," Trapper spat.

Leo sighed. He should have known Trapper's lifelong resentment of all things Colton would rear up. "This isn't about the Coltons, Trap. Please. If you've heard anything—"

"Not about the Coltons. Bah!" Trapper let loose with a string of expletives that would have had Leo's grandmother reaching for a bar of soap. "The first body they found, they thought Wyatt Colton himself was responsible. Sheriff even recused himself for potential bias. Don't tell me the Coltons aren't involved in this Avalanche Killer mess. They're in it up to their greedy little eyeballs."

"Can you please just focus on the details for now and tell me what you know?" Clearly, it was time to put in yet another call to the county to find out when he would have better internet access and thus civilization would be making it down the road to his land.

Every time he thought about calling, it was either too late or a weekend. That said, a quick online search could have saved him this entire conversation. "Please, Trapper. For Jane."

Trapper blinked, as if connecting his invitation to stay and Leo's request for information. "You thinking that poor girl may have been his next intended victim?"

"I don't know what I'm thinking." But the idea had followed him home from town yesterday. And haunted him every second he'd tried to sleep last night. He'd lost track of the number of times he'd gotten up to check on her, just to convince himself she hadn't been stolen away in the night. "All I know is that she turned up in my barn, bruised, battered and without any memory of who she is. Then when I go into town, I hear talk of a serial killer stalking Roaring Springs. I might not be a Rhodes Scholar, but even I can see when things add up."

"Or don't add up, depending on the case. Okay." Trapper nodded. "I see what you're thinking. What did Jane say when you told her?"

"Ah, nothing." Leo's gaze skittered to the floor. Maybe he needed to run a broom through this place.

"Land's sake, what kind of idjit are you?" Trapper slapped his hand on the table. "You're telling me you think that girl might have been attacked by a psycho and you aren't telling her? What are you going to do, keep her locked up on the ranch until they catch him?"

"Maybe I am." Leo shrugged. "Or at least until her memory comes back."

"And if her memory includes being assaulted by this

monster? And she finds out you knew or suspected? Leo, I never took you for an i—"

"Stop with the name-calling." Leo was doing enough of that himself. "Look, Trap. You have the best ears in Roaring Springs. And the best eyes. Nothing gets past you. And if you don't have any details about this case, then the only thing I have left to ask you is to stay here, on the ranch, and help me keep an eye on her. I don't like the idea of leaving her alone for long stretches of time."

"So take her with you." Trapper cackled. "Obviously she has a talent for ranch work. What did she do? Try to feed the cows by hand?"

"She tried to catch a runaway calf on her own." The memory of that was going to keep him laughing for a long time to come.

Trapper's mouth snapped shut. "Oh. Well." He cleared his throat. "Isn't that just the dumbest and sweetest thing I've ever heard. You hiring me as her bodyguard, then?" Trapper's frail chest puffed out like a pigeon on bread crumb duty.

"More like keep her busy. I can't keep being distracted. Not if I'm going to bring that herd to market next month in time to invest in some new prospects."

"What about her memory? You want me to keep poking at that? Or would you prefer she not remember?"

"What kind of question is that?" Leo wasn't the type of man who snapped at accusations. Unless of course they landed a bit too close to home. "Of course I want her to remember who she is. She has a life, Trap. Somewhere, she has a life." One that didn't include him. And the sooner he came to accept that, the better. Which meant it was time to put some distance between him and Jane. And this guy was the perfect person to do that. "Let's get Spectacle settled into her stall, shall we?"

"Oh, yes, let's." Trapper rolled his eyes, but when they stood, he added, "I'll do what I can to help with your Jane, Leo. But you need to decide what it is you really want. And given all the goings-on in Roaring Springs, I suggest you figure that out sooner than later."

Chapter 5

"Either I was starving or you, Leo Slattery, are getting better in the cooking department." Trapper dragged the last slice of white bread around the rim of his dinner plate before he pushed it away. "Did you know this boy here couldn't boil water before he left for the great north?"

"Steak and baked potatoes aren't exactly rocket science," Leo said. "Jane? What's wrong? Your head bothering you again?"

"What?" She blinked and jerked in her chair, as if just noticing she was rubbing her fingers hard against her temple. "Oh, yeah. I guess it is." The beam from the ceiling light was making her wish she was wearing sunglasses. "Sorry. Did I miss something?"

"You missed your dinner." Trapper pointed at her

half-full plate. "You're going to need your strength out here. You're too skinny, especially for ranch life. Eat up."

Jane flicked her fork under a leaf of lettuce. "I guess I'm not that hungry. I probably ate too much at lunch." She almost reached for the chai tea she'd made from a container she found in the back of a cabinet, but the smell of cloves was making her feel slightly sick.

"You're just a bit of a thing," Trapper scoffed. "Not sure you can eat too much. Protein. That's what you need, girlie. Lots of protein. Especially if you're going to be helping me with the horses starting tomorrow."

"I, uh, what?" She looked at Leo, who seemed as surprised as her.

"That was actually going to be your surprise, meeting the horses, but it looks as if I got bypassed."

"We've got four of them, you know, five now with Spectacle, who needs special care." Trapper went on as if neither of them had spoken. "I think this young man's been neglecting them with all the work he's got going on around this place. What with Gwen being away and all. Going to be up to you and me."

"Okay." Jane frowned, recalling Leo had told her about Gwen's work on the ranch with the horses. Why did she feel as if she'd been dropped off the edge of the horizon? "I don't know how much I know about horses." She didn't know much about anything, near as she could tell.

"What you don't know, I'll teach you. Been tending these horses since before I could walk. It's in my blood. Time to get it into yours. Which means you need to eat. Leo, you have anything to take the edge off my sweet tooth?"

"I picked up a peach pie at M&P yesterday. And there's ice cream in the freezer. Jane?" He gave her a concerned look. "You sure you're okay? You're not due for another pill, are you?"

Was she? She'd lost track. "I don't think so. And I'm sorry. I can't eat anything more." Her stomach was rolling. "I think maybe I did too much today?"

"Sliding around in the mud can be exhausting," Leo teased, but she didn't have the energy to laugh. Although she wanted to. "Maybe you should go to bed."

"Yeah." She pushed up from her chair and tried to ignore the way her head spun. The pounding was worse than it had been when she'd first awoken in the shed. "Yeah, I think I will. Dinner was good, Leo. Thank you for it. For everything."

"Hey." He caught her arm when she stumbled. "Hey, I don't like this." He got to his feet and moved in, pressing his hand flat against the side of her head. "If this gets worse you need to tell me. We agreed, remember? I know you don't want to go to a doctor, but that might not be your decision any longer."

Logically, she knew he was right. But she couldn't shake the feeling that once she stepped foot off his land, once she took a step into the real world, everything was going to change.

She lifted her chin to look into Leo's worried eyes. "Let me see how I do tonight, okay? If I still have the headache in the morning, I'll let you take me into town."

The very idea made her want to throw up what little food she'd eaten.

"You'll tell me the truth, yeah?" He stroked her cheek with his thumb. She shivered, and for the first time since Trapper had arrived, she wished she and Leo were alone. She felt so good around him—safe. Protected. Confident. Which unnerved her to the quick. How could she feel these things when she didn't know who she was or where she came from? "Jane?"

"I'll tell you the truth."

"And we'll take care of them horses," Trapper called over a plate filled with peach pie. "You sleep well, girlie. And feel better."

"Thank you, Trapper. I will." Still she didn't move. Couldn't move. Not with Leo's dark, searching gaze sliding over her like silk. "I'll be okay." She wrapped her hand around his wrist and squeezed. "I'll see you in the morning."

She stepped back, trying to reconcile how lost she felt when he let go of her. Every step she took back to her room was deliberate, careful. When she closed the door behind her, she dropped to the floor, curling her legs in tight and resting her head on her knees. She heard Ollie scratching at the door, then Leo's gentle call to the dog to leave her be. Jane let out a long breath, closing her eyes against the darkness of the room even as the stabbing pain settled into a dull, aching throb.

Was she prone to migraines? She didn't think so, since she realized she didn't know anything about them. When it came to cooking or the washing machine or other tasks around the house or even different topics of conversation, she knew enough to hold her own. But Leo was right. If these headaches kept up, she wasn't going to have a choice but to go to the doctor.

She pushed to her feet, feeling her way over to the bed, wondering about this strange, empty feeling she had in the pit of her stomach. She almost felt as if…as if she wasn't completely herself, as if part of her was missing or lost. "Of course you're lost," she muttered as she pulled off her T-shirt, shimmied out of her jeans and dropped into bed in her underwear, huddling under the blankets as she shivered against a sudden cold.

Cold. In the middle of a Colorado summer. It made as much sense as a woman who couldn't remember her name. *My name*, Jane thought. *What's my name…?*

And she dropped into sleep.

Glass shattered, exploding in and around her, showering her arms and face with razor-sharp shards. Jane screamed and dived to the side, the gearshift of her car digging into her ribs as she tried to disengage her seat belt.

The driver's-side door was ripped open. A figure, dark, in shadows, black against the near-midnight sky, reached in. Clawlike hands grabbed for her. Long fingers scraped into her arms as she kicked out, hard. She wasn't aiming for his knee, but that's where she hit, the needle-sharp heel of her pump causing enough damage to shove him off balance.

Cool air brushed against her now bare foot; her shoe had fallen off, but she couldn't stop now. She kicked off the other one and, while the shadowed assailant got his

*bearings, she felt nails break as she pushed the button
again on her seat belt. When the latch broke free, she
took a deep breath and arched for the passenger door.
She'd just gotten it open and was scrambling for escape
when a hand locked around her bare ankle.*

Jane screamed. A throat-scorching, lung-burning
scream that echoed into the night.

"Jane!"

She screamed again, scrambling up in bed, hugging
the blankets against her as she braced herself against
the headboard. Light streamed in through the hall, spot-
lighting Leo as he stood in the doorway.

"It's all right," she said shakily as she pressed a hand
against her face and found her cheeks damp. "I'm all
right. Bad dream." *Really, really bad dream.*

"You're *not* all right." Leo left the door open and approached the bed. "I think you might have woken the
dead with that scream of yours."

He was trying to make jokes again, trying to lighten
the mood, but it was useless. Not when all she could
see, all she could *feel*, was that monster—that man's
hand locked around her ankle. She kicked her leg free
of the blankets, pulled it in so she could touch the still
faintly bruised skin.

"What is it?" Leo came closer, leaned over to click
on the bedside table lamp.

She blinked into the dim light, saw him standing
there in nothing but a pair of plaid pajama bottoms.
She'd thought him beautiful fully clothed. Now, staring at the well-developed muscles of his chest, the way
his toned, sculpted body tapered down to the tempting

sight of chiseled hip bones…it was all she could do not to reach out and touch him. If only to prove he was real.

"Jane? Did you remember something?" He sat on the edge of her bed. Not in a particularly comforting way. In fact, he seemed determined to keep some distance between them. Not at all like he'd enveloped her in his grandfather's study the other day. The way she wanted him to envelop her now. "Jane?"

"I…don't know. It was all shadows and night. I was in a car. My car. He broke the window to get to me. Wrenched the door open. I tried to get away but the seat belt…" She trailed off, lifted the blankets off her bare stomach and stared down at the red-turned-pink welts marring her skin.

"What the… Jane, why didn't you say anything about these?" He was back on his feet, turned on the overhead light and returned to the bed to examine the bruising. His fingers brushed featherlight over her skin. Jane shivered. And not from the cold. She felt so good when he touched her. "You could have broken or bruised a rib."

"It's not that bad," she argued. But now she knew where the marks came from. She stretched out her ankle where the shadows of finger impressions had formed over the past day. "It doesn't hurt that much."

"It hurts me," Leo whispered. "Jane, darlin', why didn't you say anything?"

"Because I didn't know how they got there." She pushed his hand away and tucked herself back into the covers. "But I guess I do now." But the answers, however vague, didn't make her feel any better. If any-

thing, she felt worse. "I don't want to remember, Leo."
She didn't want to ever feel that terror again, that gut-
wrenching fear that continued to surge through her body
even minutes after the dream had ended. "I'm sorry I
woke you."

"You don't owe me an apology, Jane. But you do
need to talk to me. You need to get this out. The more
you do—"

"The more I do, the more real it becomes." She closed
her eyes and turned her head away. "There's nothing
new, Leo. I still don't know my name or where I'm from
or who I belong to. There's nothing except this mind-
numbing terror that only gets worse."

"Okay. So let's talk about that." He started to sit
down, but she held up her hand, unable to look at him.
"Let's talk about going to the police."

"No. I just want to go back to sleep. I just want to
forget all over again."

"This isn't you talking, Jane." But he remained standing. Remained at a distance.

"You don't know that," she choked out. "You don't
know anything about me. I may just be this sniveling
coward afraid to face whatever happened to me out
there."

"I don't believe that. And even if you were, I told you,
we're in this together. We're going to find out who you
are. Remember? I promised you that."

"And what if I don't want to find out?" This wasn't
the first time she'd considered the option. And right
now, it certainly sounded most appealing.

"I don't believe you." Hands planted on his hips, he

stared down at her and for the first time since she'd met him, she realized he saw too much. All the broken parts inside her that she didn't want him to see. "You aren't a coward, Jane. You're a fighter, remember? And whatever it is you have to face down, you're going to do it. And I'm going to be right there with you."

"You say that as if it's your decision." Great. Now she sounded like a whiny five-year-old.

Leo just looked at her. "It's three in the morning, Jane. Do you know what time that is?"

She narrowed her eyes. "Is that a trick question?"

His lips twitched. "Kind of. My father called it the hour of the tiger. When one day fades into the other. When the barrier between what was and what will be is caught, for a thin amount of time. It's when all those thoughts, all those fears, all the insecurities we struggle against during our waking hours come out to play. That's what you're feeling right now, Jane. Which is why I don't believe you when you say you don't want to know what happened to you. You do want to know. You need to know. And so do I." He leaned over and stroked his hand down the side of her face.

For a moment, one breathless, heart-stopping moment, she thought he might kiss her. She held her breath, licked her suddenly dry lips as she saw his face come closer to hers. Anticipation knotted in her stomach. Her hands loosened on the blankets that fell away and exposed the straps of her bra and the swell of her breasts. "Leo," she whispered.

"Starting tomorrow, we leave the fear behind. Both of us. You have to know who you are, Jane. I have to know who you are. If for no other reason than it'll give me permission to kiss you the way you're silently begging me to right now."

She whimpered as he leaned forward. But instead of pressing his lips to hers, he kissed her on the forehead. Chaste. Tender. Gentle.

All the things she didn't want.

"I'll leave the door open," he murmured against her skin. Any response froze behind her lips. "And Ollie." He broke off as the dog hopped up on the bed. "He's been waiting to do that all night. Get some more sleep, Jane. We've got work to do tomorrow."

He left her bedroom without a look back. Jane glanced at the table lamp, then at the dog before she slid back down in bed, Ollie shifting closer to curl himself around her legs.

"If I can't have him, you aren't a bad second choice," she whispered, and reached down to pet the dog. Ollie sighed.

And Jane drifted back to sleep.

"That there is Ginger." Trapper's voice carried a surprising hint of reverence as he introduced Jane to the horses the next morning. "Of the four, well, five including Spectacle, she's the calmest. Takes a lot to rile her up."

"She's stunning." Ginger sniffed the small green apple in Jane's palm before plucking it free to eat. "How old is she?" Jane couldn't stop herself from moving closer and brushing the backs of her fingers against the side of the horse's face. Big black eyes blinked down at her as Ginger turned her head slightly as if to get a better look at Jane. Her silky mane spilled forward and brushed the woman's hand.

"Going on ten." Trapper was bopping around the stable gathering up items and lining them up on a narrow table situated between Ginger and Duke's stalls. "Horses are excellent judges of character. They're like dogs that way. They see who you really are underneath all the pretense and pessimism."

"Are you a pessimist?" Jane joked, unable to tear herself away from Ginger even as she glanced back to where Ollie had taken up guard duty by the door. All of the horses in Leo's care were stunning, and even after a few minutes she could sense distinct personalities. Duke, the largest of the two stallions, had an air of aristocracy or at least leadership about him. Ginger here—Jane couldn't stop stroking her—the calm voice of reason. Then there was Bullet, aptly named, Trapper declared, as the young'un would run as far and as fast as possible given half the chance. Lastly, the smallish black mare who preferred the back corner of her stall had been named Teyla, after one of Leo's favorite TV characters.

"Pessimist? Me?" Trapper cackled. "What do you think? You ever care for horses before?"

"I don't think so." She answered the question so naturally, so automatically, it took her a moment to realize Trapper was testing her.

The old man grunted and shifted a strapped brush toward her, motioned for her to pick it up.

"You don't believe me." She slipped the strap over her hand, gripped the brush with her palm.

"That gentle a touch with no hesitation? You've been around horses at some point. Take my word for it. Go on. Give her neck a good brushing. Both sides. Then we'll bring her out and you can take care of the rest."

Jane bit her cheek, irritated and curious at Trapper's words. Obviously Leo's old friend had no idea what it was like to move through the day with a big blank spot in your brain, as if something she saw, heard or smelled would suddenly fill the gap. It wasn't until she'd fully woken up this morning that she realized she'd been hoping last night's nightmare would have jarred something loose. That somehow she'd open her eyes and her past would have filled itself in.

Instead, she'd lain there, staring up at the ceiling, trying to see beyond the spinning lights, the shadows and the clawed hand gripping her ankle. Rather than memories, she'd pushed out of bed with an odd blanket of fear still draped over her shoulders. A fear she was determined to dislodge one way or the other.

Leo was right. With the morning had come reason. Cowering under the covers and hiding wasn't going to move her life forward. Whatever else she didn't know about herself, instinct told her she was not a woman who let anything other than her own will dictate how her life would go.

"You believe me, don't you, Ginger?" Jane fell into a steady rhythm of brushing as she held the horse's face with her other hand. "If I could remember I would." At least…she thought so.

A few minutes later, Trapper unlatched the stall door and clicked his tongue, gesturing for Jane to lead the horse out. Once the horse stood, secured with cross-ties, in the center aisle, he pointed to its flanks. "Keep going."

Jane's hand was already cramped, but she found something soothing about the brushing. Ginger must have agreed because she barely moved as the soft bristles were pushed through her soft, short coat. Jane's mind cleared. The pressure that had been building in her chest over the last few days eased, and she found herself humming softly as she swept the brush over every inch of her charge. Soon, the minutes faded away and all that mattered was the moment.

A car door slammed outside. "Hello! Anyone here?"

Jane froze, her entire body going tight as she swung around to where Trapper stood. He inclined his head, held out a hand, pressed a finger to his lips. Then he walked out of the stable.

Ginger whinnied and took a step back. Jane moved closer to the horse, then, hearing the low rumble of voices outside, pushed curiosity through the fear. She set the brush down and, as quietly as she could, went to the small square window near the door. Jane stayed out of sight, popping up only enough to peek outside through the bottom corner of the window. The dark SUV that had pulled up in front of the barn was covered in mud from its tires to its sunroof, which nearly obscured the gold-and-silver decal on the front windshield. The tall, muscular figure who was speaking with Trapper looked as cowboy as cowboy could get, from his brown Stetson all the way to his silver-tipped boots. He held a map in his hands and was pointing this way and that.

"Nah, you took a wrong turn down at the highway," Trapper was telling him. "You go back out to this road, take it all the way down and fork off to the right. That'll take you by the Dunhams' place, but they're used to folks cutting through. You'll get to the highway about twenty miles after."

"Great." The man slapped the map against his hand so hard Jane jumped. He looked around, eyes narrowed like laser beams. "This is a lot of land to be running all by yourself. I might be looking to buy in the area. You interested in selling?"

"Nope." Trapper's sharp answer eased the pressure building in Jane's chest.

The visitor shifted his attention to the stable. Jane dropped to the ground, pressed her forehead against her knees and tried to stop shaking. He was just lost, she told herself. Just looking for directions. Nothing more. She squeezed her eyes shut and rocked. *Please let there be nothing more.*

"No discussion, huh?" The man laughed, but Jane didn't think he sounded amused. "I'll be moving on, then. Appreciate the help."

"Sure."

Jane didn't breathe again until the sound of the SUV's engine faded in the distance.

"False alarm. Just some jackass— Jane?" Trapper stopped near Ginger. "Little miss, where have you gotten to?"

Jane uncurled and forced herself to her feet, clinging to the wall with fingers that dug into the wood so deep she got splinters under her nails. "Here." She barely recognized her own voice.

"Heaven on earth, girlie. What are you doing over there?"

She let out a long, shuddering breath, and when she looked to the old man, saw he already knew the answer.

"Ain't no one going to hurt you here, Jane. Leo gave you his word on that, and I'm giving you mine. You believe us, don't you?"

She nodded. She had to. She didn't have a choice.

"Good. Fear's a right good thing." He picked up her discarded brush and brought it over to her. "But it'll overrun your life faster than a jackrabbit in hunting season. You good now?"

She nodded again then, at Trapper's arched brow, added, "Yes."

"Then git back to work. We've got stalls to clean."

She accepted the brush and returned to Ginger, forcing herself to find that calm again, that peace, that had descended only moments before.

"Natural touch for sure." Trapper approached with a pitchfork in each hand as if nothing had transpired. "Let's get things cleaned up for her. You can attach her halter to the cross ties over there." He motioned to an area just inside the back door of the stable. "Tomorrow you'll be on your own with this routine. Once I see you can care for these animals, we'll find out if you can ride."

"Be still my heart," Jane murmured to the horse.

The horse let out a sound that to Jane sounded like a chuckle and bobbed her head. "You're on my side, aren't you, girl." The late-morning breeze brushed against her cheeks, and she stood there, arm resting on Ginger's flank, as she stared out at the Colorado splendor. A splendor that, no matter how hard she tried, didn't trigger a solitary memory—only an overwhelming feeling of gratitude and satisfaction as the vestiges of fear evaporated.

"This is why you live out there, isn't it?" She hadn't meant to ask, but the idea of Trapper moving from land parcel to land parcel had at first seemed odd. Now, looking at the majestic beauty of the greens and yellows playing against that pristine, cloud-dotted sky, she almost understood. "It's its own home, isn't it? Without walls."

Without borders or restraints. Without anything other than instinct and respect.

And yet it was here, on this ranch, where she felt most safe.

"Ain't no better place like this in the world." Trapper's voice was softer than expected, and she looked over her shoulder to find him beside her. He'd cleaned up some since yesterday—trimmed his silver-streaked beard, combed his hair. Wore clean jeans and a pale blue button-down shirt, the same scuffed, weathered boots on his feet. Gone was the wild-looking mountain man. In his place was a curmudgeonly grandfather with a spark of defiance and a hint of humor in his gray eyes.

"I've done my fair share of traveling. Did my bit in the service back in the day. Army rangers. Leo's grandfather, now, he was a navy man, but Leo's pop?

He upped into the army as soon as he could, much to Leo's mama's dismay. We might have had our differences, but the three of us all agreed, ain't nothing like a Colorado view. Brought us all back. Led us home." He inclined his chin toward a fenced section in the distance before the first hill rise. "They're resting out there, beneath their sky. All of them but me."

There was no mistaking the sadness she heard in Trapper's voice, no matter how hard he cleared his throat.

"Leo's spoken of his grandparents. And you." Jane frowned. "But he's never mentioned his dad." An odd pang struck, and she pressed shaking fingers against her sternum. Did she have parents? A family? People who were missing her? She didn't know. Not for certain.

But if she had to rely on her feelings? On this odd longing hovering inside her? She'd have to say…

"Difficult topic, Leo's folks." Trapper coughed and shook his head. "And you might be able to charm one certain young man with that smile of yours, missy, but you won't be pulling any family secrets out of me. You want to know about Leo's pop, you'll be asking him yourself. Now, let's get back to work."

"Yes, sir." She didn't take his admonishment to heart. If anything, their conversation had endeared him to her. Trapper might be many things, among them cantankerous and ornery, but he was loyal to Leo. And that was something she couldn't blame him for.

Leo couldn't remember the last time someone waited for him to get home. All day he wondered if he'd find

Jane sitting on the back porch, shelling fresh peas from the garden like his grandmother used to, rocking in the old chair he had yet to repaint and seal.

"Because the 1950s are calling," Leo muttered to himself around a laugh. Why did he have the feeling if he mentioned that to Jane she'd dump said bowl of peas over his head?

Finding Trapper leaning against the back porch railing looking as if he'd swallowed an entire flock of canaries reminded him of the times he got caught sneaking in after curfew. Leo glanced up at the sky currently bathed in the promise of twilight. He wasn't that late, was he?

"You done stalling?"

Leo felt his face go hot. "Why would I be stalling?"

"Hmm." Trapper motioned for him to stop, and headed toward him. "Beautiful woman in your house, can't imagine. Before you head inside," Trapper said as Leo headed for the back door, "something you ought to know."

"What? Did something happen? Is Jane all right?"

"Nothing like proving my point," Trapper mumbled, and held up his hands at Leo's growl of frustration. "She's fine. Just, how did you put it? Spooked. Someone took a wrong turn, stopped for directions."

Leo frowned. Trying to bank the combination of concern and suspicion. "That's strange."

"I thought so, too. No one's coming out here who doesn't know what or who they're looking for. Big fella. Dark hair, darker eyes. Drove one of those gas-guzzling behemoths that shouldn't be allowed—"

"Trap," Leo warned.

"Got the plate number." Trapper rattled it off along with the make and model of the vehicle. "Might have been nothing. Then again, like you said, odd, stopping here. Given all that's happened."

"Did you tell that to Jane?"

"Not after I found her curled up on the floor in the corner of the barn, I didn't." The old man's eyes sharpened. "Whatever happened to your girl, you were right. It was bad. She's working to shake it off, but this might have set her back a bit. She might be needing some space. And you might need to think about going to the sheriff yourself."

"Yeah." Unease took root deep in his gut. Somehow he needed to convince Jane that the police were their best bet. Otherwise he was going to have to do something he swore he'd never do: break his word.

"That said," Trapper went on, "I did a little searching this morning before breakfast."

Leo scowled. Talk about information overload. Right now all he wanted to do was see Jane and prove to himself she was okay. "What kind of searching?"

Trapper rolled his eyes in a way so similar to Leo's grandfather that he wondered if Trapper had been taken over by the old man's ghost. "The kind of searching you've been asking me to do. About your girl."

"She's not—" Oh, what was the use. Leo swallowed the sigh. "What did you find out?"

"Nothing for certain, but I'm guessing you might find some answers over at the old Preston place. From the description you gave me and the direction you think your Jane came from, that's your best bet."

"Preston. Paul Preston?" Leo pulled off his hat and slapped it against his thigh. A plume of late-summer dust rose and coated the only clean spot on his jeans. "Didn't he die a while back?"

"About five years ago." Trapper nodded. "Left the land to some distant relative. Nephew, cousin or some such. Place is as derelict as it could be. Not that I got that close. Didn't want to stay gone too long."

Leo gnashed his teeth.

"Don't you get to fussing." Trapper narrowed his eyes. "Needed to take Spectacle out to stretch her legs. Didn't take much to do some investigating. Wasn't gone more than a couple of hours and by the time I got back, you were on your way out. Besides, Jane's been in with the horses all day and Ollie's nearby. Doing fine, by the way. Girl's got a real way with them. The dog and the horses."

"How did she seem? Before the guy in the SUV?" It had taken far more effort than expected not to come back and check on her throughout the morning. That nightmare she'd had last night had taken years off him. But that effort was nothing compared to the determination it took for him to walk out of her room. The terrified expression on her face, the way her entire body was trembling, had drawn him like a moth to a flame.

And could have burned him just as badly.

He'd wanted to sink onto that mattress beside her. He wanted to pull her into him, wrap her in his arms and promise nothing was ever going to hurt her or scare her again. But he couldn't do that. He wouldn't make promises he couldn't keep.

And he wouldn't give in to the desire that had gut-punched him the second he saw that she'd only worn her underwear to bed. All the more reason to keep his distance.

"How did she seem about what?" Trapper's assessing gaze locked on to him like a scanning device.

"About…things," Leo said. "Did she seem anxious? Out of sorts? Headachy?"

"Girl's mind is as blank as a new chalkboard. Might not have thought so before." Trapper scrubbed a hand along his face. "Can't say about being in pain, but there's a sadness about her. Given her reaction to strangers, makes sense. Poor thing. It's like she's lost."

"She *is* lost." Which was why Leo couldn't give in to any of the thoughts that had been coursing through his mind for the entire day. She didn't know who she was and until she did, he had no right to any part of her life other than to get her home. "But the horses helped?"

"You knew they would," Trapper said. "Just like they did with your pop."

Leo's heart stuttered and he glanced away. He knew what Trapper wanted to say at the end of that statement, what Leo could have said for him. The horses had helped stabilize his father until they hadn't. Mitch Slattery had come back from his tours in the Middle East physically capable, but mentally damaged. Whatever he'd gone through in the Gulf War hadn't only haunted Leo's father—who manifested severe PTSD—but had also destroyed whatever was left of the man Leo had known. Day by day. Hour by hour.

It had been Leo's idea for his father to work exclusively with the horses on the ranch after he'd seen a story on the national news about a ranch out West open exclusively to veterans with war-related psychological issues. Thankfully, the idea had been one Leo's grandfather had wholeheartedly supported. The quiet and solitude, the routine, the caring for a creature that would only look to him for nurturing and attention had done wonders.

Until the demons had started screaming again.

And driven Mitch over the brink.

He wasn't going to let Jane tip over the edge. No matter what he had to do.

"Whatever that girl of yours has gone through, I'd be hard-pressed to say it's as near as horrific as what happened to your daddy, Leo." Trapper's voice called him back from the fog of the past. "But we've all got ghosts. She's just more haunted than the rest of us right now."

"Maybe a trip out to Preston's place might be a start." Leo hated the idea of dropping Jane straight into what must have been a nightmare for her, and there wasn't any guarantee she'd go for it. But they had to start somewhere.

Regret pressed in on him and a longing he'd never felt before, but it didn't matter. Jane mattered. He'd promised to get her home.

Because home was where she belonged.

Chapter 6

"I've got an errand to run tomorrow. Thought maybe you'd like to come with me."

Jane glanced up from where she'd curled up on the couch, the tattered paperback romance she'd fallen into after dinner resting on her lap.

Leo stood over her, two steaming mugs in his hands. He offered her one, an expression of expectation on his face. A face she had to admit she'd missed the past weeks. She'd brushed the horses down so often she was afraid they'd go bald. She'd baled more hay than possibly existed in the entire state, and listened to enough wild-man Trapper stories she could start her own nature program on cable. But other than the occasional breakfast in the morning and dinner every evening, she'd barely seen Leo other than the occasional hello. And even those greetings sounded…strained. With Trapper and Ollie around, she didn't feel lonely but she did miss him.

"Thank you." She accepted the mug and sipped. The citrus notes of the tea danced on her tongue, while the hint of whiskey almost made her smile. "Why?"

"I thought you could use something to help you sleep." He sat in the leather recliner at the end of the coffee table and crossed a bare foot over one jean-clad knee. They'd finished dinner—singed chicken breast, sweet potatoes and fresh roasted corn—a little over an hour ago. Long enough for Trapper to finish up the dishes before he ambled back to the bunkhouse, grumbling that he was going in search of what he called real food.

"Not the tea. Why would you like me to come with you? Wouldn't that make it harder to avoid me?" The accusation had been poised behind her lips for longer than she cared to admit. Every time she came anywhere near him, anytime she inadvertently touched him, he jumped as if she were a rattlesnake.

Inclining her head toward him, she narrowed her eyes, silently daring him to deny it.

"You're right," he said finally. "I have been avoiding you."

She set her mug down, closed the book. "And?"

"And what?" He drank what she strongly suspected was boosted coffee and shrugged at her.

"You aren't going to apologize?"

"For avoiding you? No. I'm not."

"Oh." Well, she'd played that completely wrong,

hadn't she? Here she'd assumed once he'd apologized they could move forward and get beyond whatever had gotten between them. "If you've changed your mind and want me to leave—"

"I don't." His calm, matter-of-fact response snapped her patience like a twig. "That's not it, Jane."

"Then what's going on? Look, if this is about my nightmares waking you up—" Ollie let out a whine and rose from his place in front of the fireplace. He walked over and dropped his chin onto her drawn-up legs.

"He doesn't like raised voices," Leo told her in a tone that told her neither did he. "This isn't about waking me up, Jane. I'm a bit offended you think it is."

"Then what *is* it?" She gently pushed Ollie away, then uncurled from the sofa. "Did you find out something about me? Is it bad news? Has it changed your mind about helping me?"

"I didn't think you wanted help." He sat forward as she stood to approach him. "You've been attending the horses, cleaning up the house, doing just about anything you can it seems to avoid finding out who you are. Which is one reason I've been leaving you to it. So do you?" He dropped his loosely clasped hands between his knees and tilted his head up to look at her. "Want my help?"

"You know I do," she snapped, and shot to her feet. "We aren't in the, what did you call it? The hour of the tiger? You were right. I can't keep hiding from whatever is out there." No matter how much she preferred holing up in the house or in the stable with the horses. The encounter with the lost motorist had rattled her more than she wanted to admit, but he was right. Maybe it was time to charge ahead again. "I need to find out what happened to me. It might be the only way—"

"To figure out who you are. I agree."

Wait. Jane stopped pacing.

"Which brings me back to my original question," he said. "I have an errand to run tomorrow, and I think you should come with me."

"Oh, my God. You just *played* me." Jane's hands tightened into fists, and she actually felt a growl build up in her throat. When she let it out, Ollie whimpered again and moved closer for inspection. "That wasn't just reverse psychology. That was... I don't even know what that was."

"That was me letting you take the lead." Leo stood up and reached out to lay gentle hands on her shoulders. "How's your head?"

"How's my head?" Ready to spin off her shoulders. Shoulders that were far more warm than the rest of her. Shoulders that relaxed beneath his touch. She'd missed him. So much. "It still hurts. But not as bad as it did." Truth be told, she'd been so irritated with Leo and so focused on helping Trapper with the horses, she hadn't been paying that close of attention. "What do you mean that you were letting me take the lead?"

"You have to want to get your life back, Jane. I can't make it happen for you. So I gave you some space. But it's been long enough. You needed a push." His lips curved into a grin that ignited a flame of irritation.

But that flame flickered into something else as she looked up into his eyes. Eyes so dark, so deep, so fathomless, she wanted to drown in them. Her stomach fluttered, as if something burst to life. The feel of his hands on her shoulders, the warmth of his body radiating against hers, slipped through her, soothed her. Tempted her.

If he knew what she was thinking, he'd probably run for the hills. But he wasn't that quick. He couldn't be. Because the slingshot impulse that kicked through her had her raising her hands to clasp the sides of his face. Before she went up on her tiptoes and kissed him.

Feeling Leo's surprise was as intoxicating as it was empowering. The shock of her action had her smiling against his mouth, a mouth that softened against hers as his hands moved off her shoulders, skimmed along her sides and came to rest against her hips.

Jane knew when reason shot through him; she felt it in the hesitancy of his kiss. But instead of demanding more, which she craved more than her next breath, she lowered her heels and pulled herself away. She didn't move. Instead, she simply stood there, her heart pounding hard against her chest as she still clasped his face in her hands.

"What was that?" he asked in a hoarse whisper that nearly had her kissing him again.

"Me taking the lead." And then she did kiss him again. Quick. Hard. And felt his fingers flex against her flesh. "Best get used to it, cowboy. 'Cause you asked for it."

Leo's plan had been to head out to the Preston place after lunch the next day, but moving the herd into the next pasture and a routine check of fence line had gone quicker than expected. Probably due to the fact he'd headed out even earlier than normal, anxious to get the day started and find some answers for Jane. The sooner they found out what happened to her, the sooner they'd unlock whatever door her mind had closed on her. The sooner she'd be…gone.

Yeah. Leo grimaced and tightened his hands on the steering wheel. Yeah, that's what was pushing him out the door. Getting Jane home. He certainly hadn't been avoiding the prospect of facing her the morning after she'd kissed him.

In all his years he'd never tasted anything as sweet as Jane's lips—like the summer wind and strawberries, laced with a touch of that whiskey he'd added to her tea. Rather than quenching a desire he'd hoped was a passing fascination, having her so close, feeling her so near, had righted something inside him he hadn't realized was wrong. No. Not wrong. *Missing*.

He slipped the truck into its usual space between the house and the stable, and caught a flash of movement over in the paddock.

Fascinated, stunned, Leo pushed open his door, bent down to greet Ollie, who bounded over to him with an excited bark, and then escorted him over to the fence.

The world around him slowed. The air stilled. And there she was…long red hair braided down her back, a too-large hat on her head, galloping around the pen on Ginger's back. Jane's face radiated utter and complete happiness.

He had to remind himself how to move, but move he did, closer even as he saw her almost in slow motion.

He'd lived in one of the most beautiful parts of the country, amid the glaciers and waterfalls and forests of Alaska. The quiet, the solitude, even among the machinery and boisterous male population, had been his solace, and yet nothing could compare to the breathtaking sight before him.

"She's a natural."

Leo started as the world came back into focus. The sound of Ginger's hooves beating into the ground echoed against the occasional laugh or comment coming from Jane's smiling lips. "She sure is," he told Trapper.

"I'm betting it's gonna be tough, getting her out of the saddle. She had a bit of a rocky start, but now she rides like that's where she belongs."

"Except it's not." The last of the fantasy faded. Leo's heart tipped as he straightened his spine. "She's not ours, Trapper." *She's not mine.* He could feel it in the deepest part of his soul. As much as he wanted to believe, as much as he wanted her, she didn't belong here. Besides, Jane wasn't anyone's until they found out who she really was.

"Could be ours. Just sayin'." Trapper shrugged. "You headed out to the Preston place?"

"In a few, yeah." Why couldn't he stop watching her? Why couldn't he stop imagining…

"Nothing stopping you from changing your mind, you know." Trapper braced a foot up on a fence rail and slung his arms over the top. "She doesn't seem to be in any rush to get answers."

"Maybe I am." Maybe it was foolish, maybe he was living in a dream, but he found himself clinging to the thin thread of hope that it wouldn't matter who she was. That their kiss last night was only the beginning. "I gave her my word I'd get her home, Trapper. I mean to keep it."

"Stubborn as your granddaddy." Trapper shook his head before he removed his hat and waved it at Jane and Ginger. "That's enough for today, little girl. Let's cool her down and get her settled back in."

A plume of dust rose around Ginger's feet as Jane brought the horse to a stop in front of them. "Oh, come on. Just a few more minutes?" She pretend-pouted at Trapper before turning those pleading eyes on Leo.

"Don't look at me." Leo held up his hands in mock surrender. As beautiful a sight as she was from a distance, she stole his breath close up. Skin glistening and damp with sweat, her eyes alive and bright, the way her jeans and shirt clung to every curve of her body had his fingers itching to discover what she might have worn beneath the denim and red plaid. A streak of dirt crossed her cheek and her nose, and dust coated her skin. "Trapper's in charge of the horses these days. Besides, we have a lunch date."

Jane grinned. "We do?"

That hadn't come out quite the way he'd meant it, but what the heck. She'd started it last night, hadn't she? "We do. You take care of Ginger and get cleaned up. I'll make some sandwiches and load up a cooler."

"Where are we going exactly?"

Trapper eyed Leo over one shoulder, daring him to tell her the truth—that this wasn't some romantic romp through the mountainside, but an investigative trek to where they believed she'd been held hostage.

"It's a surprise." Leo managed a quick smile. He was keeping his promise so far. He hadn't lied to her. "Do you still like surprises?"

"I do today." She grabbed the saddle horn and swung a leg behind her to dismount.

It was then he noticed the boots. "Where'd you get those?"

"Trapper found them for me." Jane kicked a heel up behind her and beamed at him. "Aren't they marvelous? I love the silver stitching detail. I can't believe they fit."

"Almost like they were meant for her." Trapper arched a brow at Leo. "Hope you don't mind. I thought I'd take a look through the attic boxes. See if there was anything Gwen and Lacey might be able to use once they're back."

Leo looked the old man dead in the eye. "You were looking for stuff for Gwen and came across the box of my mother's things?"

"Oh." Jane's smile faltered. "Oh, I'm so sorry. I didn't—"

"It's fine." Leo pushed up the brim of his hat as he caught a glint of sparkle off the boots. "It's just been a long time since I've seen them." And the last time certainly wasn't a moment he wanted to remember. Watching his father box up his mother's things was one of his earliest memories—the day he'd watched a man who had been through so much, finally break. Here? Now? She'd just turned that sadness into light. "Really, Jane. Trapper's right. They were made for you. And I'm sure my mother would have preferred them on someone's feet than sitting around in a box. I'm going to head inside and clean up."

"Now, don't you be giving me the evil eye like that." Trapper wagged a finger at Jane once they were back in the stable.

"You didn't tell me these were his mother's." Jane unbuckled the girth and drew Ginger's saddle off. "Why not?"

"Gives you two something to talk about, don't it?" Trapper reached for the saddle, but Jane slapped his hands away. "You wanted to ask about his folks, now you have a reason."

"I've got this." She glared at him when he tried to help again. "And since when do Leo and I need help finding a topic of conversation?" She grabbed hold of the saddle and pulled. Too hard apparently because her head went light and the room spun. "Uh-oh." Her knees buckled and she hit the ground. Hard. "Oh, wow. Ow."

She squeezed her eyes shut as nausea washed over her and pain sliced through her head. For the second time, she saw an image of herself, but not herself, laughing and singing and carrying on before she flipped her long hair over her shoulder.

Jane shuddered, tried to cling to the memory even as the sight vanished behind her eyes. That emptiness, that void she'd been so determined to ignore, had filled, before evaporating again.

"Lordy, little girl. What did you do?" Trapper yanked the saddle free of her other hand while Ollie moved in to press his nose against her suddenly clammy face. "What hurts? Is it your head? Did you knock it again?"

"My head's been fine," Jane reassured him and reassured Ollie with a pet. That image was so odd. It looked like her, but didn't *feel* like her. Didn't sound like her. But then, did anyone ever sound like they expected themselves to? "I'm fine. Just…maybe you're right. I did too much today." She'd been nervous at first, climbing on Ginger's back, but the second she was settled in the saddle, she'd felt…free. The beating sun hadn't mattered. The dust and dirt didn't matter. All she'd wanted to do was ride.

"I'll get Leo."

"You will not." Jane locked a hand around the old man's thin arm. "I mean it, Trapper." She took a long, deep breath and willed the pain in her head to go away. No such luck. The throbbing, bass-deep thudding was back. "There's nothing Leo can do except drag me into town to the doctor, and I'm not ready for that." She winced. "Not yet." But she knew the time was coming. The headaches hadn't stopped. She'd just gotten used to them. And the last thing she needed was dizzy spells.

"You trying to get me killed, little girl?" Trapper crouched in front of her, and for the first time since she'd known him, she saw genuine concern in his gray eyes. "Leo finds out about this, I'll be a pelt on that living room floor of his."

"Leo isn't going to find out because neither one of us is going to tell him." And if she had to, she'd leave Trapper out of it. "Please, Trapper. I'm feeling better already. If we tell him, he's just going to plunk me on that couch for the rest of the day, and that might just drive me out of my mind."

The temptation to do just that was something she had to fight against every day. Inside that house she felt safe, where nothing—and no one—could touch her. This morning had been the first morning in over a month where she hadn't looked over her shoulder after stepping outside. "I'm already antsy for something more to do around here. No offense to the horses and you."

"You'll take one of those pain pills when you go inside?" Trapper didn't look convinced. "And you'll take it easy the rest of the day?"

"I will. Cross my heart." She made the motion to be safe.

"This happens again, I'll tell him. I don't take to keeping secrets. You understand me?"

"I do. And it won't happen again. Now, help me up." She was still feeling a bit shaky, but once she was on her feet again, her stomach righted itself. But her head still hurt. "Let's get Ginger—"

Trapper cut her off. "You get yourself inside and clean up. I'll take care of her." He shooed her away as if she was a hoard of flies.

"I told you, I'm fine." But she didn't feel fine. Her ears were ringing, and she swore she heard sirens in the distance. Her imagination again. Her mind playing tricks on her. She was getting really tired of the tricks.

"Fine enough, you can do as you're told," Trapper ordered. "Now git. Ollie, you, too."

Ollie whined and pushed his head up under Jane's hand.

Because she knew it would irritate him, she gave him a quick hug and kiss on the cheek. "You really are a sweet man, Trapper."

"I am not," Trapper grumbled after her, but that only made Jane laugh as she headed into the house, Ollie by her side.

"Hey, Daria." Sheriff Trey Colton rapped a knuckle on Deputy Daria Bloom's door and poked his head in. "Heading out for lunch. Can I bring you back anything? Since it looks as if you've cemented yourself to that chair."

Daria blinked herself out of her Hunting the Avalanche Killer trance and reached for the stone-cold coffee she'd forgotten to drink. "Sorry, lost in thought. Was there something you wanted?" She sniffed at the cup and decided she wasn't that hard up. Yet. Daria leaned back in her creaky, wheeled chair and shoved her fingers into her tangled, curly hair.

When Trey stepped inside and closed the door, her feet hit the ground and she sat forward. "Uh-oh. What have I done?" Her mind raced through the past twenty-four hours, wondering if she'd said something to someone that had hit the front page of the paper. Or worse, was circulating through town. Did he know? Had he somehow found out she was a Colton? She wasn't ready to deal with all that. Not yet. Not until she had thought out every fallout scenario.

"When was the last time you were home?" Trey crossed his arms over his chest and turned those dark, laser beam eyes on her.

"Ah, a while ago." She scrubbed tired hands over her face, hiding her relief. "Long enough to grab a shower and a change of clothes."

"What about sleep? You thinking about getting some?"

Daria chewed the inside of her cheek and reminded herself that while they were technically related and she considered Trey a friend, he was also her boss. "I'm always thinking about sleep," she said with a too-innocent smile. Translation: she'd sleep when they put the case to bed. "Hey, it's lunchtime, right?"

Trey's jaw locked. "Figured you didn't hear a word I said. I'm actually on my way out, and I'll be bringing you back something."

"What?" Knowing Trey and how he liked to tease her, he'd slide an avocado club sandwich under her nose. Daria shuddered. She hated avocado.

"I think that's what I should be asking. You heard about Levi McEwan, right?"

"Small-time drug dealer we've put away at least three times?" She'd had a few run-ins with him over the years. Harmless for the most part. Except for the fact he was selling poison on the streets. "What's he done now?"

"Something that got him killed, apparently. Hikers found his body in the woods near the gas station off

Roundabout Road. Stabbed enough times to make Caesar jealous. They think he's been dead a few days."

"Rage killing from a dissatisfied customer?" Try as she might, Daria couldn't quite bring herself to feel sorry for the loss, other than for Levi's grandmother. Someone was going to have to tell her he wasn't coming home.

"Probably. Forensics should have fun with the scene. Either way, it's on the books if you need a palate cleanser."

"I don't, but thanks." The Avalanche Killer was more than enough for now.

"What's going on? You keep staring at that board as if it's going to speak to you." Trey pushed off the door and approached the magnetic whiteboard Daria had wedged into her office. But it wasn't the topography images, forensic photos or the newspaper headlines that he was focusing on. He stared at the photograph of Sabrina Gilford. "What's it saying?"

"Truthfully?" Daria gnawed on her cheek. "I don't think the Avalanche Killer killed Sabrina."

"What's your evidence?"

Daria let out a laugh. "Oh, that. Yeah. Don't have any. What I do have is—"

"Your gut." Trey didn't miss a beat. "One of the reasons I knew you'd be able to handle this case. You mention this to our FBI friend?"

"Stefan?" Daria resisted the urge to clear her throat and fidget. "No. Not directly, anyway." Whenever she was around Very Special Agent Stefan Roberts, talking wasn't the first thing that came to mind. Compartmentalization was a talent of hers. Or at least it had been before Stefan had turned up. Easy on the eyes and honorably dedicated to the job, Stefan was also fairly uncomplicated to work with. For a Fed. If Daria was completely honest with herself, uncomplicated worked to her advantage. Stefan was someone with access to information she wanted—information she needed—if she was ever going to track down her mother. Daria had exhausted all her database possibilities, but a Fed had other avenues...

"Did I lose you again?"

"Sorry, what?" Daria blinked again.

Trey just arched that brow again. Feeling her cheeks warm, she shook her head and refocused. "With each of the bodies we found, there was this odd feeling of caring about them. The way the arms were crossed, as if they were sleeping. And look, here. The necklace on her is perfectly centered. It's all the little details. But with Sabrina..." She stood up and joined him at the board, gestured at the image that showed how Sabrina Gilford had been buried. "She looks tossed aside. Discarded. As if he was angry. Even though location and manner are perfect."

"Too perfect?"

"Maybe." Daria shoved her hands in the back pockets of her navy uniform slacks. "Sabrina's different. And different, to me, says someone else killed her, but that someone else must have known the details. How else would he have known where to leave her? *How* to leave her." She looked to Trey for guidance, for reassurance she wasn't totally off the rails. "He knows who the Avalanche Killer is, Trey. He's using him to cover up his own crime."

Trey shifted slightly, his accessing eye catching on the image of Skye Colton tacked to the top left corner of the board.

Daria's stomach twisted. She knew what the sheriff was thinking. The same thing she'd been thinking when she'd garnered the courage to put up Skye's photo in the vicinity of the Avalanche Killer. She hadn't wanted to. The very idea that his cousin might be the murderer's latest victim made her sick to her stomach. Skye was one of the bright, shining beacons of the Colton family. A heart of gold with a mind like a steel trap. Whip-smart, determined and savvy. For the most part.

Hooking up with record producer Brock Madsen hadn't been Skye's most impressive move, especially not with her social media presence being so prolific and attention-grabbing. As far as Daria was concerned, putting your entire relationship up for public consumption spoke more of insecurity and desperation than social interaction. Disappearing the way Skye had after getting very publicly dumped probably hadn't been the best course of action, either. Now it had been weeks since anyone had heard from Skye. Normally Daria wouldn't be concerned, but given how close Skye and her twin sister, Phoebe, were…

"Any word?"

"On Skye? No." Daria swallowed the fear. "The missing persons alert hasn't earned us anything other than false leads and people looking for gossip, and these days people barely notice missing persons fly-

ers. We have an APB out for her car, which, since it's
red and impractical, stands out like two sore thumbs.
We've got a warrant request for her banking records and
credit cards. I've got Gerard going up to The Chateau
today to talk to Phoebe and other members of the family again in case they've remembered anything more
that might help." Gerard might not be the most likable
of the other deputies in the department, but he got the
job done. They had the best deputies in Colorado on the
job. "We're rolling out patrols to the outlying areas and
smaller towns. We'll find her."

"Yeah, but will we find her alive?"

"I hope so." Daria's gaze slipped back to the other
victims. If she was right and there were two killers,
Skye's chances of survival seemed nil. "I really hope
so."

The lunch of tuna sandwiches, coleslaw and BBQ po-
tato chips didn't sit well in her stomach. And it wasn't
the burnt chocolate chip cookies Leo had made for dessert. Truth be told, Jane wasn't entirely sure why she
was feeling sick, but the sensation had struck the second they turned onto the highway after lunch.

Leo had driven them to a beautiful picnic spot over-
looking the edge of the town. He'd pointed out other
farms and ranches and helped establish her bearings
as far as what was where in Roaring Springs. He told
her as much history about the town as he knew, from
its founding by historic families, including the Coltons
and Gilfords, to the still-bitter emotions that ran as deep
as a Roaring Springs lake over the family's commer-

cialization of the area. An odd feeling panged in her stomach, as if the name or even the story should mean something to her. If Leo noticed her self-imposed and confused silence, he didn't let on.

As it was a weekday, they'd been alone. Ollie had probably enjoyed the stop the most as he spent his time bounding about chasing bees and butterflies, and the occasional dandelion tuft. If Leo had been biding his time and watching the clock, she hadn't noticed. Except now she began to wonder…

As they bounced along the highway in Leo's truck, Jane dug her fingers into Ollie's coat and the dog turned his head toward her, his expression asking what was wrong. "Where are we going, exactly?" Her throat felt tight, as if the question was going to snap under the pressure of her growing anxiety.

"Since the police still aren't an option, I'm testing a theory."

Leo's explanation didn't help. If anything, it only raised more questions. "How is that an errand?" An errand was grocery shopping or picking up ranch supplies or…honestly? She'd thought he was trying to trick her into going to the doctor.

Every time she looked at the road ahead, she felt dizzy again. Nauseated. She tried to focus on the tree line as they sped past, but even that was making her a bit carsick. The farther they drove, the more nervous she got. Her skin prickled as if a million fire ants had skittered up her spine.

"Stop." She gripped the door handle and might have

snapped it open if the lock hadn't been secure. "Leo, stop the truck, please."

He glanced over at her before doing as she asked. The tires ground in the dirt and rocks as he pulled over to the side of the road.

Jane jumped out and dived for the trees, where she threw up her lunch. Humiliated, cold and sweaty, she stepped back, bracing one hand on the trunk of a nearby tree and caught her breath. Leo was right there, cold water bottle in hand, Ollie at his side.

"Darlin'?" Leo stroked her back soothingly. "You okay?"

"Sorry. Better here than in your truck." She tried to make light of it after washing out her mouth and drinking, but couldn't. Maybe Trapper was right. She should have told Leo about the dizzy spell. And that the headaches weren't getting any better. And that she couldn't stop hearing…

She looked over Leo's shoulder. The road. The curve of the road. The trees… "I know this place. I've…been here." Her gaze shifted back to his. "That night. This was where I was running from. After the shed, I broke through the trees. There." She pointed before facing him and narrowed her eyes. "You knew. How?"

"I suspected." The cursory nod killed that anxiety she'd been feeling and replaced it with irritation.

"You knew and you didn't tell me? You didn't warn me this is where we were going?"

He shook his head. "I've dealt with trauma before. What the mind loses, or chooses to forget, sometimes the body remembers. I was watching you in the truck.

The closer we got to this place, the more antsy you became. I could feel it. Ollie could, too. And now we have a place to start."

A place to start. "Guess you're in a rush to get rid of me after all."

"You know I'm not."

That same growl of frustration built up in her throat again. Was there anything that got under his skin? Did he always have to be so freaking calm all the time? So rational and reasonable and... She sagged back against the tree. Did he always have to be so *right*?

She couldn't keep living this way. She couldn't keep biding her time taking care of horses that weren't hers on a ranch that wasn't hers with a man who... She swallowed more water along with the regret. A man who wasn't hers. She couldn't keep hiding. She couldn't let the fear win. "Where are we?"

"About a quarter mile from the Preston farm. Paul Preston. He died a while back. After I filled Trapper in, he looked into a few things. Found this place. Thought it was worth checking out."

"How much did you tell Trapper?" No wonder the old coot had been so solicitous and concerned back in the stable. He'd probably been waiting days for her to snap or fall apart.

"I told Trapper what he needed to know. Are you feeling better? Are you ready to push further and see where this goes?"

Was she? Jane's gaze skittered back to the highway, then in the other direction. She could hear the past sounds of her feet crunching in the leaves and twigs and debris littering the ground as she'd run from the shed, run toward the only direction she could find. This highway. This road. Which meant...

She walked past Leo and Ollie, keeping close to the trees as she headed down the side of the road. The traffic was as sporadic as it had been that night, with only an occasional passing car. It made sense. Earlier Leo had told her this was one of those out-of-the-way roads that while it got you to the heart of Roaring Springs eventually, only those who lived on the far outskirts of the town knew about it or even used it.

"There were lights that night." She didn't have to turn to know Leo was right behind her. He had her back. Just as he had from the moment he'd first found her in his barn. And that knowledge pushed the last tendrils of fear aside. "The night I got away." Her voice sounded hollow, detached. "Down that way. Far in the distance, but I could see them." She shivered. She could *feel* them.

"What kind of lights?"

"Red. Blue. Spinning." Blinding. Just thinking about them made her head hurt. She pressed her fingers against her temple as if doing so would help her remember more.

"Police."

"Yes." The fear was back, a hot bubble pressing into her throat, blocking her air. "They scared me. Drove me the other way." She turned and pointed across the highway. "There was a truck. White I think? A young man was driving. He, I think he tried to help me but I just kept running."

"Maybe he reported seeing you to the police."

She shook her head. "Maybe." For some reason she hoped not.

"That's something we can look into. Do you want to get back into the truck and drive on or do you want to walk?"

"I don't know where—" She turned along with Leo and found the narrow road beneath the undergrowth leading deep into the trees. Deep into the darkness.

Big enough for a truck to pass through.

Small enough to contain her fear.

"I'm right here, Jane." He brushed gentle fingers down her arm, as if afraid of startling her out of a trance. "Whatever you decide—"

"I know." She held out her hand and blinked back tears of relief when he didn't hesitate. The sensation of his fingers sliding between hers, clasping her hand securely in his as Ollie came around to her other side, comforted her beyond measure. "I know you are. Let's go."

He didn't say another word. He simply squeezed her hand.

Together, they stepped onto the road.

Chapter 7

"You sure this isn't a set from some old creepy horror movie?"

Jane's voice carried more than a hint of the frustration Leo was feeling. Only when he realized this place did nothing to trigger her memory did he realize how much hope he'd been holding that it would.

The dilapidated, weatherworn cabin situated in the back corner of the property could very well have been used as the perfect setting for an ax-wielding murderer bent on ridding the world of pesky, hypersexualized fictional teenagers. Trees and shrubs and weeds had overgrown to the point of dangerous, with thick roots popping up out of the ground and waist-high debris overtaking the property. Whatever natural paths had once existed had been obliterated by the years of neglect.

"Whoever owns it now certainly could rent it out as one." Leo tried to keep his tone light. They needed to make some progress, if not regarding who Jane was, then at the very least who might have left her tied up in the shed and why.

"Should we go inside?" She was already on the rickety front porch, clearly having answered her own question.

"Up to you."

Ollie whined and dropped to the ground to rest his chin on his paws.

"I don't think Ollie's particularly anxious to do so." Leo bent down to give the dog a good scrub on the top of his head. "You stand guard, okay, boy?"

The German shepherd heaved a sigh and turned his face into the sun. Leo followed Jane, who pressed her hand flat against the door and pushed it open.

The hinges creaked so loudly, they may as well have been a burglar alarm. The skittering and scampering inside conjured images of all kinds of rodents, and they both covered their mouths and noses with their hands to stop from breathing in the stench coating the interior. Leo's eyes watered as he walked across the filthy kitchen to push open one of the windows.

The midafternoon sun could barely find its way through the grimy glass, but the sliver of light he managed to find removed some of the shadows from the large space that held both the kitchen and sitting room. Rusted springs had escaped the fabric-encased sofa. One of the legs of the wooden coffee table had been gnawed off by something with a set of teeth Leo wouldn't want to encounter. What was left of a shattered mirror and its frame hung crooked above the brick fireplace that contained more ashes than a crematorium. Warped doors stood on either side of the fireplace, but only one had a shiny new knob and lock glowing against the sudden invasion of sun.

"How long has this Preston fellow been dead?" Jane pushed her foot through an old stack of magazines that dropped apart at the barest touch.

"Five years from what Trapper said."

"Smells like it," she muttered.

"You haven't been here before, have you?" Given her reaction to the highway, he had a pretty good idea of what her reaction would have been had she recognized anything.

"No." She uncovered her mouth, picked up the poker by the fireplace and bent down to dig through the ashes. "Nothing is familiar. Maybe with the shed it'll be different."

"Might need an industrial Weedwacker to get there." Leo turned the knob on the bedroom to their right, and cringed at the sight inside. "Clearly this place will not be featured in *Good Housekeeping.*"

"Do you have a flashlight or something?"

"Back in the truck." One of the few apps he actually missed using on his cell phone, but he'd gotten used to not having it at all these past few months. "Let's try this." He found a box of long matches on the mantel, struck one, and then crouched beside her as she reached into the pile of ash and removed what was left of a plastic card. "Looks like a driver's license. There's the state seal." He angled the flame closer. "Careful. Don't want to light your hair on fire."

"Would give me an excuse to cut it off," she muttered.

"Don't you dare."

Her head snapped around and she looked at him, eyes wide. "Okay." She smiled, one of those all-knowing female smiles he'd bet had frustrated men for a millennia, before she returned her attention to the ID.

Leo felt his cheeks warm. Why'd he have to say that out loud? But he wasn't wrong. The very idea of hacking off that gorgeous red hair of hers was unacceptable. Not that he had any say in the matter. But he'd lost track of the minutes—or was it hours—he'd found himself daydreaming about what it would be like to feel that hair sliding between his fingers. Of diving his fingers deep as he held her to him, as he kissed her. Made love to her...

"Leo? Did you hear me?"

"Nope." And he wasn't going to apologize for it. How could he when hot fantasies about Jane were as close as he was ever going to allow himself to get? "What?"

"I can't make out the name, can you? L-E-V—" She squinted and shook her head. "Maybe outside."

"We could do with some fresh air, that's for sure." Leo glanced over his shoulder to where the kitchen table was piled high with food-encrusted plates and buzzing with flies and other insects. "Dirty dishes mean someone's been here recently. Let's just check one more thing before we head out."

"Tell me you have a decontamination shower back at the ranch," Jane joked as she set the poker down.

"If only." Leo guided her to the side after determining the second door wasn't going to budge. "I always wanted to do this."

"Do what?"

Leo held out his arms and braced himself as he kicked hard against the brass lock and door frame. The wood splintered and broke apart. Then the door shot open. "Okay, that was kind of awesome."

"It kind of was." She started in ahead of him, but he stopped her with both his hands and a look. "What?"

"There's a lock on that door for a reason. Let me go in first."

"Why?" Her brow arched in a way he had come to recognize when she was challenging him.

"Because I'm a man and I have—"

"A penis?" She blinked so quickly her lashes looked like tiny butterflies.

"I cannot believe you just said that." But he laughed. Harder than he had in a long time. And when she joined him, his heart lightened considerably. If he'd ever heard a more wondrous sound, he couldn't recall. "Point taken. Compromise. We'll go in together."

"My hero." She sighed at him before they stepped inside. And froze. "Oh, boy."

"Yeah." All humor drained out of Leo as he looked at the half-dozen waist-high lab tables displaying remnants of what looked like chemistry supplies. A yellow powder coated the edge of one table. The windows had been spray-painted black, and the floor was splashed with what looked like bleach. "Someone was using this as a drug lab." He took hold of Jane's arm when she started to go in farther. "Let's not."

"But what if—"

"What if this is a crime scene?" Leo cut her off. "Actually, there's no what-if about it. It *is* a crime scene."

"Yeah, you're right."

"We should go back to the ranch and call the sheriff."

For the first time, Jane seemed to consider the option, but any hope that her situation would resolve sooner than later evaporated when she shook her head. "No. Not yet. I want to know more myself before we bring the police in."

"Jane—"

"What am I going to tell them? Nothing. Because, other than waking up here, I don't have any memory of what happened before. They'll only ask questions I can't answer. I want to be able to answer at least some before we call them."

Leo's head ached from clenching his jaw. "All right. But this can't go on much—"

"Maybe we can still get some information out of this." She held up the ID. "Maybe someone knows who this is? And if we can find him, maybe he knows what happened to me."

"You really think removing potential evidence is the right way to go?"

"I think it's either move forward with this or stop looking. Worst case, someone else reports this and they find our prints. We can answer questions then if we have to."

"Listen to you, Miss CSI." But Leo was already backing out of the room and bringing her with him. He detoured to the fireplace and used his shirt to wipe the handle of the poker handle, then did the same with the doorknob on the second bedroom.

Fresh air had never smelled so good. "Hey, Ollie. Chase anything good while we were in there?" He bent down to scrub his hands into the dog's fur. Ollie turned his nose and tried to get away. "Yeah, I know. We stink. Proving you were most definitely the wisest among us."

"I think the last name is McEwan?" Jane held the ID up to the sun at different angles to get a better read. "Does that sound familiar?"

"No, but then, I've only been back here a few months. Is that the shed?" He pointed across what looked like an apocalyptic weed field. She looked in the direction he indicated and nodded.

"Yeah. That's about how this place looked once I got out."

"Okay, then." He walked beyond the main cabin, looking for a break in the weeds. "Here. This should do." Along the back edge of a fence was a narrow path. "I'd see if maybe one of those tractors over there work, but who knows what kind of attention we might bring."

"Nothing like a walk through the weeds to win a girl's heart." She offered a stiff smile. "The next time you have errands—" she gave him the deadly air quotes "—feel free to refrain from issuing an invitation."

"Noted."

They weren't very far into the trash-strewn weed

patch when she spoke. "Someone would have to know about this place to have left me here."

"Maybe we can find out at the county registrar's office who inherited it." Leo kept a sharp eye out as Ollie led the way down the path. To him, the width and placement seemed worn out deliberately, as if it had been used multiple times before. "This can't have been a one-person operation. There were too many tables set up in that room."

She hurried forward and took hold of his hand as the dead weeds and shrubs seemed to close in. "You're thinking there's some kind of drug gang working out of Roaring Springs?"

"As much as I'd like it to be, Roaring Springs isn't some kind of safe haven from the rest of the world," Leo said. "There's demand everywhere. Even when I was up in Alaska, if you had need of something in the pharmaceutical arena, there were people with connections. Not labs like that, of course. At least, not that I knew of." Some things he was happy to live in ignorance of. "Legal or illegal, prescription or manufactured on-site, if you had the money, you could get it."

"Would what we found back there make a lot of drugs?"

The path curved, and for a moment Ollie was out of sight. He let out a sharp bark, only one, as if commanding them to hurry up.

"I'd bet yes," Leo said. "Colorado's just like any other part of the country. If there are buyers out there, they'll find a way to manufacture and distribute. Might be an-

other avenue to explore if that ID doesn't get us anywhere."

"With a last name of McEwan, someone has to know
him. I can't imagine it's very common."

"I imagine not." But Leo didn't think rushing out
and asking anyone in town if they knew this guy was
a good idea. Although…if he was looking for a way to
push Jane into going to the police, this could be the excuse he needed. "Let's not get ahead of ourselves. First
the property owner, then the ID guy."

"No." Jane cleared her throat and tugged him to a
stop. They'd come to the end of the path and there,
standing before them, like some big hulking wooden
specter, stood the garden shed. "First we deal with this."
She released his hand and moved past him, stopping beside Ollie, who had sat down in front of the door. "Do
we need to go inside?"

"You don't need to, no." Once again, he'd seen no
indication that she was having a flash of memory. In
fact, maybe it was better she didn't go in. "I want to,
though. Maybe I'll see something you didn't."

"I wasn't looking for anything other than a way
out." Jane sank to the ground and curved her arms
around Ollie. "The window I broke is over that way."
She pointed to the left. "Although if you want to break
the door down again, go for it. I'll have a better view."

How he loved a woman with a sense of humor.

"I'll take the window this time." He had enough ego
to know when a second chance might turn into a complete embarrassment. "Ollie?"

His dog woofed.

"We'll be fine," Jane assured him. "Just…hurry up."

"Yeah, way ahead of you." Leo was as ready to be done with this field trip as she was. Climbing in through the small square window through which she'd escaped only days before proved more difficult than he expected. Jane's slight build and frame had given her an advantage. The few shards of glass in the frame didn't take kindly to the disturbance, and scraped against his upper arms after he used two wooden crates to boost himself up and through. His booted foot landed solidly on the seat of the old mower, but it was a balancing act to find his way across to the floor. He landed with a louder thump than he expected.

"Leo? Are you okay?"

"Fine." He could tell by the closeness of her voice she'd come to the door. The ancient table saw had been moved recently, by Jane if memory served correct. He leaned over and ran his finger lightly against the circular blade. He saw slight traces of red on the metal. Jane's blood. His stomach clenched around the image of her desperately trying to cut herself free. He looked slowly around the small shed, the suffocating stench of old dirt and rusted tools penetrating his nose and mouth. To think this was where she'd woken up. Alone. Restrained. Terrified.

She'd gotten herself free. She hadn't let the terror win. She'd gotten out. And found him.

He was right the other night in her bedroom. She was a fighter. Seeing this place proved it.

A wave of emotion nearly doubled him over. That she trusted him even an iota after surviving this added another layer of responsibility to his already burdened shoulders. She didn't deserve this. No one did, but especially not Jane. She deserved to be back home, with the people who loved her, knew her. Would care for her.

"Leo?"

"Yeah?" He barely heard his own voice.

"What do you see?"

He looked to the door and imagined her standing on the other side, fingers pressed against the wood that had kept her trapped, as she faced the little bit of her past she could remember. "Looking now. By the way, when I do get you to a doctor, you're getting a tetanus shot."

Her response was a long time coming. "Okay."

Sunlight streamed through the holes in the beamed roof, brighter than they would have been that day. He headed for the door, and first thing ran his fingers along the edge of the frame looking for a key. Nothing. He tried the knob and when it didn't budge, he frowned and crouched, examined the make and model.

"Did you find anything?"

"Yeah." He hit the side of his fist against the door above the fixture. "There's no way you could have gotten through this without a key. It's steel reinforced. Each lock only has two keys and they're trademarked so even key makers can't create new ones." Not that the criminal element couldn't have found a way. His boss up on the pipeline had used a lock like this on the supply room.

But why the need for such safeguards? It was an old garden shed. Nothing in here other than unused and forgotten equipment and tools. Other than Jane, what on earth could they be keeping in here?

Leo got to his feet and walked to the other side of the small structure. The plank flooring was rough and uneven. But some planks seemed newer than others. He started stomping as he walked, listening to the sound of his boots against the wood. Harder here, softer there. Boards creaked. Nails whined. And then…bam! His foot went right through one of the boards.

"What on earth are you doing?"

"Testing another theory." He bent and plucked the broken pieces apart, tossed them aside. "Found where they store their drugs." Leo looked down at the remnants of a plastic bag that had duct tape around it and a few small yellow pills the same color as the powder back in the lab. He sighed. A few questions had been answered. But larger ones remained. Including the biggest one of them all.

Why was Jane still alive?

"Tell me again why we're here?" Jane tucked her hair up under her hat as Ollie jumped out of the truck. Leo had driven behind the bank of stores on the main drag of Roaring Springs, meandering between buildings like a pro. Driving into town, seeing all the cars and people, had set every nerve in her body on edge, maybe not as badly as back at the Preston place, but enough she heard the edge in her own voice.

"We are here because I'm tired of living in the world of the caveman." He headed to the open back door of a brick building that looked as if it had been built around the time of the gold rush. "If you don't want to talk to the police about this—"

"I don't." When was he going to give up on that? "And you promised me, Leo."

"Right." He winced as if it was the worst deal he'd ever made. "Then we need some help putting all these pieces together. And nothing is more helpful than the internet." He hesitated and looked back at her. "You do remember the internet, right?"

"I can't tell if that's a joke." At his arched brow, she sighed. "Yes, I remember the internet." But the very thought of it made her slightly nauseated. Why did everything about the past make her feel sick?

"So you can't argue it's not our best bet at this point."

"No." As much as she might want to. She straightened her hat, pushed the brim farther over her eyes. "But why here?"

"Because Lucky D's serves the best burgers in town, and I don't feel like burning dinner tonight."

Her stomach growled, reminding her she'd lost her lunch a few hours ago.

"See?" Leo grinned and pointed at her stomach. "You can't argue with that, either."

"I don't want to be around people." The very idea of it had her breaking out in a cold sweat. She thought she'd done pretty well so far, going along with him in searching the Preston property and not holding a grudge when he'd essentially tricked her into facing that night. "You're pushing your luck, cowboy." She shoved her hands in her pockets and set her jaw. "How about I wait in the truck with Ollie?"

Ollie perked up and got to his feet.

"How about we decided to stick together? It'll take

fifteen minutes, tops. Come on." He held out his hand. "I promise, it'll be painless."

"Then we can go home?" She couldn't even begin to explain how anxious she was to get back to what she knew, what she felt comfortable with.

His grin faded for a moment. "Yeah." Then his mouth curved into a genuine smile. "Then we can go home."

"Fine." She slipped her hand into his and let him tug her inside.

In one breath, one blissful, lung-coating breath, Jane realized he'd brought her into hamburger heaven. Had she not been worrying her nerves outside, she might have noticed earlier the pungent, salivating aroma of grilled onions, frying bacon and a greasy grill top. Even the low hissing of the orders currently sizzling to perfection on the ancient stove brought her an odd sense of calm. "Oh, wow. I can feel my arteries clogging already."

"Totally worth it. Miss D, you're back!" Leo moved in front of Jane, whose head was all but spinning as she took in every inch of the diner's kitchen. White tile and stainless steel seemed to be battling out for domination. The pass-through window had one of those circular holders for the order tickets currently flapping in the breeze from the nearby fan. Metal scraped on metal as burgers were flipped, veggies were grilled and the deep-fat fryer bubbled with oily goodness.

"Leo Slattery, is that you?" Even before the owner of the voice peeked around the corner of the double-shelf counter, Jane knew the woman would have a smile on her face. A face that had seen even more years than

Trapper, if Jane had to guess. She was short and on the stout side, and her gray hair was pulled back in a bun on the top of her head in a way that accentuated the bright blue of her eyes. "Been back about a week and wondering when I'd be seeing you again. You stay right there, young man! I've got burgers to flip."

"Yes, ma'am. How was your vacation?"

"Vacation? Ha!" Miss D's eyes glinted when she looked over her shoulder. "Two days after I got to my sister's, she and her husband got into a four-car pileup on the highway. I ended up playing nursemaid and wrangler to them and their grandbabies. Then I get back here and find my kitchen's a disaster, and no one's been doing the bookkeeping. I haven't had two seconds to breathe in the last week."

"Miss D was one of my grandmother's best friends," Leo explained. "Rumor has it her award-winning blueberry cobbler was actually my grandmother's original recipe."

"Don't you go blabbing that nonsense around here," Miss D ordered as she swooped around the corner and pulled him into her arms for a hug. "And here I thought when you moved back to Roaring Springs I'd be seeing more of you. You thaw out yet from all that time in the icy north?"

"Just about. Been busy up at the ranch," Leo said. "I'll make it a point to come more often."

"You'd better. Now. Who's this?" She waved her spatula up and down as if sizing Jane up. "Never known you to come pouncing in through the back door."

"Jane doesn't like crowds." Leo motioned through

the window toward the nearly packed diner. "I told her you'd accommodate her."

"Don't blame you, young lady." Miss D moved in closer and peered up at Jane, eyes narrowed and assessing. "One reason I love this kitchen. Keeps out the riffraff, and keeps me from having to deal with them. You look familiar. You new to town?"

"Yes." Jane bit the inside of her cheek, trying to keep her nerves in check.

"Hmm." Miss D nodded slowly, then took her arm and led her back to the grill. "Since I'm betting Leo here came for a reason other than food, and seeing as my help has absconded across the street to take her fiancé to an early supper, I'll put you to work minding these patties." She whipped an apron off a hook and tied it around Jane's waist before pushing another metal spatula in her hand. "Now, don't you go pushing down on them. You just watch. You see those edges start to turn dark, you flip over here, to the cooler part. Okay?"

"Um, sure." Jane turned slightly panicked eyes on Leo, who only flashed that breath-stealing smile at her. And that dimple. Maybe it was the fluorescent lights, but how had she not noticed how deep that dimple in his cheek dipped? Her heart fluttered. Hospitals wouldn't need a defibrillator with him around.

"What brings you by, then?" Miss D hefted her body onto a tall stool and fanned herself with a menu. Jane did her best to keep an eye on the patties as well as an ear on the conversation.

"Can I borrow your phone for a bit? Just a few minutes. I need to do some quick searches and—"

"You telling me they still haven't gotten those lines run up to your place?" Miss D shook her head. "You know how many letters your grandmother wrote to the town council about that? Course that was just because your granddaddy kept going on about it. Poor woman passed before she ever got that FaceTwit or whatever you call it loaded on that computer of hers. Here." She set her spatula down long enough to dig through her purse stashed under the counter. "Don't have much use for it myself, save for emergencies. You might have to charge it up. What food are you ordering?"

He accepted the phone with a quick smile. "You know I'm partial to your burgers. Double decker with fries? And onion rings? I've got Trapper up at my place for a time, so might as well make that two."

"Three," Jane added. The more she stared at the grill the hungrier she got. "And is that lemon pie?"

"Banana pudding icebox cake," Miss D said with a touch of admiration. "Makes an old woman happy to see a flit of a thing like you longing for pie. You got what you need, Leo?"

"Yes, ma'am." Leo was already tapping on the screen of the smartphone. "But you're right. It needs charging."

"Over there, by the walk-in."

"I think these are ready." Jane bent over and pried up the edge of one of the patties. Was it wrong of her to wish the online connection would crash? How much easier things would be if they just stopped looking for answers, if things could just stay as they were.

"You'd be right about the burgers," Miss D declared over her shoulder. "See how that juice is puddling on the top? There's your sign. You sure you're new to town? I swear you look just like—"

"Hey, Miss D!" Someone banged on the pickup bell at the counter. "We've got orders piling up!"

Miss D went still for a moment; then, after giving Jane a slow, purposeful smile, she patted her arm. "You just move those over like I said. I need to go teach that new server of mine some manners."

"Have you found anything?" Jane asked Leo as she carefully placed three burgers into the corner of the grill and, just for fun, moved the spatula through the charring onions.

"Maybe. You okay here for a few minutes?" He held up the phone and turned in a circle. "I think I'll get better reception outside the kitchen."

"Sure." Jane frowned, unfamiliar with the expression on Leo's face. Distracted? Confused? By the time Miss D came back, grumbling under her breath about "this younger generation," Jane was whipping up burgers faster than any assembly line in a factory, including their take-out order.

She jumped when the swinging door burst open and a young woman rushed in, dirty plates balanced on her arms.

"We're hitting an early dinner rush, Miss D."

"Nothing unusual about that, Sylvie. You just keep doing what you're doing, and if young Benny out there—"

"I'm watching him." Sylvie gave a passing curious look to Jane, who must have looked ridiculous in her hat and ranch wear standing at the grill. Jane turned back to the grill.

"You've done great, Jane. Thank you."

Taking Miss D's words as a dismissal, Jane replaced the spatula and was about to remove her apron when she noticed the plates.

"Feel free to scrape those down and stack them there by the sink."

Jane shrugged and brought the garbage can over, but she hesitated over the more than half a steak left on one plate. She shifted to the side slightly and looked out at Leo's truck. Ollie, as if sensing her return, moved into the doorway, tongue sticking out. His eyes were clearly pleading with her to come back outside. "Would you mind if I took this for Ollie?" She stabbed the meat and held it up.

"Not at all. People who come here should know they're going to get a belly full of food. Feel free to take whatever you think he'll eat."

She should probably check with Leo first. After all, Ollie was his dog. But she had seen Trapper sneaking Ollie bits of his steak the other night during dinner and assumed it was okay.

She finished scraping the rest of the plates. "I'll be right back." She hurried outside with the meat and held it out to the dog, who let out an odd whine before chomping it down. "I bet I just won you for life, didn't I, Ollie?" she cooed, scrubbing at the dog's neck. The sudden blare of a siren had her jumping back, and with a cry, she clutched her hands to her chest. A flash of red and blue shot down the narrow footpath between Miss D's diner and the building next door.

Jane's ears roared. Her head felt light. But she steeled her shoulders, forced herself to move toward the fear rather than cowering against the back of the truck. In the distance, she heard Ollie bark, but it sounded dim, foggy almost, as did the bang of a screen door. The sound of her name being called.

Still she moved on, one step, another step. She felt the brick of the wall scrape against her fingers, and when she reached the street, she gasped. Her chest tightened as all the air in her lungs evaporated. The police station just across the street was teeming with officers. Uniformed officers with shiny badges on their dark shirts. Patrol cars buzzed in and out of parking spaces, the spinning lights making her dizzy.

Badges. *Ow!* Pain sliced through her skull as if she'd been stabbed.

"Jane."

She cried out, covering her mouth with her hands as she backed into the wall, knocking her head as she looked up at Leo.

"What happened?" He reached for her, ran his palm against the back of her hair as if checking for injuries. "Why'd you take off…?"

She shook her head, unable to form words, barely able to breathe. Everything hurt. Her fingertips and toes prickled as if she was dying a slow, agonizing death.

"It's going to be okay, Jane," he soothed. "The police can help. We can go inside, talk to someone about what's happened to you. They might know something already." He moved in front of her, grasped her upper arms in a gentle but firm hold. "I'll be right there with you."

"No. You promised. No. Police." She shook her head, hating the tears that sprang to her eyes. Hating the fear that pressed in on her from every angle. He didn't understand. She wasn't safe here. She had to get out of here. Out of this alley. Out of this town. Away from… everyone. "I c-can't…c-can't b-breathe." She pounded a fist against her chest, trying to feel something, anything other than the terror that made every part of her tingle like sharp needles were piercing her skin.

Leo glanced behind him. For an instant, she swore she saw regret pass across his features, as if he was debating whether to listen to her or not. "Please, Leo." She could hear her breath rattling in her chest. "Please take me home."

"Okay, darlin'." He smoothed a hand down her back and murmured softly, "Let's go." He wrapped an arm around her shoulders and pulled her in close. They made their way back to the truck, where she climbed inside and clung to a concerned Ollie like a life preserver. She closed her eyes, pressed her face into the dog's fur and willed the shaking to stop.

"Everything okay out here?" Miss D appeared in the doorway with two large paper bags in her hands.

"Fine," Leo assured her. "Appreciate you letting us stop by. How much do I owe you?"

"Not one red cent." Miss D tsked. "Told you when you got back, you're family, Leo Slattery, and I don't go charging family to keep their strength up. You bring that girl back sometime soon, you hear? She's a good grill minder. And probably has a better head on her shoulders than that ridiculous great-nephew of mine."

"Thank you, Miss D." Leo took the bags and kissed her cheek. From her seat in the car, Jane blinked the tears free and wondered if he had any idea how people looked at him. As if he lit up their day. Her heartbeat eased only to skip a beat as he approached the truck. He secured the bags in the cooler in the back seat— no doubt to protect them from a snooping Ollie—then climbed inside. "You doing better?"

Jane nodded and buried her cheek in Ollie's fur. "I just want to go home."

Chapter 8

Leo had been standing silently in the doorway to the stable for the past few minutes, watching Jane wrangle a line of rope into some kind of knot he would never attempt. The second they'd gotten back to the ranch she'd bolted out of the car, Ollie hot on her heels, and vanished into the stable. To the horses. Where she felt safest.

His instinct had been to follow her, especially since she hadn't uttered a word on the long drive back to the ranch, but he'd held back and left her alone. Mainly because he'd needed some time to erase the image of utter terror he'd seen on her face as she'd looked across the street to the police station.

It had taken every ounce of control he had not to override her protests. His cursory online search—cut short by too many interruptions in the diner and a slow connection—had produced a modicum of information that both eased his mind and raised new concerns. Instead of answers bringing him comfort, the questions he had now convinced him they needed help. Help he was going to demand she ask for. Until he caught her in mid panic attack, staring horror-struck at the police station.

Something more was going on. He was convinced of that now. Her reluctance went deeper than the fear of being discovered and made to face something she wasn't ready to remember.

He hadn't meant for her to confront all her other fears today, either. The Preston place was more than enough. But if he'd had any doubt whether her issues connected somehow to the police department, they were gone now. There was no faking a reaction like that. And he wasn't in any rush to provoke another one.

That said, the day wasn't over yet.

And so he stood. Silently. Watching her. Memorizing the sight for the day when she was no longer here. He suppressed a smile as she turned around in circles. She was so focused on the rope, she didn't notice him.

"So if I put this this way, and then that way—" She stuck her tongue out slightly between her lips, chin tipped down just enough to obscure her eyes from his sight. "Aha! I got it." She tugged the two ends of the rope and solidified the knot. "I was faster this time, Duke. What do you think? Will Trap approve?"

The horse nickered and bobbed his head up and down, and Ollie let out a yelp of greeting before bounding over to Leo.

His heart swelled as Jane raised her eyes to look at him. She fit. Despite how she'd arrived, despite having no recollection of who she was, she fit. Here, on the ranch. Here. *With him.* He wanted her, not just in his bed, but in his life. She didn't just make his days better, she made them brighter. And it wasn't just the loneliness talking; but that ache, that longing for what he had come to accept might never be, had been eased. All by this woman. And not even the Colorado sunset could compete with his current view. "You do have a way with them."

"Trap bet me I couldn't get this one." She whipped the knotted rope around. "He owes me a beer. I have a witness." She gave him a shaky smile. The fear was still there. The aftershock, for want of a better word. Leo hung one of the discarded ropes on a peg and walked over to give Duke a pat on the neck. "You about done?" Polite conversation had become their mainstay. It had to be if he was going to keep the distance he needed to maintain. "Dinner's ready."

"You mean dinner's unpacked." She glanced at the clock on the wall. "I'm sorry. I didn't realize I'd been out here so long."

"No harm done. Miss D's burgers reheat great." It was a small lie, and the only one he'd told her. So far.

He loved watching her. She had an elegance in the way she moved. He looked down at the boots on her feet. Made of richly dyed, gray leather with the silver stitching, they'd barely been worn. His mother's boots, Leo mused and not for the first time was grateful that while his grandmother had been a practical woman and not one to keep too many possessions, she'd kept enough memories of the mother he didn't remember for the day he was ready. And what better time than to help Jane? And that's what he was supposed to be doing: helping her. Not wanting her.

"I'm sorry."

"For what?" He didn't care for the uncertainty clouding her beautiful brown eyes.

"For running away like that. For being a coward." At first he thought she was afraid to meet his gaze, but she inched up her chin and her eyes flashed. "I can't explain—"

"You don't have to explain."

"Of course I do," she snapped. "For crying out loud, you're putting your life, your work, on hold to babysit me and I can't even bring myself to step inside a police station. Could I be any more pathetic?" Jane unbolted Teyla's stall door and guided the haltered horse into the center of the aisle, snapping cross ties to the noseband before grabbing a brush.

"You dealt with a lot today," Leo told her. "Clearly taking you into town was a mistake and pushed you too far."

"I'm not some delicate flower who's going to break in the wind." Jane smoothed the brush over Teyla's flank. "At least I sure don't want to be. But every time I get the chance to move past it—"

Her block hit whenever she came anywhere near the police. Something he needed to find a way around. "Whatever happened to you was traumatic, Jane. We all deal with events like that in our own way. There's no one solution. Trust me, I know."

Her hand stilled. She took a step to the side and looked at him. "You really do, don't you. You aren't just saying that?"

Leo took a deep breath. "My father." He'd never talked about it. Not really. There hadn't been a reason to, but there was now. Not to help himself, but to help Jane. He cleared his throat as the grief surged. "He never was able to deal with whatever happened to him in the war. Other than being diagnosed with severe PTSD, there wasn't much that could be done so my grandparents brought him home. Here. My grandfather always said there wasn't anything a Colorado sky couldn't fix. It took some time, but we thought he was doing better. He was working with the horses, seemed to be adjusting after his latest stay at the VA but we missed the signs. Maybe we were too hopeful, I don't know."

He looked her square in the eye because looking anywhere else would mean falling back into the memory of a day he'd spent a lifetime trying to forget. "He shot himself. Out next to my mother's grave." Out where his grandparents had later buried their only son. "I was seventeen. He got up that morning, had breakfast with us, said he had a full day planned and then…" Leo waited for the sympathy to erupt in her eyes, the patronizing pity he remembered so clearly from the days surrounding his father's death: the funeral, the reception. The church services for months after. Instead, what he found on Jane's face was sincere empathy shining in those glorious eyes of her. "We heard the shot a few minutes later. He was just…gone."

"I'm sorry, Leo."

"Me, too." Leo managed a wan smile. He didn't tell her the rest—that in some ways, his father's death had been a relief. A release. For all of them. Whatever bitterness and anger Leo might have felt over losing his father had been tempered by the memories that had been good. Memories his grandparents had been determined to focus on. "It's not something I like to talk about. For obvious reasons, but if you're ever wondering why I'm so determined to help you get beyond this—"

"Whatever *this* is."

"Whatever this is." He stepped closer, took the brush from her hand and set it aside. Every nerve ending in his body burst to life. That's what she did to him: brought him to life. He should walk away. He should run, but didn't want to. What he wanted, what he needed, was to be with her. If only for the breath of a moment. For a moment, this moment, he wanted to give in. "There is more to this than me wanting to help you, Jane. A lot more."

"I didn't mean to complicate things between us last night. You know, by kissing you."

Complicate things? Massive understatement. But it wasn't the kiss that complicated things. It was the memory of the other night, after her nightmare, the image of her in bed wearing only a bra and panties, clutching thin blankets against her rising chest as she stared up at him with eyes filled with…longing. Longing he shared. Longing he was finding more difficult to deny. He stroked a finger down the side of her face, felt a bolt of desire hit him straight in the gut before it moved lower and settled, heavy and throbbing as she leaned her cheek into his touch.

"Things were complicated before then."

"Since when is complicated a bad thing?"

"Jane—" He lifted his other hand, brushed his fingers along the length of her arm before coming to rest against the side of her neck. She closed her eyes. The softness of her skin, the absolute trust on her face stirred him to the core. He gazed down at her, memorizing every feature. The shadows of the attack had faded, but hadn't fully disappeared. The jagged scar along her hairline was constant evidence of that. "Jane," he whispered as reason tried to retain its hold.

"I thought I was wrong." Her voice swept through him like a warm breeze on a winter's day. "I thought maybe it's just me who feels this way." She straightened and looked him straight in the eyes. Eyes that were as clear and as coherent as they could possibly be. "I think perhaps we should find out for sure. Make sure last night wasn't a fluke. That way if I'm wrong—"

He kissed her. The first brush of his lips against hers set everything inside him aflame. The faint pressure, featherlight and questioning, as if asking permission, shot through him even as he heard a soft moan escape her throat. "It's not just you," he murmured before kissing her harder. Longer. He wanted this. Wanted her. And as her hand slid up his side, fingertips dancing along his hip, his ribs, around to the back of his shoulder, he fought for control.

"FAST FIVE" READER SURVEY

Your participation entitles you to:
✳ 4 Thank-You Gifts Worth Over $20!

Complete the survey in minutes.

Get 2 FREE Books

Your Thank-You Gifts include **2 FREE BOOKS** and **2 MYSTERY GIFTS**. There's no obligation to purchase anything!

See inside for details.

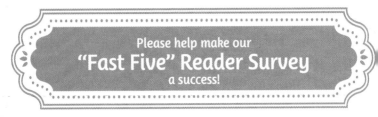

Dear Reader,

Since you are a lover of our books, your opinions are important to us... and so is your time.

That's why we made sure your **"FAST FIVE" READER SURVEY** can be completed in just a few minutes. Your answers to the five questions will help us remain at the forefront of women's fiction.

And, as a thank-you for participating, we'd like to send you **4 FREE THANK-YOU GIFTS!**

Enjoy your gifts with our appreciation,

Pam Powers

To get your
4 FREE THANK-YOU GIFTS:

✳ Quickly complete the "Fast Five" Reader Survey
and return the insert.

"FAST FIVE" READER SURVEY

1	Do you sometimes read a book a second or third time?	○ Yes ○ No
2	Do you often choose reading over other forms of entertainment such as television?	○ Yes ○ No
3	When you were a child, did someone regularly read aloud to you?	○ Yes ○ No
4	Do you sometimes take a book with you when you travel outside the home?	○ Yes ○ No
5	In addition to books, do you regularly read newspapers and magazines?	○ Yes ○ No

YES! I have completed the above Reader Survey. Please send me my 4 FREE GIFTS (gifts worth over $20 retail). I understand that I am under no obligation to buy anything, as explained on the back of this card.

240/340 HDL GNPN

FIRST NAME	LAST NAME

ADDRESS

APT.#	CITY

STATE/ PROV.	ZIP/POSTAL CODE

READER SERVICE—Here's how it works:

BUSINESS REPLY MAIL
FIRST-CLASS MAIL   PERMIT NO. 717   BUFFALO, NY

POSTAGE WILL BE PAID BY ADDRESSEE

READER SERVICE
PO BOX 1341
BUFFALO NY 14240-8571

NO POSTAGE
NECESSARY
IF MAILED
IN THE
UNITED STATES

◄ If offer card is missing write to: Reader Service, P.O. Box 1341, Buffalo, NY 14240-8531 or visit www.ReaderService.com ◄

"Leo." His name on her lips was as close to a plea as he'd ever heard. A plea he couldn't bring himself to deny.

He drew her closer, wrapped an arm around her waist and tugged her against him as his mouth covered hers again. He dived in, devoured every inch of her that he could as she sank into him. The softness of her drove him instantly to the brink of sanity. In all his life he'd never wanted for a thing. Until this moment. Now, all he wanted was Jane.

Her hands fisted in his shirt, tugged him further past reason, deeper into that abyss of desire he wanted to dive into. His hands moved over her back, to the waist-band of her jeans, pulled the hem of her shirt free so he could touch the bare skin beneath. Soft. Silky. Feminine. His fingers pressed into her flesh, and Jane moved into him. He stepped back until he felt the wall at his back and, bracing himself—bracing both of them—inched his hands up to beneath the fabric of her bra.

She gasped into his mouth as her hands released only long enough for her to curve her arms up and around his neck. There wasn't an inch of his body that wasn't burning. Every part of her that pressed into him fired then fried the synapses in his brain as his hands moved down and around, cupped her waist and pulled her hard against him.

She tore her mouth free, which gave him full access to the side of her neck. He trailed his lips to the pulse point throbbing beneath her skin, and felt a power punch of pride that he was the reason for its erratic beat.

"Leo." Never had a moan and a prayer merged so

beautifully. "Please." She ducked her head and caught his mouth again with hers, her breasts crushing against his chest to where he could feel her hardened nipples pressing against him. It would be so easy, so very easy...

"Jane," he murmured when she came up for breath. He looked down at her, cupped his hand around her cheek and knew those passion-glazed eyes that struggled to focus were all for him.

Jane...

Reason descended in an instant, crashing through his desire. Leo squeezed his eyes closed and tilted his head back until it knocked against the wall. His body was so tight he thought his bones might snap. He was hard, everywhere, for her, but this wasn't right.

"Leo?" The sound of his name on her lips nearly drove him over the brink. He shook his head. He couldn't look at her. Not now. Not again. Because he knew if he did, this wouldn't stop with a kiss.

Her name wasn't Jane.

"We can't do this." He reached up to pry her hands from around his neck. "I can't do this."

"Could have fooled me," Jane said with a bitter laugh that scraped along the edges of his heart.

"Jane." He did look at her now and saw the disappointment descend, erasing the desire that only moments ago he'd been stoking. And that, beyond everything else, made this even more difficult. "I'm not going to deny I want you," he murmured gruffly. "That I want to be with you. I care about you." He stroked her cheek as defeat rose in her face. "But we can't. Not like this. Not before we know who you are. For all we know you—" he had to take an extra breath to push the thought free "—you could have a family. You could be married." The very idea was like a knife in his heart.

"I don't think that's true," she countered without hesitation.

"You're making my point. You don't know. Not for certain. And neither do I." He shouldn't, *couldn't* care this much. Not this fast. And not about a woman who, because of some crazy, violent attack, had memories only of a few weeks. "Until I'm certain you know your own mind, whatever is happening between us isn't going to go any further. I can't let it."

The passion that had been shining in her eyes seconds ago vanished beneath a flash of anger as she stepped out of his hold. "You think I need a memory to know what I want?"

"I think that until we know who you really are, you're not in a position to make this choice. Not when you can't comprehend the potential consequences." For either of them. He lifted his hand, wanting nothing more than to stroke that sudden tension from her face, to feel the heat of her skin beneath his fingertips.

She stood there, hands on her hips, fingers tangled in the cloth of the shirt he'd tugged free of her jeans, and stared at him. And all he could do was hope the wall would support him. "Well, then. There's only one solution. We need to find out who I am."

"I agree." He took a steeling breath. "Which is why I need to ask you something."

"What?"

Leo knew what he needed to do. What he didn't

want to do. Once he started down this path, there was
no going back. Once he asked her the question, it was
only a matter of time before she walked away. But he'd
made her a promise: to get her home. "Does the name
Skye Colton mean anything to you?"

Skye Colton. Skye Colton. Skye…

Jane repeated the name over and over again in her
head as if it was some magical mantra destined to unlock the mysteries of her memory.

For a man seemingly preoccupied with her identity,
Leo certainly didn't seem to be in any rush to dive
deeper into the question he'd posed. Every time she attempted to start the discussion over dinner, he shifted
his attention to Trapper and their conversation about
which outbuilding on the property they thought would
be best for Gwen once she and Lacey got home from
their honeymoon.

Jane's anger simmered, low and steady as she ate
pretty much in silence, doing her best to curtail her
sighs of frustration and refrain from rolling her eyes.
He was stalling. She knew it. And given the looks he'd
shot her across the table, he knew she knew. Who was
this Skye Colton? And why did she have this nagging
desire to prove him wrong?

"I don't know, Trap." Leo shook his head and finished his beer. "I think they need space. Not just around
the house, but inside it."

"Well, if it's space you're looking for…" Trapper
mumbled and dumped another spoonful of sugar into
his coffee.

Jane finally pushed her plate away, then snatched one last fry. "Sounds to me as if you need a female perspective."

The men dropped into silence.

"Yes, that's right. I'm still here." She wiped her mouth and stood, picked up her plate, then slapped Trapper's hand when he tried to sneak Ollie another handful of fries. "Stop that. He's had enough treats today."

Trapper scowled. Ollie whined.

Leo grinned. "You heard the lady."

"Since it seems we need this settled before we latch on to other topics." She glared at Leo before she carried the dishes over to the sink. Ignoring Ollie trailing behind her, she retrieved the icebox cake from the fridge. "How many outbuildings do you have on the property?"

"Half a dozen or so. Mostly they're used for storage during the winter," Leo explained. "There's also the original foreman's house out on the outer edge of the property, but I haven't had a chance to check that out since I've been back."

"Buck's old place?" Trapper asked.

Leo shook his head. "No, he wanted to be closer to the main house and stable. I'm talking about the old stone cottage on the upper ridge."

"Ah." Trapper's eyebrows shot up so high they disappeared beneath his scraggly gray hair. "That was originally where your granddaddy was going to build that fishing cabin he always talked about, but then Essie got involved. It ain't no cabin."

"Is cabin code for something?" Jane cut three pieces of cake and rejoined them.

"Could be code for a lot of things." Leo sank his fork into the creamy cake. "You know?" He took a bite and nodded. "I think this is another of my grandmother's recipes."

Stop stalling, Jane mouthed.

Leo looked at her for an extra beat, then ducked his head.

"Cake like this is why Essie Slattery was queen of the church social," Trapper cackled as he attacked his own dessert.

Finally. A lull. "So are you going to talk about who you think I am or are you saving that for another meal?" She popped her fork in her mouth and leaned over to took him square in the eye.

Leo swallowed so hard she heard it.

"You find something out, young'un?" Trapper frowned. "I'm disappointed in you. Thought you'd be chomping at the bit to share that tidbit of information."

"Yes," Jane said even as those knots in her stomach tightened. When were they ever going to go away? They'd loosened for a bit, just a while ago when she and Leo had been kissing in the barn. No doubt because being in his arms, losing herself in the feel of him, in the taste of him, was the only time her brain actually turned off. And every other part of her turned on. She might not know who she was or what her life was about, but she knew she wanted him. "Leo seems to believe I'm Skye Colton."

Trapper swore. "You can't be serious."

"I am," Leo said. "I didn't have a lot of time on Miss D's phone, but when I did a search for local missing persons, Skye Colton's name popped up." He turned expectant eyes on her. "She's been missing since early July."

Jane wanted to shrug off the coincidence along with the sudden chill, but couldn't. She wanted answers, didn't she? She wanted to know who she was. So why was she suddenly so afraid of knowing the truth? "If you're waiting for me to suddenly have an identity epiphany, you're out of luck. I haven't had so much as a blip since you mentioned her name in the stable. So which one of you want to tell me who these Coltons are?"

"Allow me," Leo cut Trapper off before he could speak. "The Coltons own a big—"

Trapper snorted.

"Let's just say they own a good portion of Roaring Springs." Leo silenced him with a look.

"Russ Colton calls it the Colton Empire, if that tells you anything," Trapper muttered. "And that's just one branch of the family tree."

"Trap, knock it off," Leo snapped.

The old man held up his hands and resumed eating his dessert.

"The Roaring Springs Coltons started off with a small ski business," Leo explained. "And grew it into a five-star resort that stretches from the valley to the mountains."

"Fancy fallutin' place if you ask me," Trapper mumbled into his plate. "That lodge is a monstrosity and don't get me started on that *Chateau*."

Jane blinked. "And you think I'm one of them? You think I'm this Skye?"

"Jane." How she hated the careful way he said her name. "How can you not be? The timeline fits. The clothes you were wearing when I found you scream money. Like I said, I didn't have much time to look very deep, since I was looking into that other matter first."

Jane pressed her lips tight. The ID they'd found in the abandoned property. She'd almost forgotten about that.

"Young lady, you are not a Colton." Trapper stabbed his fork at her and for the first time, she saw open hostility in the old man's eyes. "You know how I know? You've got a soul. You're connected to this land. To those horses out there. You've a natural touch and a gentle nature. Them Coltons don't know nothing but takeovers and buyouts. Water rights, sky-high prices most regular folk can't afford. They haven't made many friends with us regulars, that's for sure."

"Regulars?" Jane looked to Leo for an explanation even as her insides began to roll.

"Regular folks. Townsfolk." Leo shook his head. "It's just a guess, Jane. I only got a glimpse of the missing persons list before Miss D told me you'd run off. I didn't see any photos, but the pieces fit pretty firmly. It's enough of a lead we should pursue it."

"How, exactly?" Jane abandoned her dessert and crossed her arms over her chest. "Another trip into town to use Miss D's cell phone? Or would that just be pretense to try to get me to go to the police again?"

Leo shook his head. "Jane, I promised I wouldn't do that and I don't—"

"You don't break your promises. Yeah, I got that the first ten times you told me." That was one of the few certainties in life she knew she could count on. "So, what? We just sit on this information and hope my brain kicks in and proves you right?"

"How about we sleep on it for tonight and look at it again in the morning," Leo suggested in that calm, rational tone that grated on Jane's last nerve. "I don't want to go assuming anything just yet, and you've already dealt with a lot today. Just…let it sit. And we'll go from there."

"Fine." Someday he was going to be wrong. But today, tonight? She'd let it sit.

A creak echoed through the house. Leo blinked up at the ceiling he'd been staring at for the better part of the night. The second he saw the name Colton pop up on his missing persons search, he knew however crazy his life had become since Jane's arrival, it was about to take a whole new turn. A soft bang cut through the night.

Leo frowned, confused for a moment as to what he was hearing. "Jane." Was she running away? Taking off to find out the truth without him?

He was on his bare feet and out in the hall in seconds, heading straight for her room. Those internet stories about the Avalanche Killer had seeped into his sub-conscious, creating waves of worry that continued to flow beneath the surface of his forced calm. But those weren't the thoughts keeping him awake. No. Those thoughts had everything to do with the beautiful woman residing down the hall from him. "Jane?" He flattened his hand against her door and pushed it open. The bed was empty. "Ollie?"

The dog had taken to sleeping with her now, something Leo tried not to envy. He missed the constant companionship the dog had given him. But Ollie wasn't there, either.

Another squeak, another softer bang and Leo was heading through the kitchen to the back porch. The relief that surged through him when he saw her, Ollie close by, robbed him of breath. She was still here.

She hadn't left. Yet.

Leo gripped the door frame. Desire ripped through him like a summer storm as he looked at her, sitting on the top porch step, leaning against the railing. She was barefoot and wearing only boxer shorts and a skimpy blue tank top. The moonlight shone bright enough to catch against that glorious red hair of hers; hair that spilled around her shoulders, curling at the very tips as if tempting a man—tempting *him*—to catch them between his fingers. Liquid fire. Both the woman and her hair.

She turned her head toward him. "Did I wake you?" Her voice wafted over him, drew him outside where the Colorado summer night grazed over his bare torso. The loose-fitting pajama pants were a gift at the moment, hopefully hiding his instant reaction to the sight of her against the mountains tipped with darkness. "Ollie isn't the quietest dog on the planet." But she smiled as she said it.

"I wasn't asleep. What about you?" He sat on the same step, determined to keep some distance between them. But when he braced a foot on the step, he noticed it was scant inches from hers. It would be so easy, he knew, to slip his arms around her, to kiss her again and draw her back inside, where they could pass the rest of the night together without a moment of rest.

"Nightmares again." She ran her hand up and down her arm as she turned her gaze back to the mountains. "They're getting worse. More intense. It's like I can feel him grabbing me." She pressed her foot flat. "Even though the bruises are gone, I can still feel his hands."

Rage bubbled low in his stomach, and Leo actually wondered what would happen if he ever got his hands on the man who had attacked her. "I'm sorry."

She shook her head. "No reason for you to be. But I can't give in to them anymore. I'm finding this—" she motioned to the night "—a very good cure to nightmares." She took a deep breath, and Leo's gaze dropped as her breasts pushed high against the deep V of her tank. He bit back a groan as her nipples contracted against the fabric. Did she even know what she was doing to him? "Do you hate them as much as Trapper does?"

"Who?" Leo tried to get some of the blood back into his brain.

"The Coltons. Do you hate them, too?"

"No." Leo could answer honestly. "I remember my grandfather and Trapper having the same argument while I was growing up. Don't get me wrong. I understand where Trapper is coming from. The small-town feel is gone for the most part. Those independent businesses in town, they struggle a lot more than they used to. It's become a bit of a competition, trying to draw customers from the resort into town. People who come to Roaring Springs, they want to experience all the town has to offer, but to do that they have to choose. I like to think there's enough for everyone if some kind of balance could be found."

"So you haven't been to…" Jane frowned. "What did Trapper call it? The Lodge?"

"Ah, no." Leo laughed and shook his head. "No, that's a bit out of my price range. Besides, I've got the best view in all of Roaring Springs. The view my grandparents fell in love with more than fifty years ago."

"And you think I'm one of them."

He knew an answer had to be found, but he also knew, once she knew who she was, she'd be leaving this place. Leaving…him. "I do." And because he'd made her a promise, added, "One step inside the police station, and we'd probably find out for sure."

In the dim glow of moonlight, he saw her jaw clench.

"It couldn't hurt to ask, Jane. All it would take is one phone call. I can have the sheriff come out—"

"No police." Her voice shot like bullets into the night. "If I'm a Colton, we'll figure it out. Or I'll remember. Now that I have a possible name, maybe something will shake loose. Until then, we have work to do on the ranch."

"Oh, we do, do we?" Leo liked the sound of that entirely too much. He was sure going to miss her when she left. He was already dreading the mornings when he walked into the kitchen and she was not there waiting for him. He was already… His hand froze on his knee. He was already in love with her. He swallowed hard, but found it impossible to dislodge the epiphany. It wasn't going anywhere. Because he did love her. Her name didn't matter, not when he'd been dealing with, living with, whoever she was at heart. "Have plans for this place, do you?"

"Maybe." Her eyes sparked in the darkness. "I want to take a ride tomorrow. On Ginger. See this place and those buildings and this land the way you do. The way your grandparents did. And I want one more thing." She slid across the step and covered his hand with hers. "You."

"Jane—"

"Sleep, Leo. That's all." But the way her hand curved around his, the way her fingers slipped between his, told him he was going to have a difficult time denying her. "I'm tired of feeling so alone. That bed's too big. It lets the nightmares in. Please, Leo. I won't ask for more. I just want to be near you. Close to you."

He looked down at their clasped hands, which was torture enough. But sleeping in the same bed with her, feeling every curve, every inch of her luscious body pressing against his…?

"Are you tired now?"

She nodded, and the action did what he'd seen in his dreams so many times. Her hair spilled forward, brushed against his legs.

"You okay with a chaperone?" He glanced at the dog. Ollie heaved a sigh and rolled his eyes as if telling Leo to get on with it already.

Never one to ignore advice from his dog, Leo stood. And held out his hand.

*** * ***

The face in the mirror wasn't her.

The face looked like her. Mostly. A bit rounder per-
haps, a bit softer. Kinder? But as she looked closer into
the rearview mirror of her car, she wondered—

Glass exploded against her side, showering her with
hot, sharp shards. Her skin stung where they struck as
the door was ripped open and the hand reached inside.

She screamed. That throat-ripping, from-her-
toes scream only desperation and terror evoked. She
kicked. She clawed. She struck out, breaking nails as
she grabbed desperately for the latch on her seat belt.
Just as the hand locked around her bare ankle...

"Help me! Phoebe, help me!"

She twisted and turned, searching the back seat,
hoping to find what—who—she was looking for. But
found only herself looking back at her.

"Help me!"

"Jane!"

She was shaken so hard her teeth almost rattled. A
dog barked in the distance.

"Jane, come out of it. Come on. Wake up."

She was lifted up and pulled out of the dream so
firmly, the ghostly images of her attacker vanished like
smoke.

"That's it. Open your eyes, Jane. Look at me. Look.
At. Me." A hard, firm arm encircled her back while a
strong hand caught her chin, turning her face so that
as she blinked awake, she saw the only thing that could
ease the fear.

"Leo." The whisper caught on a sob and she leaned

into him, clung to him. Wrapped herself around him so tight she wasn't sure where either of them ended. A cold nose pressed into the base of her spine and she jumped. "Ollie," she breathed and reached back to touch the dog.

"You scared him," Leo chided gently. "I think they might have heard you down at the state line."

"Oh, no. No." She squeezed her eyes closed, but choked back the tears. She would not cry. She would not shed another tear over what she couldn't remember. "The dreams were supposed to stop."

"No." Leo pressed his lips to the top of her head. He was so gentle, so kind. So good. She almost broke her vow not to let a tear fall. "No, they were supposed to get better. And they are. If you think about it, you know they are."

If she thought about it? What on earth was he…? Jane frowned, forcing her mind back into those moments, back into the car. And the mirror.

The eyes. Brown eyes. The same as her own.

"Phoebe? Who's Phoebe?"

"Who are you asking?" Leo stroked her back, rocked her gently. "Me or yourself?"

"Both." Neither. The residual fear was fading faster now, faster than it had before. Her fingers curled into his bare skin. Jane took a deep breath and inhaled the now familiar scent of him. She smelled the clean air of Colorado, the hint of leather and the faint hint of citrus. Strong. Sturdy. Masculine scents that when combined seemed made just for her.

"Are you Phoebe?" Leo whispered into her hair.

Was she? She frowned, allowing herself another moment in the dream, imagining the woman, whoever she was, to answer the question. "Phoebe." Jane shook her head and sat up, but not far enough to break his hold on her. She didn't want Leo to let go of her. Ever. "No. It doesn't feel…right." Close. But not right. "I'm sor—" Her apology was silenced by Leo's mouth as he kissed her. Kissed her so completely, so thoroughly, that the last vestiges of the dream fractured and drifted away.

And just like that…she settled.

When he lifted his lips, he replaced them with a gentle fingertip that stroked along her swollen mouth. "That's the last time I want you to apologize."

"But it was such a nice way to tell me to stop." She couldn't help it. She smiled. The sweat dotting her face evaporated in the cool breeze drifting in through the open window. "Is it time to get up?"

"Not yet. A few hours to go." He shifted and sat back against the wooden headboard that reached up half the wall. But he didn't release her. He pulled her with him and she curled up, tucked securely into his side, her head resting on his shoulder. "Go back to sleep, dar-lin'." He kissed her forehead, stroked the side her face. "Just close your eyes and go back to sleep."

Easy for him to say. Jane's mouth twisted in frustra-tion as she thought about how much she wanted to touch him, to kiss him, to explore every inch of this glorious, honorable, sexy man. It would be so easy. Her fingers warmed at the thought. Or maybe it was due to their pressing into the space just below his heart. Bare skin. Taut skin. It wouldn't take much to just—

As if reading her mind, his hand caught hers and brought it up to his shoulder. "Go to sleep, Jane."

She sighed. Then smiled.

And slept.

Chapter 9

"Oh, this is the one." Jane all but jumped out of the saddle and was moving across the path before her feet hit the ground. She pulled off the riding gloves and stuck them in her back pocket as she approached the single-story ranch house. "How was there ever any question?" She glanced back at Leo as he dismounted and tied both horses' reins over the porch railing.

"Gwen said she and Lacey didn't want that big a place. She thinks it's too much work." He patted his hand on the railing behind her as Jane admired the wood-carved front door.

"To get it ready or maintain?"

"Ah." Leo shrugged. "Don't know. Didn't ask."

"Men." Jane rolled her eyes and walked to the window, where she cupped her hands around her eyes to peer in. "Oh, there's really good bones to this place, Leo. It's perfect for a newlywed couple. It's quiet, romantic and, from what I can tell, quite practical."

"Are you sure Buck's old place—"

"No." She shook her head and moved to the door as if that settled the matter. "Nope. I mean, that place is great and all for a single cowboy, but this, I'm betting…" She trailed off as she pushed open the door. The first thing she saw was a cobblestoned fireplace. "Oh, yeah. This is it. I love this floor. And it's in pretty good shape. Just needs some sprucing up." She stomped her foot in a few places to prove her point. "When are they due back?"

"End of September I think. I have the date back at home."

"Okay, okay." She nodded and circled the kitchen, pulled open a few cabinets, ran her fingers along the dusty butcher-block countertop. "I think we can make that work. Let me see the rest."

"Have at it."

He was humoring her and she knew it. She'd scared the crap out of him with that nightmare last night. But the second she'd woken up this morning, well after Leo as he'd already been up and dressed and drunk half a pot of coffee, she'd thrown the memory of the nightmare aside and was ready to plow ahead into the day. Which she did, tending to the horses in the stable while Leo went out to take care of the herd. They'd met back at the main house by noon and set out to explore on horseback soon after lunch. Trapper, being Trapper, was packing up to take off for some, as he called it, "alone time." Who knew when he'd be popping back around.

"So Gwen's going to be your fore—person." Fore-woman sounded so odd. "What does Lacey do?"

"She writes historical novels. Big sweeping epics like Larry McMurtry. There was talk about turning one of them into a movie a while back, but it didn't happen."

Jane emerged from the bedroom she'd been examining. "What's Lacey's last name?"

"Conroy. But she writes as L. C. Hamilton."

She sagged against the door frame. "*The Prairie Before Me*. Your Lacey is L. C. Hamilton?"

"Well, she's not *my* Lacey," Leo joked.

"I loved that book. I remember sitting on the window bench in my bedroom glued to the pages. All the details about the pioneers and… What?" She broke off at the odd expression on Leo's face.

"You remember." His eyes flickered as his lips twitched. "That's the first time you said anything about your past."

She blinked. Again. A third time. "You're right. I can see that space, that room, so vividly. Blues and silvers and cream-colored fabric draping the windows." She walked over to the grimy pane of glass and touched a fingertip against it.

"What else do you remember?"

She hadn't heard him approach, shouldn't have been surprised to find he'd drawn near, but she shivered nonetheless. "Snow. So much snow I could barely see out my window. I looked up one minute and it had nearly obscured the entire pane." Elegance. Order and organization. And loneliness. She remembered feeling very, very lonely. She rubbed her fingers against her chest, just above her heart. She never felt lonely around

Leo. Even when he was out on the land. "She'll need an office."

"Who will?" Leo touched her shoulder.

"Lacey. She'll need an office where she can write. How many bedrooms are there?"

"Three," Leo told her. "Jane, let's explore this some more. Let's see what else we can get you to remember."

"Not now."

"Why not? Something's been jarred loose. It's the perfect time—"

"No, it's not." Jane cut him off. "If I remember more, I'll tell you, but for now, I'm fine with this. I'm not in any rush." She didn't want to remember more. Not yet. She wanted to take baby steps, not giant leaps. She wanted to stay here, for as long as possible. Not because of how safe she felt here. But because the idea of leaving Leo scared her more than whatever secrets her past held. "Please, let's just take this slow. I don't want to force things."

"The world won't stop just because you want it to, Jane."

"I know. But I can slow it down." She did look at him now. She had to, otherwise he'd never see the determination she made sure shone in her eyes.

"Okay." He sighed. "So this is the space, huh?"

"This is the space. Which means now we need to get down to business and discuss the budget."

"And also who we're going to hire to do the work."

"Hire?" Jane shook her head and patted him on the arm as she passed. "We don't have to hire anyone. I'm going to do it myself."

* * *

"You're doing it again." Prescott Reynolds bent down to peer at Phoebe Colton's reflection in the dressing table mirror. His hands rested on her shoulders, giving her a gentle squeeze of encouragement. Comfort. Understanding.

"Doing what?" Phoebe feigned ignorance as she flicked a finger against an errant hair band.

"Worrying. Everyone who can be is looking for Skye. They're going to find her. You have to believe that."

"I do." But would they find her in time? Phoebe pressed her fingers against the ache in her chest. The ache that had begun when Skye had taken off out of the blue after being embarrassed, humiliated and hurt over learning she'd been dumped by her longtime boyfriend via social media. It had been almost two months since she'd heard from her sister. Her hope had reignited briefly when the police located Skye's car in an abandoned salvage yard fifty miles south of town. The only reason they'd found it was because some kid had tried to pawn Skye's laptop and phone, which Trey Colton, the sheriff, had put a trace on. The kid had panicked and spilled everything.

The car had been totaled, with severe damage to the back bumper and front right side. The driver's-side window had been busted, the airbags deployed. Two types of blood had been found on the driver's seat: Skye's and one other, so far unidentified. And one of her shoes, a lipstick-red stiletto, had been found under her seat.

Skye's luggage and all her belongings, save for the laptop and cell phone, were still in the trunk. But that's where the trail, and Phoebe's hope, ended. No prints had been found on the car, including Skye's, which meant whoever was responsible for her twin's disappearance knew how not to leave evidence behind. As if disabling the GPS hadn't been the first indication. The entire thing made Phoebe sick to her stomach.

How many times had she read Skye's last text, the one that said she needed time alone, time to regroup and think? That her twin had utterly and completely vanished from every aspect of her life—how many hours had Phoebe spent scouring social media for any sign of her sister?—was simply inexplicable. Even if she was disillusioned with the rest of the world, Skye never would have cut herself off from Phoebe. Unless...

Phoebe took a shuddering breath. Skye wasn't dead. The idea wouldn't even solidify in her mind. Call it a twin thing, call it a psychic connection or call it having spent every single day with her identical sister since the moment they were conceived. She'd know if Skye had left her behind. And right now, that was the only thing keeping Phoebe sane. "I dreamed about her again last night."

"I know." Preston took hold of her hand and led her over to the small settee by the window and pulled her down beside him. "You were talking in your sleep."

Phoebe curled into him, overwhelmed by love for this man who had taken not only her on, but pretty much the entire Colton family when the two of them had gotten...involved. Phoebe almost smiled. Funny way to explain whatever had happened between her and Prescott. Somehow she, stuck-in-the-corner Phoebe

Colton, had landed in the spotlight with one of the most eligible bachelors in Hollywood. All, when she stopped to think on it, because of Skye.

"I keep seeing horses." Phoebe toyed with a button on his crisp white shirt. "Lots of horses. And this beautiful dog. It's so strange. I can't explain it."

"You don't have to," Prescott told her. "But what you do have to do is focus on the moment. We need to get to the hospital before visiting hours are over and meet the newest Colton."

"Mmm." Phoebe managed a smile now. "I'm betting Molly and Max's little girl is simply gorgeous." A pang of envy struck just below the ache. "It's bittersweet, isn't it, that they named her Sabrina?" The body of Molly's sister, Sabrina Gilford, had been discovered after the avalanche, a suspected victim of the Avalanche Killer. Phoebe and Molly had talked about Molly's grief over her child never being able to know her aunt. But being her namesake should help heal the wounds of loss.

"It's a lovely tribute," Prescott agreed. "A way to bring a bit of light to the darkness."

"I suppose. This Sabrina certainly won't be lacking for love or attention. She'll be getting boatloads of both." Beginning with the huge teddy bear Phoebe had ordered to be delivered to the house when the new family arrived home.

"Maybe we can stop and talk to Daria? See if there's been any progress?"

"We can do that." Preston sank his hands into her long hair to rub her neck. "I don't want you giving up hope. Your sister will come back."

He didn't promise. He wouldn't, Phoebe understood as she squeezed her eyes shut against the pain. Preston would never promise her something he couldn't deliver. Which meant he knew what she did.

With every day that passed, it was becoming less and less likely she'd ever see her twin again.

"Come on! Hurry up! I can't go without you!"

"I'm coming!" Jane's response was automatic. Just as automatic as her following the long-haired, red-headed girl running along the path in front of her.

"Careful, girls. Presentation, remember." The stern warning triggered a bout of eye rolling that gave Jane a headache. "Those are new shoes. No scuff marks, please."

Jane looked down at the shiny black patent leather Mary Janes. For a moment she considered scuffing them on purpose, just because. Presentation was everything to her mother, but presentation came with a cost. It took a lot of the fun out of life. Pretty is as pretty does, her grandmother used to say. What did that saying even mean? Why couldn't they just play and have fun without anyone telling them to stop?

"Where are we going?" Jane called as the girl disappeared around the bend. The paved road gave way to gravel, which gave way to dirt. Rocky soil. Soil that hurt her feet as she ran after her. Night snapped on, plunging her into darkness. But there, in the distance, bright red hair. A beacon. A guide.

But she stopped running. It hurt to breathe now. It hurt to think. The light in the distance began to spin. Not

*red anymore but blue. Then white. Then red. Then...
She stopped.*

*Her child self had been transformed into the woman
she was now. No. Not the Jane she was now. The Jane
she'd been that day she'd woken up in the barn. The
white silk and linen clothes. The bare feet. The bruises
on her arms, her wrists. She kicked out a foot. Her
ankle.*

*"Come on, already!" the voice in the darkness
called.*

*Jane shook her head. No. No, she wasn't going any
farther. She was going home. She was going to the
ranch. She was going to find Leo and... She turned.*

And slammed into a solid, male body.

*"Leo." She sighed, but the relief snapped away as
clawed hands locked around her arms and squeezed.
She opened her mouth to scream, but held back, tilted
her chin up to see what man, what monster had caught
her. But he had no face. He was only a shadow. A blue-
uniformed shadow...with a badge that blinded her as it
glinted against the darkness.*

*And a name tag on his shirt. She wrenched free, rac-
ing past him and running back down the road. Breathing ragged, she looked over her shoulder and saw he'd
dropped to the ground and, on all fours, was running
after her, as if an animal racing after escaped prey.*

*"Run, Skye! Run!" the voice from the darkness
yelled.*

This time, she did as she was told.

She ran.

Jane shot up in the chair, a scream lodged in her throat, Ollie's head in her lap.

She drank in large gulps of air, scrambling to her feet as she plucked a sticky note off her cheek and tried to shake off the remnants of the nightmare. Ollie whined, a familiar sound that brought her far more comfort than she liked to admit.

"Boy, you must be getting as tired of this as I am." She crouched, brought the animal in for a hug, then pushed to her feet and returned to the desk. The cold sweat on her face had dried and she shivered, moving her shaking hand from one pile of paperwork to another— her task for the day while she and Leo waited for the last few supplies she'd asked him to order so they could put the finishing touches on Gwen's new home.

Routine had descended with far more ease than she would have expected. She found herself rising early with Leo, unable to sleep without him beside her. They'd eat breakfast together, and he'd drive her and whatever tools and supplies she needed to the house before he headed out to tend the herd.

Thanks to some old home-care manuals she'd found in his grandfather's office, she'd learned how to use a floor sander so she could refinish the wood floors, a power sander to refinish the cabinets in the kitchen and bedrooms. Whatever she couldn't do on her own, she made a list and she and Leo tackled the jobs together.

By the time September came along and the temperature began to dip into fall, she was looking for another project. Another distraction. Another… Oh, why didn't she just call it what it was: a stalling tactic.

Today she'd sent him into town to the nursery to hunt down some suitable landscaping flowers and shrubs, not only for Gwen's front yard, but also for another idea that had been percolating for a while. In the meantime, she could help tackle some of those items on Leo's list—the list he'd been ignoring for, well, as long as she knew him.

The man was nothing if not determined. Too bad he was determined to restrict their sleeping arrangements to just that: *sleeping*. But that didn't mean boundaries weren't tested. And pushed. And strained to the breaking point. Who knew morning wake-up kisses could leave her so…wanting?

Excitement bubbled inside her. Trapper leaving—though she missed the old coot—had definitely opened some doors she didn't think she and Leo would be walking through, and for that, she needed to remember to thank him when he turned up again. But first, she needed to get this office in shape.

More than once Leo had lamented the fact he hadn't had a chance to go through his grandfather's paperwork or had time to even update the computer, which had sat dormant since last year. Not that it would do much good, given the unreliable internet connection. There hadn't been any real need for the machine other than to make note of expenditures and income, and given the season, there wasn't much of the latter. Besides, she'd seen him write in figures in the record-keeping journal he kept in one of the kitchen drawers.

It took a few hours, but she organized all the stuff piled on and around the desk into neat stacks, then labeled them with sticky notes until she decided what to do with them. That left mementos, books and the computer to deal with. The knickknacks, including more photos of Essie and Leo and Leo's father, she put in a box and set to the side. The computer? She planted her hands on her hips and sighed. No router. No external lines. It was time to go Stone Age. She circled and bent down to examine the old tower unit, tugging on cords and plugs to see what was what. A phone line was twisted and piled on top.

She uncoiled it and held it in her hands. "I wonder..." She bit her lip and followed a matching cord from the desk phone. She wasn't exactly tech-minded. That she knew of. "It's worth a shot." She unplugged everything and started over, making the final connection to the ancient internal modem on the back of the tower unit.

When she sat down and turned on the computer, the screen slowly blinked to life. A few minutes and a few settings clicks later, she hovered the mouse around the "connect to internet" icon and...

The beeping and screeching had her covering her ears. Good heavens, how had people dealt with this constantly back in the day? "I will never complain about slow internet or Wi-Fi again." She frowned, the idea of doing such a thing both familiar and foreign.

The screen bleeped and burped, flickered a few times, then settled on a home page for email.

"Oh, here we go. Internet, I am back." She froze, fingers hovering over the keyboard. What did that mean? An odd thrill had shot through her at the mere thought of clicking on to social media, not that it would be easy with such outdated technology. But that thrill was quickly doused by her determination to get her life—this life—on the track she wanted.

Leo wanted to know who she was. She had a name. A place to start. An answer was close by.

Now all she needed was proof.

His truck loaded with enough flowers, potted shrubs and even a couple of miniature trees to give a pharmaceutical company allergies, Leo found himself pausing in downtown Roaring Springs before climbing into the cab. He was going to miss Jane. Not just the routine and the contentment he found sharing his days with her, but how much he looked forward to seeing her. But their borrowed time was ticking away.

Whether she wanted it to or not.

He looked over his shoulder toward the police station, his stomach knotting in that way it had when he knew he was considering something he shouldn't.

One thing he and Jane hadn't discussed was what he'd discovered online about Levi McEwan, owner of the burnt ID they'd found at the abandoned Preston property. It hadn't taken much to learn that McEwan was dead and that his body had been found just on the outskirts of town near a gas station. He'd made occasional stops at the library to catch up with the local paper. What had taken effort was not sharing what he learned with Jane. He'd planned to keep the information to himself. He'd prefer she focus on recovering her own memories, not focusing on whatever distraction she could cling to next.

His next stop had been at the county clerk's office, which resulted in him having to fill out a form to request information on who had inherited Preston's property. As the office was currently understaffed, the request was filed along with hundreds of other documents. The anticipated response time was two to four weeks. Which put him right back where he'd started.

Frustrated, Leo continued to stare at the glass doors, debating whether McEwan was the way for him to glean any information about Jane... No. Not Jane. Skye. Not that she didn't give him the stink eye anytime he tried the other name on for size.

It would be so easy to step inside and ask to talk to Sheriff Trey Colton. Now that they were fairly sure Jane was connected to the Colton family, Leo was discovering family members everywhere. Including the police department.

Leo frowned. Was that why she was so afraid of the police? Was Trey or someone else in the family involved with her abduction? Was he the reason... No. He shook his head, caught a glimpse of Miss D's diner in his rear mirror. Miss D. Now there was someone who might have some information for him. He'd only promised Jane not to talk to the police. But with small towns, it was more likely those in the know were those on the periphery. Now that Miss D had been back a bit, he'd bet she'd had enough time to catch up with all the Roaring Springs goings-on.

He entered the diner through the front door this time, surprised to see the crowd thinner than expected. The hustle and bustle of a few days ago had slowed to a trickle, meaning Miss D herself was manning the counter. Today's apron was a bright pink, almost as bright as the off-center bow in her silver-gray hair.

"Heavens, Leo. You're going to give an old woman a heart attack. Twice in one week." Miss D was already reaching for a mug to pour him some coffee. "Where's your Jane?"

Leo sighed. It was as if she and Trapper had worked out a comedy routine. "She's back at the ranch. Thought maybe I'd pick up another pie as a surprise."

"You're always so thoughtful." Miss D beamed at him. "I've got a chocolate mint that'll curl your toes. You drink up and I'll box it up for you."

"Sounds perfect, thanks." He removed his hat, set it on the counter and turned on the stool to look across the street. When he turned his attention back to his coffee, he caught sight of a familiar pair of brown eyes looking back at him from near the register. The missing persons flyer was taped prominently, full color, with contact information. His chest tightened as he stood and plucked one of the flyers from the stack nearby.

Have you seen me?

Yes, Leo thought. Yes, I have.

"Such a shame," Miss D said as she glanced over from the pie case. "Skye Colton's a pretty big celebrity around these parts. Around most parts if my great-nephew's to be believed. Some big social media star on that Snapgram or Instachat? Whatever it's called. Just up and poofed!" She snapped her fingers.

"What do they think happened to her?" That Leo managed to get the words out at all was a minor miracle.

It was Jane. Or at least a woman who looked an awful lot like Jane. Her red hair was curled and coiffed to stylist perfection, spilling over shoulders bared by a strapless, shimmering evening gown. Her brown eyes were heavily outlined and accented with mascara, her skin flawless and smooth and pink in all the right places. But it was her lips—those full, pouty lips he'd kissed, the lips he dreamed about night after night—that erased any doubt.

"Well, now, since you asked." Miss D motioned him back to his seat, where she set the pink box. "Filtering through all the hogwash—" she leaned her arms on the counter and lowered her voice "—seems she got dumped by her rich boyfriend. Man up and married some other woman right out from under her. Next thing you know, the girl takes off. Family thought she'd just taken a few days to herself, but now it seems they've called in the authorities to try to find her. Word is they're worried she's been killed and left up in the snow like those other poor girls."

"She must have cared for him a lot to disappear like that." Leo forced himself to drink the scalding coffee. And here he'd let himself believe she'd been unattached.

Miss D shrugged. "Those Coltons, they tend to keep things pretty tight. But I've been keeping my ears open. Seems she was expecting a proposal and that's what broke her heart, drove her away. Now it's been more than a couple of months since anyone's seen or heard from her, even that poor sister of hers. Those two, peas in a pod aren't closer. Can't be easy, growing up in a family like that, with all that money and expectation, to find someone to love. Me? I'm thinking the girl's just lying low, reevaluating her priorities, so to speak. Why, I wouldn't be surprised if she'd found someone she can trust, someone who might be trying to find out how to help the poor girl out of whatever situation she's gotten herself into."

Leo dragged his gaze away from the image of the woman who had been sharing his bed and looked Miss D square in the eye. "You think?"

"She strikes me as a smart one. A little lost, but not brokenhearted as the news reports would have us believe. Yes, sir, I know in my heart that girl is A-OK and safe." She reached over, covered Leo's hand and gave him a good squeeze. "You keep her safe, Leo."

"You know?" He could not have been more surprised if she'd suddenly announced she'd gone vegan. "Why haven't you—"

"Because I know you and if you haven't gone to the police, there's a darn good reason. I trust you, Leo Slattery. And so does your Jane." Miss D patted the back of his hand. "You make darn good and certain you do right by her. You done with your coffee? I'm thinking it's about time you get home."

"Yeah." Leo nodded, reflecting on Skye as an unfamiliar tendril of doubt wove through him. Maybe she'd had enough of the spotlight. Maybe she just needs someplace to…hide. Maybe… It wasn't possible, was it? His heart lurched into his throat. It wasn't possible she'd been lying to him all this time, that she knew who she was, just so she had a place to hide away from her family?

No. No, that was ridiculous. There was no denying she'd been attacked. Even a social media darling couldn't have faked those injuries or the haunted, terrified look on her face. Or those heart-stopping nightmares.

One thing was for certain. He'd been right.

Jane, *Skye*, didn't belong in his world.

Not one little bit.

"Thanks for the coffee, Miss D. And the pie." He reached for his wallet and handed over a twenty. "Don't say no," he warned when she looked ready to refuse. "Put the balance on my account for those burgers. Saved me from having to cook."

"You're a good man, Leo Slattery. Your gran would be right proud of you."

"I hope so." He folded the flyer, stuck it in the edge of the box and picked up his pie and his hat before he left the diner and headed back across the street.

"Hey, Trey, you got a minute?"

The shouted name caught Leo's attention as he pulled open the truck door. He looked over as a tall man approached the front door of the police station. In the past few days Leo had done his research on the Coltons and recognized Fox Colton, who looked a bit frazzled as Trey headed away from the police station toward his cousin.

Key in hand, Leo watched as the two men spoke. From the way Fox's hands were flying, it was clear he was upset about something, but it wasn't the words that interested him. It was the way Trey slung his arm around Fox and led him into the station.

They were family. Jane's—no, *Skye's*—family, and they were missing her.

And if they were missing her even a fraction of the amount Leo anticipated missing her when she left the ranch, he wasn't sure how they were enduring it.

As much as he didn't want to admit it, he'd run out of time. He'd made her a promise to get her home. To her family. A family that loved and missed her.

It was time to keep it.

Chapter 10

"Trying your hand at something new?"

Jane yelped and jumped, her flour-covered hand flying up to her chest as she glared at him. "Can't you just say 'Hi, honey, I'm home,' like a normal cowboy?"

He grinned and slouched against the door frame, pink bakery box in his hand. "Hi, honey, I'm home." Ollie bounded over, spun in a circle, then planted his butt on the floor, tail wagging so hard the sound echoed in the kitchen.

Jane smiled back as the warmth of his smile washed over her. The only sight more beautiful than the Colorado mountains was Leo Slattery. From the moment she'd first laid eyes on him, she thought him handsome. How could she not with that cautious twinkle in his eye and the generous tilt to his lips, that dimple she wanted to kiss? And as the days and weeks moved along, she began to accept there wouldn't come a time when the sight of him didn't make her heart trip over itself. Or for parts of her—every part of her—to tingle.

"What are you baking?" He sniffed the air, removed his hat and leaned back to hang it on the hook behind him on the porch. "Smells great."

"I wasn't expecting you just yet. I wanted to surprise you." She hefted the cover of the hardback book. "I found one of your grandmother's old cookbooks when I was reorganizing the shelves in the living room."

"Jane." Leo sighed and shook his head. "You don't have to keep finding things to do around here." He set the box down, walked over to her and cupped her face between his hands.

"I like doing it." She shrugged. "And if I didn't, I wouldn't have found this. Chicken and dumplings. Look, it says right here." She tried to turn, but he held her firm. "It says this is your favorite—what are you doing?"

"What do you think?" His mouth lowered to hers and she giggled.

"Oh, okay." She linked her floury hands behind his neck and made it easier by meeting him halfway. Then melted like the butter in the Dutch oven. She sagged into him, raised up to meet him as his lips covered hers so completely, so masterfully, her entire body heated. Jane moaned, low in the back of her throat, a sound so completely foreign to her she had to wonder if the part of her he'd found had even existed before.

He angled his head, dived deeper, his tongue sweeping over hers as he tasted every part of her.

When his hands released her face and trailed down her sides, she shivered and pressed herself higher. Closer. Tighter. "Did you forget to set the brakes?" she murmured against his mouth when the pressure eased. "Because if you keep this up, there won't be any stopping."

"I know." He squeezed his eyes shut and pressed his forehead against hers. "I know."

"Don't." She drew back far enough to trace her fingers over the lines in his forehead. "Please, Leo, don't pull away from me. Not again." She kissed him again. Softly. "It's time."

He started to shake his head, but now it was she who held fast. "I have something to show you."

"I have something to show you," he countered.

She grinned. "I'll bet you do. But me first." She stepped out of his arms, turned off the stove and led him to the kitchen table, where she'd set the file folders. "I spent the day in your grandfather's office. I did some playing around and got the computer to work. Limited internet access, but, well, whatever." She shrugged. "Besides some information on the ranch I think you'll want to read—" she slipped that folder out of reach before he could open it "—this is the one you need to read now."

"Now?"

"Right now." She flipped it open. "Or I can give you the abbreviated version. Which might just save time. Here." She pointed to the first page. "My name is indeed Skye Colton. I have a twin sister named Phoebe. Identical twin, which answers that question." The face in the mirror in her dreams suddenly made sense. "If you're interested in my family tree, it's all right here. Seems there are a lot of us Coltons around, all over the country. I work up at The Chateau with my mother and sister, where I'm in charge of publicity and planning. And not so long ago, I was dating a record producer who married another woman right out from under me." She'd been rehearsing this for the better part of the afternoon, so the words came out in a bit of a rush.

"But you don't remember it. You don't remember him?"

"No." As she'd learned from Leo, they didn't lie to one another. About anything. "I don't *remember*. Because it doesn't matter. He doesn't matter, Leo. When I look at this picture of the two of us—" she flipped the page to a society pages editorial from earlier this year "—there's nothing that hits. Nothing other than how incredibly lonely this woman looks. Tell me you don't see it?"

She did. Beneath the glitz and the glamour, the beaded gown and the champagne flute in her hand, the diamond bracelet and matching necklace. The intricate curls that must have taken some poor stylist hours to create. And yet, there, in her own eyes, Jane saw the specter of unhappiness. "She's empty, Leo. Her heart, it's utterly and completely empty." But Jane's heart wasn't. Jane's heart was full to the point of bursting. Filled with Leo. "And I know this because that's how I feel when I look at her."

"What about when you see this?" He reached behind him and plucked out a folded piece of paper from the edge of the bakery box.

She took it, looked down at the missing persons flyer with her image. Her heart stuttered.

"They miss you," Leo whispered. "They're looking for you. For Skye."

"I know." Her online search had uncovered that much at least, but try as she might, the details of the life she lived before seeing Leo in that barn didn't materialize. "But I'm not this woman anymore."

"They have a right to know you're all right. Please, Jane. Let me call the police—"

"We could." She shrugged a shoulder and let the paper drift to on top of the pages she'd printed out. "Or you can admit you're out of excuses and we can go to bed." She reached down and untucked her shirt from her jeans. "I know who I am, Leo. I know what I am. I'm not married. I'm not with anyone. I don't have children. But I know what I want." She stepped closer, reached her hand up to his face, touched his cheek. His sharp intake of breath shot through her like Cupid's arrow. "I want you. Now." She backed up. "What are you going to do about it?"

That he continued the debate with himself only endeared him more to her. His jaw clenched, his fists flexed and as she scanned him from the tip of his hair to the pointed toes of his boots, she smiled. Just as he had the day they met, the worst *and* best day of her life.

She held out her hand, palm up.

When he slipped his fingers between hers, she shivered and stepped into his arms. "About damned time, cowboy," she managed to say before he dipped his head and kissed her.

She had the sensation of spinning, falling, twirling. Breathless, excited, shivering, she gasped into his mouth as he wrapped one arm tight around her waist and hauled her against him. There wasn't an inch of her that wasn't pressed against him. Her breasts crushed hard into his chest, her nipples pebbling in an instant as she imagined the feeling of the fabric of his shirt scraping against them. They were moving, locked together so completely she didn't think they'd ever break apart. Even as she clung to him she prayed they wouldn't. This was all she wanted. This moment, with this man. For as long as it could last.

"Ollie," she whispered against his lips as he carried her down the hall to his bedroom.

He raised his head, narrowed his eyes. "Leo."

She grinned. "No, I mean—"

"I know what you mean, darlin'." He waited until they were across the threshold before he turned to face the dog that had trailed behind them. "Private time." He pointed down the hall and Ollie sighed, blinked up at Jane, then turned and walked back down the hall. Leo closed the door as Jane grabbed the edges of her T-shirt and—

"Stop." Leo said it even as he removed his boots and socks.

"You're ahead of me," Jane teased, and thrust out a hip. "No fair."

"Completely fair. You know the image I've been carrying around in my brain for weeks now?" His voice carried a gravelly sound. Primal. Possessive. Male.

"Tell me."

"You in that bed that first night. Wearing only your bra and panties."

Far less modest than his old T-shirts she'd been wearing since.

"That is what you were wearing under the sheets, right?" he pressed.

"Maybe." The deep baritone of his voice thrilled her. She arched a brow, took a step back to the bed until she felt the mattress hit the back of her knees. "Maybe not." She inched her shirt up, exposed her stomach and grinned as his gaze slipped to her fingers splayed across her belly. "I'll let you keep imagining."

"No need." He stood over her, the desire in his eyes equal to the heat she felt radiating off his body. "I've finally got the real thing in front of me." He pushed her hand away, took hold of the hem himself and in one quick move, lifted her shirt up and over her head. Where the garment landed she had no idea.

The cool breeze of the ceiling fan brushed across her skin as she sucked in her stomach, which pushed her breasts to the limit of the plain white cotton bra. He caught her, hands grasping her below her rib cage, his thumbs resting beneath the edge of the underwire, and she trembled, the promise of feeling his hands over her almost too much to bear. He rubbed against her nipples over the fabric and she moaned.

"More," he demanded, and kissed her again. The softness, the hesitancy, the caution had vanished somewhere between the door and the bed. He devoured, he took, he challenged and she answered every thrust of his tongue with her own.

"Off," she managed to say on a gasp of breath. She could feel him hard and ready against her, straining against the jeans she'd admired for weeks. The way they fit, the way he moved in them. She'd lost track of the ways she imagined getting them off him. "Get this off. I need to feel you." Her fingers fumbled for the buttons on his shirt. He laughed against the side of her neck between nibbling bites when they wouldn't cooperate. She swore, struggling, until her frustration took over and she grabbed at the sides and ripped. Buttons landed with tiny clatters on the hardwood floor.

"That's my favorite shirt," Leo said on a chuckle. "May it rest in peace." He kissed the sensitive spot behind her right ear. "Tell me what you want."

"Everything. I want it all." But for right now, all she wanted… She gasped as she pushed the shirt off his shoulders and finally pressed her hands flat against his chest. Smooth. Taut. Toned. She could feel his heart pounding against her as she trailed her fingers around his pecs, down his abs, lower. So much lower.

A surge of power shot through her when he sucked in a breath, his hand covering hers as she flicked open the button of his jeans. "You're moving too fast, darlin'." He kissed her again, drawing her tongue into his mouth for a duel she surrendered to. "Let's enjoy this."

"Oh, I plan to." But he was going too slow. All these weeks of watching him, longing for him. Wanting him. She wanted him now. Fast. On her terms. Sense of honor be damned, he'd kept her waiting long enough. "Next time we'll go— Wait!" She flattened a hand on his chest when he reached for her hips. "Tell me you got protection."

"Darlin', I got it two days after I saw you in nothing but your underwear." He hooked a finger into the loop of her jeans and tugged her against him. A second later, he had her unbuttoned. Another second, unzipped. He turned her in his arms, one hand pressing against her stomach, holding her tight against him as his free hand drifted lower. She whimpered as his fingers slid firmly beneath the fabric of her panties and cupped her, the tip of his finger rubbing hard against that tiny nub of pleasure.

"Oh!" She reached a hand up, caught the back of his neck, parted her legs to give him better access as he pressed and rubbed and circled, pleasure and pressure building inside her until she couldn't breathe.

"Go over, Jane." His command was hot in her ear and echoed through her fracturing mind. All she felt was him, all she wanted to feel was him. Higher, higher, he drove her higher until she couldn't help but soar. She came, trembling, vibrating in his hold as her knees went weak and she sagged against him, the ripples of pleasure seemingly endless as he held her close. "Gorgeous." He turned her to face him again, kissed her lips. "Now, that was worth the wait."

She sank to the edge of the bed and watched, dazed, as he removed her jeans, and she shimmied out of her panties, then reached back to unhook her bra.

"Slowly," he urged, unzipping his jeans and stepping out of them.

"Not my favorite word, cowboy." But she loved the passion she saw in his eyes as she drew the straps down her arm. "You need help there?" He wasn't naked yet and she was done waiting.

"Not even a little bit." He walked around to the nightstand and opened the drawer. The foil package in his fingers boosted her anticipation. "Hold on to this. There's just one thing…" He dropped to his knees and for an instant, Jane's entire body went fire hot. He was right there, kneeling between her legs. Legs that were trembling to open as he reached up and pulled the elastic from her hair. "I've been wanting to do that for weeks." He drew the long waves down and over her shoulders, the tips teasing her already tightened nipples. His fingers sank deep, trailing through her hair before his hands caught the back of her head and he drew her in for another kiss.

Tears burned the back of her eyes as she sank into him. He was so tender, and yet she had no doubt in her mind he wanted her. She slipped her hands down his sides, over his hips to where the thin fabric of his shorts stretched around him. Jane drank him in, drew him closer and slid her palms against his skin, her fingers inching down, dragging the fabric with her.

"Skye," he whispered as he maneuvered out of them.

She froze, grabbed his wrists and squeezed until he looked at her. Whoever she was before, she wasn't that person any longer. Memory or no, it didn't matter. She knew who she was now. And that was all she wanted to be. "Jane," she insisted. "Your Jane. Always." She pressed her lips against the pulse in his wrist, then kissed him again. Before he could argue. Before either one of them could think.

She sank back on the bed, drawing him with her, hands clenched, the foil packet caught between their palms. Her other hand continued its exploration and found him, hot, hard and ready for her. "I want you, Leo." As if there was any doubt. She needed him to believe, for him to know, she knew what she was doing. "Now, suit up."

He grinned and tore the packet with his teeth. "You've got it, darlin'."

Had she any memory of before, she might have wondered if there was a sexier moment than watching the man she loved cover himself.

The man she loved. Peace—*rightness*—flowed through her in that moment, taking up residence in that corner of her heart she suspected had never been full. She loved Leo Slattery. Whatever had come before, whatever would come later, it wouldn't matter. For now, for this moment, accepting that she loved him, would always be enough.

She didn't need to wonder about anything, not as the sight of him reignited the ache between her thighs, an ache that had her hips writhing in anticipation. And then he was over her, one arm braced on the bed, the other hand stroking her hair before trailing down her side, over her hip, to tease the cleft at her core to ready her for him.

She moaned, the sound vibrating against her throat

as she arched her back, pressed her breasts high to where he could lower his mouth. His finger slipped into her, stroking, firm, but not enough. Not nearly enough. Jane squirmed beneath him, unable to ask for what she wanted, what she *needed*, as the pressure built to the point of bursting.

"Please," she panted, reaching down for him, finding him with her hands and wrapping her fingers around the length of him. "Please, Leo." Her legs fell open as he moved in. She abandoned her hold on him as she gripped her fingers into his forearms. He rocked his hips forward, slightly, just enough for her to feel him against the part of her that would give her what she desperately craved. "Leo." She cupped his face in her hands and drew him down as he thrust into her.

She cried out, the sensation of him filling her too overwhelming to comprehend all at once. He was inside her, pulsing, heavy, straining. When he moved, gently, slowly, as if giving her time to adjust to the feel of him, she didn't think she'd ever feel more wanted, more desired. More ready to abandon all control.

Jane lifted her legs, wrapped herself around him as tight as she could, held him as close as she could as he thrust. Tears seeped from her control, trailing down the sides of her face as she moved with him, surrendering to the pleasure and wonder of this man who had become so much of who she was.

Her hands trailed over and around his back, her fingers pressing against the tension she felt in every inch of his body. "Leo, let go." She could feel another orgasm building, but she didn't want to go alone again.

She wanted… She tried to catch her breath as his pace increased. "Leo, come with me." The last word ripped from her lips as she cried out, her climax pulling him with her, over the edge. Into utter and complete bliss.

Chapter 11

Leo tried to recall a moment that was more perfect than watching the woman he loved explode in pleasure around him. His dreams, his fantasy hadn't come close to the reality of making love with her, and that was saying something considering the potency of those imaginings had sent him to more than his share of cold showers.

He rolled to his side, pulling her with him, but instead of settling into his side, she ended up half on top of him, her leg thrown over his as she sank into him.

"So two months of foreplay worked pretty well." She pressed her lips against his shoulder, licked the sweat from his skin before shimmying up his body. "Imagine all the time we've wasted."

"We can make up for it." Right now, all he wanted

was to extend this moment, memorize the feel of her in his arms, the way her hair spilled over the two of them, tangled tresses of liquid fire as her hands became restless and began to search his body. "I need to tell you something."

"Okay," Jane purred as his fingers trailed up and down her spine. Then she kissed him, so deeply, so completely, he suspected she stoked the fire in his soul. "What is it?"

He waited until she inched back, just enough for him to see her complete face, the deep brown eyes he longed to wake up to. The full, swollen-lipped smile he knew was only for him. "I love you, Skye Colton."

Her eyes narrowed.

"Jane," he added with a smile. "Sorry, but it's important to address the facts. This bubble we're in won't last forever. You are, to everyone else in the world, Skye Colton. You're going to have to accept that." He stroked a finger down the side of her face, silently pleading with her to understand. "But you'll always be my Jane."

Her smile returned, as did the twinkle in her eyes. "And to think I thought that a horrible name when you gave it to me."

Another kiss. Another touch. Another exploration had him groaning into her mouth. But as he tried to roll her under him, she pushed against his shoulders, pinned him to the mattress and straddled him. The groan in the back of his throat sounded more like a growl as she arched her back, jutting her breasts as she ran her hands through the length of her hair, letting it fall all around her.

"Jane…"

"This time's my turn." She rotated her hips, lifted herself up and shifted slightly even as he was reaching for the box beside the bed. "Ah!" Leaning forward, she tapped a finger against his hand and removed one of the foil packets. "Good thing you got a whole box." She moaned as she settled back into her spot, then arched her neck, biting her lip in a way that told him this time wasn't going to last as long as she might like. "By the way…"

She was killing him, with each movement, each rotation of her body, she was draining the life out of him. And nothing had ever felt better.

"By the way what?" He gripped her hips in his hands, stilled her motions until she looked at him, her eyes glazed, dazed, and smiling.

"Oh." She gasped then moaned. "I love you, too, cowboy." She dropped the packet on his chest. "Now, are you going to do this or am I?"

Jane managed to stifle the scream before it ripped out of her throat. She shot up in bed, the terror of the dream following her into the darkness of Leo's bedroom, but in an instant, the fear began to fade as Leo's arms came around her and pulled her into his chest.

"It's okay. I've got you." He stroked her hair as her breathing eased. The wheezing in her chest faded as she squeezed her eyes shut. She focused on him, the strength of him, the warmth of him. The knowledge that he was, perhaps had always been, the only person she could rely on. "Tell me," he murmured into her hair before he pressed his lips against her temple. He settled back against the headboard, drew her close. "Tell me what you saw this time."

She swiped at her cheeks, but found them dry. No tears this time, and the fact she hadn't sobbed herself free felt like a badge of courage. "Same thing. But... different. I could see something."

"His face?"

"No." She sat up straighter, but didn't move out of the circle of his arms. "No, not his face. But his name. Letters. Initials." She squinted into the darkness, trying to pull the dream from her memory. "GG. Sounds like some psychopathic grandmother. Gigi." She might have giggled if she hadn't been trying to concentrate so hard. "The uniform he was wearing, it wasn't black. It was blue. Navy blue."

Leo's hand stilled at the base of her spine. "The Roaring Springs Police Department sometimes wears navy-colored uniforms."

"Do they? No wonder I freak out every time I see one of their officers."

"Was there anything else new? Where were you?"

"I'm not sure. The road was empty. Then the spinning lights in my rearview mirror blinded me. I couldn't see. That's when he hit me."

"With his car?"

"Mmm." She nodded. "From behind. I think I hit something, got knocked out. I could hear the sound of his boots crunching in the glass. That's what brought me to consciousness. I couldn't get out, couldn't get the seat belt off." She was trembling now, the adrenaline coursing through her system draining the more she thought about it. "He broke the window to get to me. I tried to get free, claw my way to the passenger door, but he grabbed…"

"Your ankle." Leo sat up and scooped her into his lap so he could replace the now invisible bruises with his own hand.

"He dragged me out by my foot. That's when I wake up. Every time." She sank into him with a sigh. "Every time I wake up in the same place."

"Maybe because that's all you remember."

"But do I? Remember?" she asked. "Is it a dream or a memory?" She winced as the throbbing in her head began again. Jane pinched her lips tight, forcing herself not to complain. He'd been concerned enough about her headaches before they'd made love; she could only imagine the demands he'd make now.

"I think it might be both. We should have you write down everything you said."

Whatever warmth she'd been feeling vanished. "You mean so we can go to the police with it."

"Yes."

"Even though in my dreams, it's the police who attacked me."

A second of hesitation, then, "Yes."

"Brilliant idea." She scrambled off his lap and clicked on the bedside table lamp. "Let's just have me turn myself in to whoever tried to kill me."

"Jane—"

"No! I do not want to go to the police. I don't trust them. Any of them." His expression barely shifted from one of calm placation. "And don't look at me that way. You don't get to humor me. This is my decision, Leo. *Mine*. It's my life. What happened, happened to me and you don't get to decide how I move forward." She searched the floor for her underwear and dragged it on.

"Except you aren't." He folded his hands in his lap, on top of the beige sheet, and crossed his ankles. "You're still hiding."

"I'm doing a bit more than hiding now, aren't I? What happened today doesn't change my mind about the police, Leo. What happened today doesn't give you any say over my life."

"Does loving you?"

"What?" When she realized she couldn't wear his discarded buttonless shirt, she yanked open a dresser drawer and grabbed one of his T-shirts.

"Does loving you give me any say over anything?"

"I…don't know." She kept her back to him. He had a point. "I don't know about a lot of things. Why do we have to spoil this? Why can't we just— Oh!" He'd moved silently, out of bed and to her side without her hearing him. "Might have to put a bell around you or something," she grumbled.

His hands settled on her shoulders, gently squeezing until she relaxed beneath his touch. He bent his head, pressed a kiss against the back of one shoulder. "I don't want to spoil this, either. But we can't hover here for very long. The real world is going to come calling, Jane. Your family, this GG person, the police. You can't stop it from happening just because you want to. You've got to face it."

"I will." *But not now. Please not now.* "Can't I just be happy, here, with you, for a little while longer?" She faced him, turned pleading eyes to his.

"I didn't fall in love with a coward, Jane." He shook his head. "If you want any kind of future with me, if we're going to try to make this work, that's my price." He pressed his mouth to hers. "The decision is yours."

"Will this do?" Jane dropped a legal notepad with pages of scribbled details onto the kitchen table in front of him. "I wrote it up this morning when you were tending the herd."

Leo set his lunch plate aside and, abandoning the material he'd been reading, scanned what she'd written. "Should." He didn't want to reread the details of Jane's nightmares, of the images she had spinning through her head. Because if he did, the rage toward whomever had attacked her, hurt her, tried to kill her, would reignite and, truth be told, he wasn't entirely sure what to do with it.

"Can we forget about it now? It's written down. That's enough, right?"

Leo sighed. "Will you let me phone the sheriff?"

"You can do anything you want," Jane snapped. "Call the sheriff. Don't call the sheriff. What I want doesn't seem to matter."

"Of course it matters. But that doesn't mean you're right."

"You promised me, Leo. You promised me you wouldn't call the police. It's the only thing I've asked of you."

"No," he said after a moment. "It's not."

"What are you—?"

"The headaches are back, aren't they?"

"I— What— How—?"

He narrowed his eyes at her, a muscle ticking in his jaw. "I've lived with you for a while now. I know when you're in pain. I also saw you down three painkillers when I got back, so unless you want to break your promise and lie to me now…"

"Fine. Yes. They started again this morning. After the nightmare."

"Thought so." He picked up his plate and carried it to the sink. "Seems to me we had an agreement, didn't we? That if they came back or got worse, you'd go to the doctor."

He heard the kitchen chair scoot as she sat down. She mumbled something under her breath.

"I'm sorry, what?"

"Oh, for crying out… Fine! Yes, we had an agreement." He could see her reflection in the kitchen window. She was rubbing a finger hard into her temple, as if trying to relieve pressure in her head.

"I can take you to the clinic this afternoon, Jane. A quick stop in town."

"Can't the doctor come here? Don't some of them make house calls?"

"Funny enough, this is not *Little House on the Prairie*. And I'd prefer not to make extra work for Maxine if I don't have to."

"Maxine? Your doctor's name is Maxine?"

"She was one of Gran's…"

"Friends, right. Boy, your grandmother was one serious social butterfly. I'll go get my shoes." You'd have thought he was going to be taking her to a firing squad.

"Jane." While he didn't like the distance between them, he wasn't going to give up on doing what was right for her. Even if she wasn't happy about it.

"What?"

"Brattiness does not become you." He set his dish to dry, wiped his hands and walked over to her.

"I'm not a brat!" But she caught her lip in her teeth, cringed. "Oh, jeez. Oh, man, I am a brat, aren't I?" She covered her face in her hands. "What is wrong with me?"

"You're in pain." He caught her wrists and pulled her arms to her sides. "Your attitude was clue number one. But I did want to thank you for the files you left for me containing the plans my grandfather was looking into for the ranch before he died."

"He was going to take your advice," Jane murmured. "He was going to shift to stud servicing and divest in the herd to buy bulls. Did you see—"

"The other ranches and businesses he'd already been in touch with? Yes." And because she'd unearthed those notes and typed them up for him, it wouldn't take long to get the ball rolling again. "You've done a wonderful job with his office, Jane." He kissed her. "Thank you." He kissed her again.

His body charged when she took the kiss deeper and cupped her hand around the back of his neck. "I know a better way you can thank me," she murmured against his lips.

"I bet you do. Later." He drew back and tucked a strand of hair behind her ear. "Right now, you have a headache."

This was just stupid. Jane bit the inside of her cheek to stop from saying the words aloud. Lord help her, but she did sound like a spoiled brat. So much so she was irritated with herself. She could only imagine how Leo felt, but then as she'd learned since living with him, he had the patience of a saint. Her hair tied back in a braid, her gray hat tipped low over her face, she sat in the hardback chair in Dr. Maxine Monroe's waiting room in Juniper Grove, which also happened to be her living room as the medical clinic was run out of her house.

Must be a slow day, she thought, as she caught the eye of a sullen-looking teen glaring into the screen of the phone in her hands. Her mother, looking particularly strained, sat beside her and gave Jane a tight smile in greeting before turning her attention to her daughter. "Your eyes are going to be burnt sockets if you keep staring at that thing, Delaney."

"Mom." The eye-rolling commenced.

"Yeah, yeah, I know. Whatever. Teenagers." The mother sighed. "Kaitlin Sommars."

"Leo Slattery," Leo volunteered. "This is Jane."

"Nice to meet you both," Kaitlin said before sighing at her daughter again. "We missed our appointment this morning, so we're waiting to be fit in."

"Whatever," Delaney muttered.

Jane sat up straighter, the idea she may as well be looking in a mirror sliding through her. She glanced over at Leo, who was grinning at her. "Oh, shut up," she laughed, and felt as if a bubble popped inside her. "Don't you ever get tired of being right?"

"Not about some things." He reached over and knocked a finger against her hat, pushing it up. "That alone makes it worth the drive."

"Jane?" The nurse-receptionist stepped into the waiting room. "Dr. Monroe is ready for you."

Jane stood up so fast her hat fell back. She ducked to pick it up, and saw something akin to shock cross the teenager's face as she straightened. The next instant, she was typing away on her keyboard, eyes wide. "Darn thing won't stay put," Jane joked around the odd sensation of descending dread. And the pounding behind her eyes. "Leo, you coming?"

"You want me to?" Now he looked surprised.

"You're the reason I'm here, aren't you? Can he?" she asked the nurse, who shrugged.

"Yeah, sure. Husbands are always welcome."

"Oh, well, he's—" Her face went hot.

"Come on, darlin'." Leo slung an arm around her shoulders and they headed down the hall. "Don't want to keep the good doctor waiting."

Dr. Maxine Monroe ducked her chin, tipped down her glasses until they barely stayed on her nose, and turned laser-beam bright eyes on Jane, who felt like a kindergartner caught eating glue. A slight angular woman, Dr. Monroe reminded Jane of one of those featherless birds who got kicked out of its nest. She'd certainly been thorough in her examination. They'd already been in here for over an hour, and other than the occasional tsking and mouth twists of disapproval, she hadn't said much. "You've had these symptoms for how long?"

Jane kicked her socked feet back and forth against the exam table. "Since late July."

Dr. Monroe arched a brow. "I see." Her gaze flickered to Leo.

"Don't blame him," Jane said quickly. "He'll be the first to tell you he's been bugging me to come in for weeks."

"Yes, well." Some of the disapproval vanished from her face. Some. Not all. "I'd have thought the complete loss of memory would have been an indication you should have sought medical treatment."

"And yet, oddly enough, it wasn't."

"Jane," Leo warned.

"Right. Sorry." She pinched the bridge of her nose. This was a compromise, right? A trip to the doctor for him not pushing her on going to the police. "He wanted me to come in. I didn't. End of story. Are the headaches and amnesia connected? I only know who I am because we found out. Not because I remembered."

"The mind protects us the only way it knows how." The doctor set her file aside. "Whether you're Skye or Jane, doesn't make a difference to me from an examination standpoint. Your blood pressure and heart rate are both normal. The bruises and cuts have healed, obviously. I didn't see any issues with your eyes or your ears. No ringing or dizzy spells?"

"Ah, one. A while ago." Jane avoided Leo's gaze

when he straightened in his chair. "Sorry. I was in the barn when it happened. Just thought I'd moved a saddle too quick. The day we went, ah, exploring."

"Looking for answers," Leo explained as Dr. Monroe stood up to check Jane's neck and spine again, along with the almost healed wound on her head. "She got the shakes real bad when we got close."

"I'll bet you did." Dr. Monroe clicked her tongue. "Well, I'm willing to bet you had a minor concussion, but I can't be sure without an MRI. I'll have Colleen call and get you an appointment for later today. And no." She cut Jane off before she could argue. "You can't get one for a later date. You'll go today."

"Thank you, Doctor," Leo said.

"The results will take few days. Colleen will let you know when I want to see you again. If we find what I expect, there's nothing to do beyond what you're already doing. Just take it easy, get plenty of rest, and the over-the-counter painkillers should work just fine. If you'd come in a few weeks ago, I'd have said stay off any horses, but as that ship has sailed…"

Jane couldn't imagine having gotten through any of this without being able to saddle Ginger and ride out onto the spread.

"Continue to try to stir some memories, but don't push it. It'll come back when it's meant to. And I'll be expecting you back here, at least once a week until it does." She left them for Jane to get dressed.

"Told you there was nothing to worry about." Jane shot him an overly bright smile.

"That's not exactly what she said." Leo opened the

door for her and led the way out to the receptionist's desk. Raised voices had them slowing. "What's going on?"

"Where is she?" a young man only a few years older than Delaney demanded as he held up a cell phone as if recording the exchange. "Skye Colton. She's here, isn't she? The—"

"Leo." Jane's voice shook ever so lightly as she walked over to him. Her stomach rolled. Leo spun her around, but the one word from her had been enough to catch the man's attention.

"Is that her?" the man demanded and moved in. Dr. Monroe put herself between them and the interloper. "Come on, Skye. Everyone thought you were dead! Your fans miss you. Where have you been? Why are you hiding? Is this your new boyfriend? Do you have any comment about—"

"How did he get in here?" Dr. Monroe demanded of Colleen, who looked both shaken and furious.

"He came in to make an appointment."

"Given my specialty, you're not properly equipped," Dr. Monroe snapped at him. "Leave. Or I'll call the police."

"No police." Jane gripped Leo's arms, her entire body shaking. But not from fear. From bone-snapping anger. "Get out." She ducked around Leo and advanced on the man before Leo could stop her. "Get out of here, now." She swung out a hand and knocked his phone free. It clattered to the floor. "Before I sue you for invasion of privacy."

"But…my phone! You're Skye Colton! You've lived your entire life online. You owe us an explanation!"

"I don't owe you a thing." She took another swing at him as Colleen backed up and pulled open the door. Jane stomped her foot as if she was going to dive at him and sent him scampering back outside. She swooped down and picked up the phone, tapped a few icons to delete the recording. "How did he find me?"

"Not he. They." Leo peeked out the drapes in the reception room. "At least a dozen of them are gathering. And right now they're getting an earful from whoever that was."

Unease prickled the back of Jane's neck.

"Reporters?" Colleen joined him. "Bloggers, too, I bet. Lots of them. And there's a news van pulling in across the street. There. I haven't seen this many people in town since last year's homecoming."

"Jane's question stands. How did they know where…" He trailed off, looking to where Delaney was tapping on her phone. "Excuse me, young lady."

"I didn't do anything!" The teen jumped back and turned wild green eyes on her mother. "It's just…no one's seen her in forever!" She gestured to Jane, who took a step back as her entire body went cold. "Everyone's been saying she's dead or missing or something, and I saw her sitting right there! I mean, it's Skye Colton! Do you know how famous I'm going to be?"

"What did you do?" Kaitlin asked in a tone that Leo remembered never liking being on the receiving end of. "Give me your phone."

"What? No! Mom!" Delaney all but shrieked as her mother snatched the smartphone out of her hands.

"We need to get out of here." Jane didn't have the time to be angry at the girl. Not with the way her stomach was rolling and her head pounded.

"I don't believe this," Kaitlin gasped. "You posted her picture on your page? You tagged her and this office?" The woman looked horrified as she glanced up from her daughter's phone. "Oh, I'm so sorry! Delaney, this is a doctor's office. There are privacy laws. You had no right."

Delaney shrugged, but Leo could see a hint of remorse in the young girl's eyes.

"It won't matter that I deleted the video." Jane's eyes went wide as she looked up at him. "Leo, whoever's looking for me... GG. He's going to know—"

"It's up to you, Jane." Leo did what he always did when she was worried or upset. He set his hands gently on her shoulders and squeezed. "We can end this now, get you home to your family. All we have to do is walk out that door and it'll all be over."

It would all be over. But she didn't want it to be over. At least not any part of it that involved Leo. The second she gave in, the second she agreed to walk into the truth, there would be no going back. Not to Leo's ranch, not to the horses and the sunsets. And not to Leo. She searched his face, his clear, focused eyes for an answer, for guidance, but she found no hint of help. Because he was doing what he always had: he was letting her decide for herself.

"Jane?" Leo gave her a little shake.

She wasn't ready. Not yet. She wanted more time. Time to remember. Time with the horses. Time with him. "I want to go back to the ranch."

"Okay." He pulled her in and tucked her head under his chin, but she caught the flash of relief on his face. And the thought of that made her smile a little. "Okay. You've got it. Is there a back way out of here?" he asked Dr. Monroe.

"Give me your keys." She held out her hand to him. "There's a gate behind the garden shed. It'll take you into an alley behind the house. Head east, then another two blocks. Colleen will be waiting at the corner with your truck."

Jane blinked. That seemed awfully…prepared.

"I will?" Colleen blinked doll-size amber eyes at her boss.

"You will. Get to it. Act casual when you drive away. You." Dr. Monroe pointed a stern finger at Delaney. "Exam room two. March. You and I are going to have a discussion about privacy and social media addiction. Unless you object?" She turned those birdlike eyes on Kaitlin.

"I most certainly do not. Have at her." She sat back in her chair, popped open the back of her daughter's phone and removed the battery. "I'm so sorry for whatever trouble this causes you," she said to Jane.

Jane could only nod. In a matter of seconds, all the security and peace she'd found with Leo began to slip through her fingers. It wouldn't be long before everyone knew where she was…knew she was… Wait.

Jane frowned. Why would everyone have thought she was dead?

"This way," Dr. Monroe instructed them as Colleen headed out the front door. Shouts and screams ensued, and the clicking and flash of cameras flew through the door.

An odd light exploded in front of Jane's eyes. She gasped, lifted her arm to shield her face as she turned away. The pain that had settled in her head the moment she opened her eyes in that shed popped and trickled away. She would have gasped in relief, but there wasn't time.

Leo grabbed her hand and pulled her toward the back door. She knew to move, knew how to move, but she felt as if her feet were trapped in cement, slogging and slow. Those empty spaces in her head began to fill, as if a faucet had been turned to full blast. So much, too much, so fast. Too fast.

"Jane? You with me?" Leo tugged her arm.

"Y-yes. With you."

"You call me in a few days," Dr. Monroe ordered. "If the headaches haven't subsided and you can't get her into town, I'll come to you."

Jane smirked and aimed an *I told you so* look at Leo.

The shouts coming from the front of Dr. Monroe's clinic faded as they hurried out the back gate and down the alley. They slowed down as they reached the street, hands clinging to one another as they followed the doctor's directions. Sure enough, Colleen was waiting for them at the corner.

Jane's ears buzzed as she climbed into the truck.

She closed her eyes and leaned against the headrest as the pieces of her life fell back into place. Each one a stepping-stone on the path home. A home without Leo.

It wasn't until they were well out of town that Leo sagged back in his seat and let out a small laugh. "Now, that was unexpected. What's wrong? Jane?"

"I remember." She turned her head and looked at him, waited for him to process what she said. "I remember everything."

Chapter 12

"Thank you."

Leo handed over the mug and sat beside Jane on the sofa. "It's just tea." Tea he certainly couldn't stomach. Which was why he'd brewed a pot of coffee.

"That's not what I meant." She sipped from her mug, a bit of the color coming back to her cheeks. "I meant thank you for not pestering me with questions."

"Well." He shrugged, toed off his boots and stretched his legs out, all of which presented a picture of calm and contentment. A complete facade. Inside he was a roiling mess of emotions ranging from relief to panic to utter and complete dread. "Personally, I'm dying to know all about your second-grade teacher and whatever trouble you and Phoebe might have gotten into."

"Mrs. Burke. And any second-grade mischief honestly pales in comparison to later entanglements. And you're doing great not pestering me."

He forced a smile. "You've got enough rolling around in that head of yours. No need to add me to the mix."

"But you are." She set the tea down and curled her legs under her. "You are part of the mix, Leo. A big part. Just because I can fill in most of those blanks now, that doesn't erase you. Nothing can. I love you."

And he loved her. More than he thought possible. Finally, because of Jane, he felt as if he understood his grandparents so much more. The way his grandmother would smile whenever Isaac would walk into the room; the way she'd pretend not to be waiting for him to come home at night, distracting herself with fixing dinner or cleaning or organizing his office. His grandfather's words of advice, most of which had revolved around embracing love when it presented itself and the gifts it brought, the changes it caused. Changes for the better. He'd cherish these months he'd shared with her. Quite possibly for the rest of his life.

"Leo, talk to me." The slight tremor in her voice broke through. "Please. This doesn't change anything between us. I won't let it." She had slid across the sofa, pressed herself into his side as she stroked his hair, traced the side of his face. "I'm still who I was when I woke up in your arms this morning. I might have filled in the blanks, but there's nowhere else I want to be."

"Jane—" His chest tightened with the pressure of what needed to be said.

"No." Her voice cut through his resolve. "No. Leo Slattery, you are not pulling away from me. Not now. Now when I need you the most." She plucked his cup from his hand and set it on the table next to the sofa. The next thing he knew, she was over him, legs on either side of his thighs, hands planted on the sofa behind his head. "You're not hearing me. I know who I am now. And it doesn't change what I want. And I still want you. Promise me I can stay, Leo." Her eyes darkened as his hands gripped her hips. "Promise me."

He smiled, unable to resist temptation as his hands slid up and down her back. She arched against him, that low purr emanating from the back of her throat.

"No fair," he managed. "You know how to get what you want."

"Indeed I do." She moved against him, shifting her hips enough to fog his mind and harden his body. "Say it, Leo." Jane nipped at his ear, caught the lobe between her teeth and bit gently. "Promise me I can stay."

He caught her face, brought her mouth to his and kissed her, hoping the distraction would be enough to push the request from her thoughts. But she pulled back, just enough, to silently pose the question once more.

There wasn't anything he wouldn't do for her, he realized in that moment. Nothing she could ask that he would deny. She held his heart not only in her hands, but in every cell. In every look. In every smile. "I promise." But that was all he said. There were no more words.

Not while she was kissing him and not, he thought later, while she made love to him. Or when he made love to her again in the moon-splintered darkness. But the words he couldn't utter were still there, hovering behind the overwhelming desire to hold on to her.

And the knowledge that he had to let her go.

* * *

"Anything else you need in town?" Leo asked her the next afternoon as he motioned for Ollie to jump into the cab. The dog inclined his head, let out a bark, then circled back around to stand beside Jane.

Jane, who looked as radiant and perfect as she had every day she'd been on the ranch. Jane, who had her arms loaded with some of the plants he'd brought back from the nursery for her. Jane, who was currently frowning at him as if he'd lost his mind. "That's the third time you've asked me that. No, we don't need anything. Will you go already? The sooner you leave, the sooner you'll be back, and I need your help with dinner."

"Don't you mean I need your help?" The teasing banter normally made his heart lighter. But today, the words weighed him down.

"It's amazing how well you know me." She walked over and tilted her head up for a kiss, which he willingly did. But not the quick brush of lips she expected. He cupped her face, dived deep and committed the taste of her, the feel of her, the sound of her, to memory. "Now you really have to hurry back," she moaned against his mouth, then pushed a hand against his shoulder. "Go."

Ollie trotted after her, but not before tossing Leo a questioning look. Darned dog was too smart for his own good.

Leo watched as she disappeared around the corner of the house, no doubt on her way up to Gwen and Lacey's place, before he climbed into the truck and drove into town.

He waited for the doubt to descend, for his conscience to kick in and tell him he was making the wrong decision. The guilt was there, hovering, but even that didn't dissuade him. Nothing would. Because he knew he was doing the right thing.

He parked in front of the Lucky Diner, gave Miss D a quick wave as he locked up his truck. But instead of heading in for a cup of coffee and an order of pie, he walked across the street.

And into the police station.

It took over an hour and three trips from the house to the family cemetery, but Jane was finally ready to get started. The fencing outlining the area needed a coat of paint, but that would have to wait until after the weeding, the cleaning and the seeding next spring. She'd purposely requested late-blooming flowers so there would be some color to the area through the winter. Or at least until the first snowfall. For now, this would do.

It didn't occur to her until she stood amid Leo's family that there were five graves. She'd expected four: his mother, father and grandparents. But there was a fifth grave. A smaller marker stood between his mother's and father's. Gabriel Mitchell Slattery. Who had died the day he'd been born. The same day, Jane noted, as Leo's mother had passed. Tears pricked her eyes as she sank to the ground, her heart breaking for the man she loved. A man who had every reason to be bitter and angry and yet spent most every day with a smile on his face.

Last night had meant everything to her. Not just because making love to Leo made her feel alive, desired and loved, but because now that her memory was intact, now that she knew what had come before, she knew, to the core of her soul, that she had never loved anyone the way she did Leo. What had he said about his grandparents? That they'd been tethered at the heart?

She tapped a finger against her chest and smiled. "I know just how that feels."

Phoebe.

Guilt clanged deep inside her, as she debated for the hundredth time about reaching out to her twin, but she wasn't ready for the questions, the suffocating attention. A few more days weren't going to make that much of a difference. She'd needed last night with him; she needed today with Leo, just to solidify plans in her mind. So she could finally move on. With him.

And yes, that meant going to the police. It had to be frustrating Leo to no end believing she wouldn't give in to that request, but once again, she knew he was right. The time would come. She knew it would. And he'd give her that time. He'd promised he would.

One thing she knew for absolute certain where Leo Slattery was concerned: he never made a promise he couldn't keep.

"Can I help you?" the dark-haired deputy on the other side of the counter asked Leo, who had been admiring the polished wood railings and cabinetry in the reception area. He'd clearly watched too many cop shows growing up, expecting to find yellowed linoleum, ancient metal desks and whining computers that wouldn't cooperate. Instead, what he was seeing was a streamlined, modern structure with attention to the town's history, including etched glass windows from when the building had been a men's fine-clothing department store. "Sir?"

"Sorry." Leo managed a smile as he removed his hat. "I was wondering if I could speak with Deputy Daria Bloom?" The second the words left his lips he felt the course of his life tip. Even if Jane never forgave him, he was doing the right thing. At least, that's what he kept telling himself.

"Do you have an appointment?" The deputy's cool expression didn't change. His obsidian black eyes barely shifted as he focused on Leo.

"I'm afraid not, Deputy—" Leo glanced at the deputy's badge "—Gates. But it is important."

"I'm sure it is. Go ahead and sign in." He gestured to the clipboard on the counter. "Can I tell her what this is about, Mr. Slattery?" Deputy Gates asked after Leo filled in his name, address and phone number.

"Um…" Leo hesitated.

"It'll help determine if she sees you today or later this week. We're a bit busy these days. You might have heard we're working a serial killer case."

"I did hear, actually. That's part of why I'm here. But you can tell her it's about a missing person case."

"Missing person?" Deputy Gates's eyebrows shot up and disappeared under his hair. "Sure. Have a seat. I'll let Daria know right away."

"Thanks." Leo chose not to sit, and as the deputy disappeared into the depths of the station, he paced up and down the aisle, skimming the missing persons flyers, most wanted listings and community bulletin board.

"Mr. Slattery?"

Leo turned and found an attractive, determined-looking woman heading his way. She was a bit older than he'd expected given she was still a deputy, but he had no doubt this woman could hold her own in any situation. Her navy-blue uniform only boosted the air of professionalism and dedication he picked up from her. "Yes. Deputy Bloom?"

"Daria, please. I understand you have some information about an ongoing investigation?"

"Sure do. Can we speak in private?"

"Of course." She nodded at Gates and motioned for Leo to follow. "Coffee?"

"Pass." One look at the ancient coffee maker had him cringing.

"Smart man." Daria grinned as she poured herself a cup. "Enough of this stuff and I won't only stay awake, I won't be wasting time blinking. Come on back." She led him into her office. "Don't mind the boards. It's a work in progress." She sat down and leaned back, eyeing him.

Leo set his hat on the chair and walked over to one of the whiteboards filled with photographs, dates and other forensic information for the Avalanche Killer. When he looked over his shoulder, he found Daria watching him. "I shouldn't be seeing this, should I?"

"Depends. Anything we might have gotten wrong about anything up there, Mr. Slattery?"

"Leo. And only one that I know of." He reached up and plucked Skye's picture off the board. "She's alive." He dropped the picture onto her desk.

"So I heard." Daria swayed in her chair. "I spoke

with Kaitlin and Delaney Sommars yesterday evening after Delaney reported seeing Skye at Dr. Monroe's. They also mentioned a well-mannered cowboy named Leo who was with her. Not many Leos around these parts, so I'm guessing that's you." She looked at him for another few seconds, then leaned forward in her chair, folded her hands on top of her desk. Tight enough he saw her knuckles turn white. "Is she okay?"

"Yeah." Leo nodded and saw tension he hadn't noticed melt off the deputy. "She is now. She wasn't when I found her."

"When was that?" She clicked open a pen and started making notes on a tablet.

"Late July." Daria arched a brow as Leo sat across from her. "Don't even say it. Believe me, I'm right there with you. She'd taken a pretty bad blow to the head. Didn't have any memory of who she was. Where she came from. And she was scared. Terrified, actually. She'd been attacked."

"Attacked how?" Daria's eyes sharpened. "Raped?"

"She said no. But that's all she remembered."

"And you believed her."

"I'm not sure I can explain it. I could just... I just did."

"So she didn't know what happened to her, but she did know she hadn't been sexually assaulted." Daria's doubt was obvious.

"That's what she told me. You can ask her about it yourself."

"I plan to, thanks. I take it she's still staying with you?"

"Yes." There it was. The final thread to his promise had been broken.

"Why didn't you bring her to us? Why didn't you call the police?"

Leo could understand the accusation in her tone. He'd been expecting it. Didn't mean he was ready for the spark of anger he saw in Daria's eyes. "Because the mere mention of talking to the police sent her into a panic attack."

"Did it?" Daria's brows knit. "Explain."

"The first time I mentioned the police was when I found her in my barn. Her clothes were ripped, torn and bloodied. She had cuts and scrapes and bruises along with the head wound. There was a welt on her cheek, from a ring I'm guessing. I could see the handprint."

"Don't suppose you thought to take some pictures."

"Didn't have a cell phone at the moment, so I didn't think of it. No reception in my area. I did put the clothes in a paper bag, though. Just in case."

"Smart. There might be some trace we can use." Daria nodded. "Go on."

Where did he start? "She's had nightmares, almost every night since she's been with me. Lights are always a part of it. Spinning red and blue lights. And a man in uniform. Dark. The last nightmare she had, she remembers a patrol car ramming her from behind, which sent her into a crash. She tried to get out the passenger side, but he broke the driver's window, opened the door, grabbed her ankle. Hauled her out of the car. Next thing she woke up in a gardening shed at an abandoned property. She got herself free and ran. Ended up on my ranch."

Daria listened without a hint of emotion flickering across her pretty features. "Any idea where this abandoned property is?"

"It's Paul Preston's place. A few miles from my spread. I took her back there. She didn't remember being there, not specifically, but I'm pretty sure that's where she was held. Her description of where she woke up fits."

"Preston's been dead going on five years now," Daria said.

"A friend of mind suggested it might be the place."

"A friend?"

"John McHugh Trapper. You might—"

"Oh, I know Trapper." Daria actually grinned. "Cranky old coot, but he's a good guy. Also a wealth of information."

"Trapper thought the place she described sounded familiar so we checked it out. Preston might be long gone, but someone's been using his place as a drug hub." He reached into his back pocket and pulled out the scorched ID. "We found this in the fireplace."

Daria looked down at what was left of the plastic card. "Levi McEwan. Well. That's interesting." She sat back in her chair, her frown increasing. Then the deputy shot to her feet and started shuffling through files on her desk. "When did you say Skye showed up at your place?" She yanked one free and flipped it open.

"Late July. The twenty—"

"Twenty-fourth?" She tapped a finger against the notes inside.

"Sounds right. What's going on? What do you know?"

"Know? Nothing for certain. *Yet.* Hang on." She picked up her phone and asked someone to bring in any updated information on Levi. When she hung up, she pinned him with another look. "So it's because Skye was afraid of the police you lied to the deputy when he came out to your place looking for her?"

"I'm sorry?" Now it was Leo's turn to frown. "When who came to my what? I haven't seen anyone other than Trapper and Jane on my land in forever." Trapper. Leo sat up straighter in his chair. "But Trapper told me about a guy in an SUV who was lost and asked for directions."

"Jane?"

"Skye," Leo said to clarify. "She didn't remember her name so we've been calling her Jane."

"Zero points on originality," Daria muttered. "Thanks, Blue." She accepted the file handed to her by a young female deputy. "Do me a favor and get the log for the door-to-door on Skye Colton? And do you know if the sheriff is back yet?"

"Sure." She was so young and enthusiastic her ponytail actually bopped. "And nope on the sheriff. Want me to try his cell?"

"No. I'll take care of it, thanks." Daria flipped through pages in the file while Leo began fidgeting. "Relax, Leo. I'm just putting some pieces together. You're absolutely sure no one came out to your place to ask about Skye?"

"I'm positive. Trapper would have told me if I'd been away, and there's no way Jane could have hidden that from me. She still freaks out when I mention the cops."

"Can't say I blame her if a cop is responsible for what happened to her. Wait." Daria glanced up and he could all but see the wheels spinning in her head. "She doesn't know you're here, does she?"

"No." He shook his head and swallowed a new lump of guilt. "And believe me, she isn't going to be happy when she finds out I came to you behind her back, but I figured you were a safe bet."

"Me? Why?"

"Because whoever attacked her was a man. And you're…not."

"Who says ranchers aren't observant." Daria actually grinned. "For the record, no, I wasn't the one who attacked Skye. So Levi McEwan was a small-time drug dealer in Roaring Springs. Coke, some meth, heroin occasionally. He'd been branching out, some new poison hitting the streets in the bigger cities. They found his body in late July, near a gas station. The same gas station Skye used to fill up on the twenty-fourth according to her credit card. The coroner puts McEwan's time of death within that time frame."

Panic of an entirely new sort swirled in his chest. "You think what happened to Jane is related?"

"I'm thinking I don't believe in coincidences."

"Here you go." Blue returned, the same eager expression on her face as she handed over a thick binder. "Anything I can help you with?"

"Give me a second." Daria flipped through the pages.

"Oppenhymer, Palmer, Preston, Pullman...Slattery, Leo." She flipped the binder around, tapped the entry. "Right here. Deputy Gerald Gates recorded visiting your property. Even made note of the discussion he had with an elderly gentleman. No result."

"I don't know what to tell you," Leo said. "Like I said, the only person who'd stopped by was a guy looking for directions. Said he was looking at property in the area to buy." That bubble of unease continued to build in his chest. Something wasn't right.

"Blue, would you have Deputy Gates come in?" Daria asked.

"Oh, well, I would, but he just left." Blue pointed behind her. "Said he had a family emergency come up and needed to take the rest of the day off. He asked me to mind the counter."

Leo's ears began to ring. "You said his first name was Gerald?"

"Yeah." Daria's gaze narrowed.

"GG. Skye's nightmare last night. She remembered a name badge on the man's chest. She couldn't remember the name, but she did remember the initials. G and G." Leo swore, and bolted for the door.

"Wait, Leo! Where are you going?" Daria raced after him, Blue right on her heels.

"He had me sign in. With my name and address. He would have recognized it, wouldn't he?" He headed for the front door.

"How long ago did he leave?" Daria demanded.

"Maybe ten minutes?" Blue told them.

Leo was past listening. He needed to get home. He

needed to get to Jane. This was his fault. If he hadn't gone against her wishes, if he hadn't thought he knew better, then Gerald Gates never would have found out where she was.

"Hold up, Leo." Daria grabbed his arm and steered him away from his truck.

"You can't stop me from going. I need to get home."

"I'm not going to try to stop you. But we need to get there fast. Blue, call the sheriff, tell him we have a possible suspect for the McEwan murder and the assault and kidnapping of his cousin Skye Colton. We need backup out at the Slattery ranch ASAP."

"Right." Blue disappeared back into the station.

"You." She pointed at Leo. "In the squad car." Daria dug keys out of her pocket and ducked inside. "We'll get there faster with sirens."

Jane wasn't sure what she heard first. Ollie's low growl or the grinding of tires in the gravel beyond the house. Wrist deep in the new soil she'd put over the top of Essie's resting place, she abandoned the plantings and pushed to her feet. She swiped a dirt-caked hand across her forehead, her fingers catching in the hair that had come loose from her braid. Tires ground in the gravel by the house. She'd been listening to that sound every day for months. The same sound that brought her a sense of comfort and excitement, and the promise of Leo walking through the door.

Whoever had arrived, it was not Leo.

"Come on, boy." She smacked her hand against her thigh to call for Ollie to follow, then headed toward the house. She stepped carefully, quietly, as she drew closer and bent down to grab hold of Ollie's neck. He growled again, and this time she took his warning seriously.

Whoever it was clomped his way around the front of the house. He—it had to be a *he*, as she'd never heard a woman stomp around like that—didn't call out. He didn't make a sound, which seemed all the more odd.

Jane stopped at the corner of the barn, kept Ollie at her side and leaned over to peer around. Her heart skipped more than a beat at the sight of the police cruiser. She gasped, covering her mouth with her free hand as she gripped the dog tighter. Her skin went clammy as fear descended, but she took a moment, tried to reason it out. One cop, one person, had been the one who drove her off the road. What were the odds…

His footsteps drew closer. She struggled for breath as Ollie strained against her hold. Her stomach pitched and cramped as she inhaled the sickening scent of cloves. She became light-headed. The world spun, and she braced herself against the wall to keep from pitching forward.

She squeezed her eyes shut, but all she could see was the glint of an arcing blade; all she could hear was the sound of that blade piercing flesh. All she could feel was the terror slicing through her, sharper than any knife.

Beneath the blinding fluorescent lights of the gas station, blood spewed, spraying over the foliage and shrubs beyond the line of sight. Just beyond the entrance to the station where she'd gone in to pay for her gas.

She'd stood there, frozen, caught between the horror of the murder she'd witnessed and the knowledge that the man responsible had seen her. A tall, dark-haired man wearing a navy-blue Roaring Springs deputy's uniform. With a name badge reading Deputy Gerald Gates.

The same deputy who had started toward her, knife still in hand, blood dripping from his fingers. She'd run full-bore to her car, nearly twisting her ankle, panic making her hands shake as she opened the door, threw herself inside and peeled out of the station like the devil himself was on her trail. The sports car was fast, but the cruiser with spinning lights gave chase, growing closer in her rearview mirror as she fumbled to get her phone out of her bag. Why hadn't she hooked up the voice control? She pressed her foot down harder on the accelerator as the cruiser closed the distance.

The steering wheel vibrated beneath her death grip. Could she make it to the police station in Roaring Springs? But it was the police behind her. Trey. Trey would know what to do. Trey could help her. Or...

Home. If she could just make it home, her family would be there. He wouldn't even think about following her...

She screamed the first time he rammed her vehicle from behind. The sound of metal crunching against metal sent chills racing over her body. Her heart pounded so hard against her ribs she was afraid her chest would burst. Her car skidded one way, then the other, but she managed to get it under control. She pressed her foot harder. The car strained, but lurched forward just as he clipped her again. The outcropping of rocks closed in fast. She pulled her foot off the gas and braced for impact, but there was no preparing for the explosion of airbags when she hit. Time stopped and when it began moving again, everything shifted into slow motion.

Ears ringing, blood streaming down one side of her face, she'd struggled to stay awake. In her numbed state, she fumbled for the seat belt latch, straining against the belt as she heard a car door slam. Heavy footfalls headed her way. She whimpered, hating the helpless sound as she struggled and strained, unable to get any traction with her stilettos. She kicked them off, pressed her bare feet to the floorboards and pushed up. One more depression of the latch and the belt burst free, whipping back and catching her in the face. She dived across the gearshift, reaching frantically for the passenger door as her window exploded, showering her in glass.

His hand reached in, grabbing for her, but when he didn't make contact, he unlocked the door and ripped it open. She kicked out, screaming, shouting as his hand locked around her ankle. He bent down, his dark eyes flashing in the dim glow of the overhead light of her car. Then, yanking hard, he pulled her almost all the way out. She thrashed, punching out with her fists, landing a few blows until he yanked her one more time. Her head slammed against the bottom of the car as he pulled her free. She lay there, stunned, amid shattered glass and her own blood, unable to do anything but watch him stand over her. Lean down. He backhanded her hard, across the face, the chunky ring he wore on his hand catching her skin before he hit her again. And then...

Ollie barked, dragging Jane out of the memory. She

stood there, back against the barn, frozen, and watched her attacker step around the corner. Slowly. Deliberately. Carefully.

Dark hair. Even darker eyes in a face so pale he reminded her of death. The uniform seemed to sag around him, as if afraid to mold itself to his body. But now she remembered that sickly amused smile she saw on his face. The same face that had smiled down on her that night.

The same face of the man who had stopped here for directions a few weeks ago.

"I've been looking for you."

Ollie strained against her hold, but she clung harder, afraid of what the man would do to him. She slid away, splinters snagging on her shirt as her mind raced for something—anything—to use to defend herself. "I'm not alone." Her voice trembled. Ollie growled and barked so loudly her head hurt again. "Leo's—"

"Slattery is in town. At the police station. How do you think I finally knew where to find you?" His right hand went to his holster. He unsnapped the safety on his gun and wrapped his fingers around the butt. "You remember, don't you? I can see it on your face. You remember seeing me kill Levi."

She felt the blood drain from her face. Leo was where? No. This man was lying. Leo wouldn't lie to her. He wouldn't betray her. He'd promised not to go to the police. He'd promised...

But looking at the deputy, she knew he was telling her the truth.

Leo had lied to her.

And that, more than any knife, any punch, any bullet, hurt.

"They'll figure it out," she told him. "When they find my body, they'll figure out it was you."

"*If* they find your body." He pulled out his gun and aimed it, not at her, but at Ollie. He cocked the hammer.

"No!" She stepped in front of the dog, twisting her arm in such a way she felt the tendons strain as she held on to his collar. "No, don't hurt him. I'll do whatever you want, just leave him alone." She needed to buy time, time for her brain to start working to find a way out.

"Then chain him up." He waggled the muzzle. "Nice and tight. Then get in the car. We have unfinished business, you and I."

An odd calm descended as she caught the mad look in the deputy's eyes. The second she got into that car, she was dead. She knew that as certainly as she knew she loved Leo.

"Okay." She took a chance and turned her back on the gun so she could get a better hold on Ollie. "Okay, I'll tie him up. But the rope is in the stable. Over there." She pointed to the building that had served as her safe haven all these weeks. "It's either that or let him loose, and I'd put my money on him."

"Move."

Ollie growled again and for the first time struggled against Jane's hold. "Please, Ollie," she whispered. "Trust me." She half hobbled him over all the way to the stable, the deputy right behind her. "He has a leash," she lied. "Just there." She pointed to the narrow wall separating Teyla and Bullet. Bullet. An idea formed, easing the fear bearing down on her again.

"Then get it," Deputy Gates snapped.

"One question." She dragged Ollie over to Teyla and reached for the lead rope hanging beside her stall. "Why did you kill him?"

"What does it matter?" Gates asked. "He was stealing from me. Taking more product for himself than he was selling. No one steals from me."

"Noted." She pretended to stumble and grabbed hold of Bullet's door, slid the latch free as she pushed herself forward, dragging Ollie with her.

"Tie him up already, would you?" He glanced over his shoulder.

"Afraid you're running out of time?" She looped the rope around Ollie's neck and secured him to a nearby post.

Gates swung on her, advancing fast. She spun and yanked hard on Bullet's door, pulling it open in one fast whoosh. The young stallion burst free, his feet catching the edge of the door and sending Jane sprawling to the ground. Gates cried out as the horse didn't stop, knocking him to the ground so hard and so fast, his gun discharged into the roof. Jane jumped to her feet, grabbed a shovel and ran at Gates. She slammed the shovel down hard on his hand, dislodging the gun. She kicked it well out of reach, dropped the shovel and dived for the weapon, but Gates grabbed her around the ankle and sent her crashing face-first into the floor. She tasted blood. Her nose and mouth went numb, but she wasn't giving up. She wouldn't surrender. Not to this man.

She threw out her arms, searching with her hands, grabbing with her fingers as she found the handle of the shovel again.

Ollie was going mad, his barks so loud she could barely hear the screeching tires and slamming doors.

"Jane!"

Leo. Was she hearing things? Jane threw herself over, kicked out with her free foot, but Gates wouldn't let go. The madness and rage swirled in his eyes as his other hand locked around her calf, dragged her closer as he hauled himself up. She readjusted her grip on the shovel and hurled it around, swinging like she was going for a home run. She connected with his shoulder so hard her own arms vibrated.

Gates screamed in pain and released her. Splinters embedded themselves in her palms, but she barely felt them. She struggled to her knees, never taking her eyes off the writhing figure before her. He reached for her again. More voices. More shouts. Dozens of them. Or maybe she was imagining things. Maybe it was her mind playing tricks on her. She drew the shovel back, ready to hit him again.

"Jane, stop!" She was grabbed from behind, spun away as the shovel was pulled from her hands. "It's okay. They've got him. Shh. They've got him."

Leo. She clung to him, sank into him as he wrapped his arms so tightly around her she couldn't breathe. She didn't want to breathe. She didn't have to. Not when he was there.

"Come on. I've got you. Let's go outside." He led her

out of the stable, but she stopped him, shaking her head as she planted her feet. "Ollie. Where's—"

"Here he is." A young uniformed female deputy brought Ollie, rope leash and all, over to her. "I figure maybe you two are better off handling him than we are." Ollie hopped up and around them over and over as they brought him along.

Once outside, Jane pulled herself free of Leo's hold and dropped to her knees, hugging Ollie against her as she sobbed into his fur. "You're okay, boy. You're okay." Ollie lifted one paw over her shoulder and seemed to be petting her back. "You did so good. So, so good." She didn't think she'd ever forget the manic look on Gates's face when he'd aimed that pistol at the dog. If anything had happened to him...

"You need to tell me what happened," Leo said as he crouched beside her. He reached out to brush her hair back from her face, but she pulled away, angry tears escaping her control. "Jane, talk to me."

"You know what happened," she said as he looked into her eyes. "You lied to me."

Chapter 13

Leo straightened from where he'd been slouching against the side of the ambulance as Daria and Sheriff Trey Colton approached. In the dusk, his ranch teemed with patrol cars, deputies, and other investigators who were already marking evidence trails from the house to the stable. Deputy Blue had been charged with tracking down Bullet, who was probably halfway to the next property line by now.

Two larger deputies were hauling Gates over to a squad car while the man screamed in pain over the injuries to his shoulder and chest. Not one ounce of sympathy trickled through Leo. Part of him wished he'd let Jane take another swing at Gates, but given what he'd seen, she might have killed him. No way was he going to let her have a death—not even Gerald Gates's death—on her conscience.

She wasn't hurt. She was alive. Except for a few new scrapes and bruises, uninjured.

But to be safe, the paramedics were giving Jane—Skye—the once-over, not an easy feat as she wouldn't relinquish her hold on Ollie.

Leo had lived through a lot in his life: the loss of his parents and grandparents; on-site accidents up north that had cost men their lives. He'd taken chances where he shouldn't have and lived to tell the tale, but nothing had prepared him for the endless ride back to his ranch. The idea they might have been too late, that Gerald Gates could have killed her before...

He gave his head a hard shake as if he could dislodge the image.

If Daria was as exhausted as Leo felt, she certainly didn't look it. If anything, she looked like she'd drunk half a tankard of Red Bull. "Tell me he spilled his guts," Leo said.

"Gates has said enough we can piece it together," Daria said. "Trey, Leo Slattery. Leo, Sheriff Trey Colton."

"Belated welcome home to Roaring Springs," Trey said with a bigger smile than Leo expected. "Nice to know Isaac's ranch is in good hands. And on a personal note, thank you for all you've done to keep Skye safe. I'm looking forward to delivering good news to my family for a change. They've been going a little nuts since hearing she was alive. Not all missing persons cases turn out this well."

"I suppose they don't." Leo looked back to Jane, who had an odd, distant and almost vacant expression on her face. She hadn't looked at him. Not since she'd confronted him about his deception.

"She'll get over it." Daria touched his arm. "Just give her some time. She'll realize you were only doing what was best for her."

Leo winced. He seriously doubted that. "What's the story with Gates? Why'd he kill McEwan?"

"Levi was stealing from him," Jane said from where she sat on a stretcher. "Gates took exception. I was in the wrong place at the wrong time."

"We ran the property records on the Preston place," Daria said. "Paul Preston was Gates's uncle. As his nephew and only living relative, Gates inherited the property. When he transferred to Roaring Springs two years ago, he did so to expand his drug distribution network. From what our techs have found so far at the Preston property, he had a pretty big operation going until recently." She paused for a moment, then went on. "Probably moved it again after he killed Levi. We've been in touch with his previous department in Denver suggesting they look into his time there. I'm betting we find a connection between the drug supply chain and what we've dealt with here since he arrived."

"Being a deputy was the perfect cover." Trey's eyes went dangerously dark. "He could keep an ear out on the drug cases, know what areas to avoid. Also says something about our background check policy. Something I'm going to make sure is reevaluated as soon as possible."

"Why didn't he kill me?"

Leo's blood chilled at the detached tone in Jane's voice. She was pushing the paramedic away, shaking her head as she tucked the thermal blanket tighter at her throat and stepped out of the truck. Ollie hopped down beside her, looking between the two of them as if begging them to make up.

"We don't have to talk about that now," Daria said. "You don't need to hear—"

"I have no doubt he was planning to," Trey said, cutting her off. "I did a little digging. About fifteen years or so ago Gates's father got into a business deal with your dad, Skye. Whatever that deal was went belly up and the Gates family lost everything. They never recovered, either financially or professionally. And personally? Gates is the only one left alive. Seeing you at the gas station that night, he probably thought he'd been given a gift. What better way to make Russ suffer than by living through the loss of one of his children? By kidnapping you, by drawing it out, he was prolonging his own enjoyment. Then you escaped."

"When you didn't turn up he probably thought he'd lucked out and you'd died of exposure," Daria added. "Either way, you weren't home and that was enough pain to inflict on your father."

"He was going to rape me before he killed me," Skye whispered. "Today. I saw it in his eyes. I knew if I got in that car with him—"

Leo held out his hand, but she stepped out of reach without even looking at him. He tried to ignore the hollow pang in his gut as his heart sank. She was alive, he reminded himself. When all was said and done, that was all that mattered. The woman he loved was safe and alive. That would have to be enough.

"What else do you need from me?" Jane asked.

"An official statement," Daria said. "You can come in tomorrow morning, and we can—"

"No. I want to finish this. I want this all to be over." She swiped her hair off her face. "Would it be all right if I took a shower and changed first?"

"Yeah. We've photographed your injuries. If you could bag your clothes. All of them." She glanced down to the blood-spattered boots. "Sorry about that."

"It's fine," Jane whispered. "I'll just be a few minutes."

"I'll come with you. I left my truck—"

"I'll ride with Daria. Alone." Jane kept her gaze pinned on the deputy. "If that's okay."

Daria nodded. "Yeah, it's fine. Just give a shout when you're ready."

Jane nodded and walked back to the main house, Ollie trailing behind her.

"She just needs some time," Trey told him.

"No amount of time will make this right." Leo swallowed around a too-tight throat. "I told her when she first got here I didn't make promises I couldn't keep. But I let her down."

There was a long silence as Trey and Daria waited patiently for him to go on.

"I went against her wishes...the only one she had. *Don't go to the police.* If I hadn't, Gates wouldn't have known where to find her."

"If you didn't, he'd have found her eventually and we wouldn't have been in time." Daria gave him a reassuring squeeze on his arm. "Because of you she's alive, Leo. We all thank you for that."

Leo nodded to acknowledge he'd heard her, but didn't say a word. He turned and headed inside. The water was running in the guest bathroom. He brewed a pot of coffee and sat down at the table to wait as Ollie came over, whined and laid his chin on Leo's knee. "I screwed up, boy." He patted the dog's head and waited, heart thudding heavily in his chest, until she emerged.

She'd put on clean jeans and a T-shirt, had braided her hair again and donned the second pair of sneakers he'd picked up for her on that first shopping trip. She'd folded her dirty, bloodied clothes, placed them in a paper bag, along with his mother's boots, and set them on the washer where he'd left the other bag with the outfit she'd been wearing when she'd arrived.

"I'm just going to check if I'm leaving anything I need." She headed to the living room, but he caught her wrist as she passed.

"Jane."

She froze solid, every bone in her body stiffening beneath his touch. She looked down to where he held her, raised her eyes to his. "Skye."

He absorbed the punch as if it was an actual body blow. His entire body would have caved in on itself if he hadn't been sitting down. "Skye. I did what I thought I needed to."

"I know you did. But what I wanted didn't matter. You lied to me, Leo." She shifted slightly so she could look at him. "Of all people, you lied to me. We could have done this together. You didn't have to go behind my back. You didn't have to deceive me."

He wanted to argue with her, wanted to explain that he'd done what he had to, what she needed him to do. But no matter how he tried to rationalize it, she was right. He'd lied to her. To argue that fact wasn't only futile, it was wrong. "I promised I would get you home."

"I guess it was stupid of me to think I'd found one with you."

"You did." He could feel her try to pull away, but he tightened his hold. "You have. I love you, Skye. We can—"

"What? We can *what*, Leo?" She looked down at him. "Start over? You can make new promises, ones you have every intention of keeping until you change your mind? You know, Brock might have deceived me, but he never pretended to be something he wasn't. Which was why I was more embarrassed than hurt when he ditched me for someone else. But this? This actually hurts." She knocked a fist against her chest.

"You're really going to compare what I did to what he did?" He couldn't believe what he was hearing.

"You don't get it, do you?" She shook her head, eyes wide with disbelief. "You were the one person I believed would never, ever hurt or betray me. From the second I saw you in that barn, I trusted you. Do you know how many people I've trusted in my life, Leo? One. My sister. Even my parents and brothers have let me down over the years. It never once crossed my mind that you'd ever lie to me."

"A lie meant to protect you." The excuse drew him to his feet.

"A lie that almost got me killed. Maybe one day I'll be able to move past that. But I don't trust you anymore, Leo. And I c-can't be with someone I can't trust." She blinked away the tears that pooled in her eyes and set her jaw. "No matter how much I wish otherwise. Let me go, Leo." She raised her arm where he still held on. "Now."

He released her and stood there, unmoving as she made a pass through the house, returning only moments later. "There's nothing here that's mine. At least, not anymore."

"Skye—" He needed to try again. He needed her to understand that he'd been wrong in how he went about things. That he didn't want to lose her. Didn't want to wake up to a house where she wasn't in it. "Skye, please."

"Hey." Daria rapped her knuckles against the back screen door and stepped inside. "Sorry to interrupt, but I'm heading out. Unless you changed your mind about staying?"

"I didn't," Skye said. "I'm leaving." She reached down and gave Ollie a solid pat. "It's time I went home."

Emotionally drained, physically exhausted and sore, Skye sat curled up on the small sofa in Daria Bloom's office, a toxic paper cup of coffee clutched between her trembling hands. "Is that all you need?" she asked the deputy, who was click-clacking her way on the keyboard, transcribing her statement word for word.

"Just for you to read this and sign it. Printing now." Daria tossed her a quick smile. "You sure you don't want a candy bar to go with that? It really helps to choke it down."

"This is fine." The disgusting taste helped keep her mind off Leo. Her eyes drooped. "Hoping the caffeine will help."

"I bet you'll be glad to be back in your own bed up at The Chateau." Daria plucked the papers out of the printer and waved her over.

"Yeah. I bet I will." She scanned through the write-up of everything she could now remember and scribbled her name on the last page. "You think Gates will take this to trial?"

"I think Gates is going to cut himself a cushy deal with the Feds. Out-of-state trafficking carries a pretty hefty sentence. Add kidnapping and assault to the list, I don't anticipate you having to testify."

"Too bad." Skye smirked. "I heard the deputies saying you thought I might have been taken out by a serial killer."

"The thought crossed our minds." Daria glanced up at the board Skye was examining. "Do me a favor, huh?"

"Sure."

"Don't go running off like that again. At least without staying in touch with someone."

"Believe me, I've learned my lesson. Are you driving me home?"

"Don't think I have to. Wow." She checked her watch. "Boy, they made good time."

"Who?" Even as the word left her lips, the door to Daria's office burst open and Phoebe barreled toward her. "Oh."

"I knew you were alive." Phoebe wrapped her in a hug so tight, she stole Skye's breath. "I knew... I always knew..." She leaned back, caught Skye's face between her hands and pressed her forehead to hers. "I've missed you so much." She blinked and tears spilled down her cheeks.

"Me, too," Skye whispered as she caught a glimpse of a vaguely familiar—and quite handsome—man standing in the doorway. Before she could put a name to the face, she saw her parents heading down the hall, along with her brothers. Boy, they all must have really been worried if even Decker, Blaine and Wyatt had made the drive down the mountain.

Soon she found herself passed around into life-affirming hugs. She managed to keep the tears at bay until she reached her mother. "Mom," she managed to say before her voice broke.

"There's my girl." Mara Colton, looking as elegant as always, folded her into her arms. "We've been so worried about you."

"I know. I'm sorry." She squeezed her eyes shut, trying to block out the memory of Leo pleading with her to reach out to her family, to let them know she was okay. Until this moment she hadn't realized why she'd been so reluctant. She hadn't wanted to see disappointment on their faces. She didn't want to feel like a bother. But she didn't. What she did feel was her mother's oddly comforting embrace and her brothers' hands rubbing her back. And when she opened her eyes, she saw her father, her strong, larger-than-life, sometimes overbearing, often distant father looking down at her with... tears in his eyes.

"Skye? Are you all right?"

She nodded, accepting the question for the emotional home run that it was. But she couldn't speak. Not without lying. She wasn't all right.

How could she be when she lost the only man she'd ever loved?

Chapter 14

"Does there have to be a party?" Skye dropped backward onto Phoebe's bed and let out a sigh that might have echoed across the mountain range had the windows been open.

Phoebe glanced up from where she was painting her toenails, an odd expression on her identical face. "I'm sorry. Did I hear correctly? Skye Colton doesn't want to go to a party in her honor?"

Skye bit her lip. She had no doubt Skye wanted to attend. It was Jane who felt particularly ambivalent. And these days she identified a whole lot more with Jane than her previous self. "I'd have been happy with dinner with the family." Instead, Mara and Phoebe had decided her return was the perfect excuse to fling open the doors to The Chateau and celebrate. "Speaking of family, when are you going to give me the details on how you landed Prescott Reynolds?" She rolled over and propped her chin on her hand, kicked her stiletto-sandaled feet in the air behind her.

"When I'm sure your recently amnesiac brain can absorb it." Phoebe had developed a new expression in the days since Skye had been home. A cross between disbelief and wide-eyed concern. "Did you put on any makeup?"

Skye groaned and flopped back over. "Yes, Mom. I just didn't paint it on as usual."

"You also aren't wearing your Spanx. Mom will be horrified."

Skye looked down and pushed two fingers into her stomach. "I've got another five pounds to go before she can start using the *F* word." Still, she'd had a bit of a struggle with the gold beaded dress. She'd stood in front of her mirror for countless minutes waiting to feel…normal.

"No one is ever going to use that word for you." Phoebe stretched out her feet and wiggled her toes. "You really liked it out there, didn't you? On that ranch?"

That ranch had become code for Leo Slattery, who, thanks to Daria, Skye hadn't had to fill her family in on. She didn't want to talk about Leo, because the moment she did, she'd have to accept just how much she missed him. So much she'd curled herself up in a tight ball every night and cried herself to sleep.

"Shouldn't we be heading down soon?" She popped off the bed like a tiddlywink and headed over to the mirror where Phoebe was trying to arrange her hair.

Skye bent down, put her face right beside her sister's, just as they always had.

"Skye." Phoebe lifted a hand to Skye's cheek. "I can see it even if you can't. You miss…the ranch. Why wouldn't you, given the awesome tan you got riding all those horses."

"Just one horse, actually. Ginger." Another pang of longing chimed inside. "But Duke, oh, he was a beauty. Teyla and Bullet were like naughty children, but…" She trailed off.

Phoebe let her go. "Have you thought about what you're going to do now that you're back? You going to sell your story as an exclusive? I bet it would make an awesome TV movie. That online magazine you were supposed to be reporting for—"

"Not interested." The idea of sharing what had happened to her was nauseating. Actually, the idea of sharing any of her life these days made her wonder if she'd ever been connected to reality. She didn't want the spotlight anymore. She didn't want anything other than… "I don't want to be the family face anymore."

Phoebe arched an outlined brow. "Okay. What do you want to do?"

"You'll laugh." She looked down at an errant thread on her dress. One tug, one little pull and she bet the entire dress would collapse. Kind of the way she felt about her life right now. She needed something to focus on. Something to feel good about. Something to do!

"I will *not* laugh." Phoebe's brows knit. "And I won't tell Mom if that's what you're worried about."

"I want to go back to school. I want to take some

business classes, maybe some design. I don't know, the history of architecture. Landscape design. I found I'm actually pretty useful. I'm not as stupid as people think."

"No one thinks you're stupid, Skye."

"No one thinks I'm a rocket scientist, either."

"You've helped me and Mom run The Chateau pretty successfully. You're incredible at party planning."

How did she explain to her twin that party planning didn't come close to the beauty of a Colorado sunset or watching a golden horse race across the horizon? How did she tell a family that was so happy to have her back that she was utterly and completely miserable?

"I think you just need a reminder of how important you are to this place," Phoebe announced. "Grab my shoes out of the closet, will you? The black glitter pumps?" She shimmied out of her robe and reached for the knee-length black evening dress.

"Sure." When she returned with the shoes, Phoebe was sitting on the edge of the bed watching her. "What?"

"You're not happy."

"Why do you say that?"

"Because I know you better than anyone else in the world. Because we shared very cramped quarters for nine months one time."

"Eight and a half," Skye corrected her.

"Something's changed for you, Skye. You're different."

"Having amnesia for months will do that to a girl."

"It's not the amnesia. It's Leo." Phoebe's face softened. "Oh, Skye. Don't cry."

Skye shook her head, tried to blink the tears away. "I don't want to talk about him."

"Because you love him." Phoebe pulled her down on the bed beside her. "Anyone can see that."

"How can I love a man who lied to me?"

"From what I heard he thought he was protecting you. That's what Daria told Dad at least."

"Daria needs to learn to keep her mouth shut." Just how long had the deputy been standing outside the kitchen that day, anyway?

"She cares about you, Skye. We all do. Tell you what." She turned Skye's face toward hers and wiped her thumbs under her eyes. "Let's get through this party, and then you and I are going to have a talk. A nice long talk about men and love and all that wonderful stuff."

"Can there be ice cream?" Skye sniffed. "Real ice cream, not that fake, low-calorie stuff?"

"I think I can rustle some up. Come on. One party. Then we'll figure out what to do about you and Leo."

Leo couldn't remember the last time he'd worn a suit. He didn't even own one, but at least his grandfather had a few and one of them even fit. The black bolo tie felt as if it was strangling him as he pulled his truck up to the valet parking at The Chateau and instantly understood what Trapper had been talking about all these years. The place looked like it had been plucked out of historic France and plopped into the mountains of Colorado.

The line of cars was nonstop, and if anyone noticed the difference between the BMWs, the Mercedes-Benzes and his ancient pickup, no one said a word.

Not the valet who took his key, nor the attendant who directed him to the main lobby. Part of him felt as if he should have dipped himself in 24-karat gold before stepping foot inside. He removed his hat, giving his fingers something to do other than hide in his pocket.

The invitation he'd received from Russ Colton himself couldn't have been more surprising. Not that the Coltons wanted to celebrate Skye's safe return, but that Skye's father even knew who he was.

"It's not a firing squad, so relax." Daria sidled up next to him and pushed an open beer into his hand. "It's good to see you here."

Grateful for a friendly and familiar face, Leo smiled. "I got the impression refusing the invitation wouldn't have gone over very well." Given he was hoping to expand his presence in the Roaring Springs business world, alienating Russ Colton didn't seem the smart move. But he was fooling himself if he didn't think Skye was the reason he'd come.

"Everyone is looking forward to meeting you," Daria said.

"Are they?" He drank some beer and wished for a buzz that would deaden his nerves. "Can't imagine why." Did everything in this place have to glow? It was sensory overload to his eyes. Not that it wasn't beautiful. It was. And quite…glamorous. Everything he'd always suspected Ja—*Skye* to be.

"You kept Skye safe and protected, Leo. You helped get their daughter home. Believe me, Russ and Mara are completely predisposed to liking you."

"You seem awfully in the know when it comes to

the Coltons." Leo couldn't help but frown, especially when he saw a flicker of uncertainty cross Daria's pretty features.

"Hard not to be when you live in Roaring Springs. Okay, let's start you out on an easy one. I see her brothers over there. Let's introduce you."

"She has three brothers?" Leo swallowed more beer. "Older or younger?"

"All older. Don't worry. They're harmless. For the most part."

Thankfully, Leo found Daria was right. Blaine, Wyatt and Decker were completely welcoming and appreciative for all he'd done for Skye. Their significant others were especially complimentary and enthusiastic as he was welcomed into the throng that was the Colton family.

He was deep in conversation with Wyatt Colton, discussing his plans to expand his ranch's stud servicing, when he stopped. He felt the charge in the room, the change in energy he had met so many mornings in the kitchen before he'd snuggled against it in bed. Bottle halfway to his mouth, he turned as Skye and her sister, Phoebe, descended the staircase.

The murmurs around him faded into the distance. He barely noticed the knowing smiles exchanged between the Colton brothers and their women. How could he when all he could see, all he wanted to see, was Skye?

He stayed where he was as she made the rounds, her parents following at a distance as they followed up with greeting their guests.

"They make quite the picture, don't they?"

The unfamiliar voice had Leo nodding. He glanced over and did a double take at finding one of his favorite actors standing next to him. "You're Prescott Reynolds. Leo Slattery." He held out his hand. "I'm a big fan."

"Back at you. I heard what you did for Skye. I'm sure you've heard it enough tonight, but thank you."

"I did what anyone else would have," Leo said for what felt like the millionth time.

"It'd be nice to think so but no. Not everyone would have. There are plenty of people who would have taken advantage. Sold the story to the tabloids, exposed her to that maniac who attacked her. You went above and beyond."

"It was an easy choice to make." He knew when she saw him. She stopped speaking, her eyes widening for a moment before she took someone's hand and begged off. The way she walked toward him, the way the shimmering fabric of the gold dress swirled around her ankles, caressed her curves, had his hand tightening around the neck of the bottle. He kept his eyes on her face, looking for a hint of what to expect. In that moment, he regretted coming here. They'd made a clean break—a heartbreaking one, but a clean one. And yet he hadn't been able to stay away when the opportunity to just see her again had presented itself. "Hello, Skye." Skye. Not Jane. Because Jane was gone.

"Leo." She stood before him, her red hair spilling over her shoulders like a fiery sunset. He could remember how it felt to have those curls tumbling through his fingers, as she wrapped herself around him, clung to him. Soared with him. "I didn't know you were coming."

"We wanted to keep it a surprise. Leo, it's so nice to finally meet you in person. I'm Mara Colton. Skye's mother."

"She's our mother, too, but we're second-rate these days," Blaine joked, and got an elbow in the ribs from Matilda.

"We wanted to thank you in person." Russ Colton offered his hand, which Leo accepted with barely a glance. He couldn't stop looking at her. She was perfect. Utterly and completely heartbreakingly perfect.

"I'm just glad everything worked out for the best." How he choked the words out he didn't know. But he saw a bit of the light go out in Skye's eyes. "I appreciate the invitation, but I'm not able to stay. I have a friend staying with me, and he's not been feeling well. I need to get back soon."

"Of course." Russ nodded. "Thank you for making the time. Mara, shall we?"

"Oh, yes, I suppose…" She cast worried eyes on her daughter. "It was lovely to meet you, Leo. Please, I hope we can speak again soon."

Leo nodded.

"Leo." Skye moved toward him. Her brothers suddenly cleared their throats and found an excuse to leave. Even Daria walked off and joined Phoebe and Prescott by the stairs. "It's good to see you." Skye reached out to touch him, but seemed to think better of it. "Is it Trapper?"

"Is what Trapper?"

"The sick friend. Is he all right? Or..." She trailed off and that's when he saw it. The suspicion. The doubt. The distrust.

"I didn't lie." His temper flared, but instead of snapping at her, he shifted his attention to a spot over her shoulder. "Trapper came back two days ago. Caught a nasty virus and he's been holed up in the bunkhouse, trying to get better."

"Oh. I'm sorry to hear it. I saw a recipe in your grandmother's cookbook..." She stopped. Sighed. Her chin wobbled a bit as she tried to force a smile. "It's not going to work, is it?" She didn't have to say anything else. He knew precisely what she meant.

"No. It's not." Leo looked around at this place she called home. There wasn't an inch that didn't sparkle and shine; there wasn't any part of it that didn't encase its occupants in the finest and best life had to offer. And she fit. So beautifully, so perfectly. Skye Colton just...fit.

This was where she belonged. Here. Not with him on a ranch, tending the horses and planting seedlings and sipping whiskey-laced tea by the fire.

"Leo," she whispered as he took a step toward her. He knew people were watching them. Suspected what had happened between them. Who was he to disappoint those wanting a show? He bent his head and kissed her. Slowly. Deeply. Deliberately. Memorizing every moment because he knew it would have to last him a lifetime. When he raised his mouth, he ignored the silence that had descended. He ignored the eyes on them and looked only at her as she blinked up at him.

"Goodbye, Skye."

And he walked out of her life.

Chapter 15

Dinner with the family. Again. She hadn't seen this much of her siblings and parents since she'd sat in a high chair, and even then they'd been scarce. Skye listened to the rumblings of her father and brothers, avoided the curious, questioning gaze of her mother, and moved her legs out of reach when Phoebe kept kicking her under the table.

"The old Skye would have kicked me back," Phoebe said when she leaned over under the pretense of picking up her napkin. "You've been haunting this place like a ghost since you've been back. You want to get out of here and talk about it?"

Given Skye had begged off their ice-cream plans after the party the other night, she wasn't surprised by the invitation. The idea that her parents had invited Leo to her welcome back reception had touched her. She'd spent most of her life feeling like an afterthought to them, not surprising given she and Phoebe had been surprise babies. But since she'd spent those months away, it seemed as if distance had indeed made the heart grow fonder.

"I'd want to talk about it," Phoebe went on as if Skye were participating in the conversation. "A man kisses me like that in front of just about everyone I know on the planet and whew." She fanned herself with her napkin and earned a look of disapproval from their mother. "I don't have to ask what kept you occupied on that ranch. You know, Daria had said how handsome he was, but can I go on record as saying I think that man of yours could give Preston a run for his money? Seriously."

She slurped up some soup, a sound that usually made Skye laugh. At this moment, however, Skye was beginning to think Phoebe had lost her mind. "And those eyes. Did I mention he never said hello to me? Like I didn't even exist. Then again, I think you're the only person he saw once you walked down those stairs."

"Skye? Would you like something else for dinner?" Russ held up a hand to stop Wyatt's and his conversation. "I thought you liked seared scallops."

"It's fine, Dad. Although a rare steak wouldn't be unwelcome." Her cheeks went hot when she realized she'd said that out loud.

"Since when do you eat red meat?" Blaine asked.

"Probably since she spent time on a cattle ranch," Phoebe all but sang out. "I honestly can't imagine anything worse than being trapped around horses and steers and bulls and all that dust and dirt."

Skye blinked at her sister, catching the amused expression on Preston's face as he watched Phoebe.

"Ungodly hours, too, I'm betting," Phoebe went on. "Up before the sun. Going to bed before…well, earlier than you're used to, I'm sure. Were there chickens? Nasty creatures. Pecking all over the place, and the feathers and noise. And imagine how many pairs of jeans you'd go through. I don't think the denim industry could keep up with the way you go through clothes."

"There weren't any chickens," Skye said. "Leo plans to get some soon, though."

"Does he? Well, thank goodness you don't have to worry about that. Last thing I'd want to do is stick my hand up a chicken's—"

"Phoebe!" Mara wiped her mouth as the front doorbell chimed. "Gracious, I wonder who that might be."

"If you ask me, your entire ranch experience sounds horrific," Phoebe continued. "I mean, imagine all that work, day in, day out. You just aren't built for it, Skye. I'm sorry to drop a truth bomb, but there you have it. Nope. Skye Colton was not made for ranch living. Not in this lifetime. Not in any other. Doesn't matter how hot the cowboy might be, and he really is up there on the Scoville scale. Hey, Daria. You want Hildy to bring you some dinner?" Phoebe bit into a scallop. "Scallops. They're Skye's favorite and they're delish."

"Exactly how much wine have you had this evening?" Preston asked when she reached for her glass.

"Not a drop. Now hush," Phoebe muttered under her breath.

"Ah, no dinner, thanks." Daria couldn't have looked more uncomfortable if she'd just sat on a cactus. "I'm sorry to intrude, but I have something for Skye." She held up the silver-and-gray boots she'd taken for evidence. "As expected, Gates cut a deal, but in the meantime, I had these expedited through evidence. I thought maybe you'd like them back."

Her chest tightened. She shoved her chair back and retrieved the boots from Daria, and saw the understanding and smile in the other woman's eyes. "Thank you." Skye hugged the boots to her chest before she kicked off her sandals and shoved her feet into them. Then she hiked up her long skirt, rocked back and smacked her toes together.

"Those are…lovely." Her mother's voice drifted over her.

"They're perfect," Skye said. She looked at the table where her family sat. A family that looked inordinately confused at the moment. Except Phoebe. Phoebe looked completely and utterly content, from the encouraging arched brow to the knowing smile stretching her lips.

Love and affection for her twin swelled like a balloon inside Skye. She didn't need anyone's permission. She didn't need anyone's approval. But knowing she had it made the decision all the easier.

In that moment, as she looked at her boots, all the doubt and anger that had followed her home vanished. She loved him. Right now, the lie didn't matter. The deception didn't matter. All that mattered was that Leo

Slattery was the best man she'd ever known, and she wasn't going to let him go without a fight.

A laugh exploded from her mouth, a laugh she tried to catch behind her hand as the happiness flowed out of her. "I have to go."

"Go? Go where?" Mara started to stand, but Russ reached out, covered her hand and shook his head.

"Let her go, Mara."

"Thanks, Dad."

"Now, hang on, where are *you* going?" Russ demanded when Phoebe jumped to her feet.

"Where do you think?" Skye's twin raced over to her, grabbed her hand and pulled her out of the dining room. "To help her pack!"

"Land's sake, stop your fussing." Trapper slapped Leo away as Leo tried to set a tray of hot tea over the old man's lap. This was the fifth day Trapper had been in bed, the rib-breaking cough finally letting up. Leo hadn't been able to convince him to stay in the house, so he'd upgraded the bunkhouse room to include a small TV with a DVD player and loaded him up with old movies, preferably ones with Lauren Bacall. Trapper appreciated her beyond all others. "You ain't no pretty face to be a caretaker. I'd prefer someone of the female persuasion if you don't mind. Redhead would be nice. On the scrawny side. You know any?"

It wasn't the first time Trapper had mentioned Skye, by name or allusion. But it was the first time he wasn't going to rise to the bait. Well, maybe he'd nibble. "She's back where she's supposed to be, Trapper. She's home with her family."

"Never known you to be stupid, young'un. You know what your grandmother would do if she knew what you'd done? Letting that girl get away? She'd toss you over her knees and swat your backside but good."

"My grandmother never spanked me and you know it." Leo tried not to laugh.

"Yeah, well, she'd have made an exception this time around. Leo—" Trapper caught his arm before he could move away "—you love that woman. And I might not have the best eyesight in the world, but I could see she felt the same. Even if she is a Colton."

"No bad-mouthing the Coltons anymore, Trapper. Not when I'm looking to sell to Wyatt Colton next spring."

"Balderdash! Ain't no way—" Trapper started coughing again, released Leo's arm and sagged back against the mountain of pillows. "See? You're gonna kill me with news like that."

"Get used to it. He's coming out next week to help me map out some plans." Clearly he hadn't alienated the Coltons like he thought he would have by kissing Skye in front of darn near everyone in the county. Wyatt had called him the next day to continue their conversation about Leo's plans for the future of the ranch. "You don't like it, you can stay out of sight. But there will be no disrespecting the Coltons around me, understand?"

Trapper mumbled something under his breath.

"Sorry, I couldn't quite hear—"

"I said, fine!" Trapper shouted and earned a whine of

despair from Ollie, who had been sticking to Leo like a fly on bug paper ever since Skye had left. "I'm tired. Let me get some sleep. We can talk about this more later."

"No talk needed. Decision's made. But I'll check on you in a bit." Truth be told, Leo had been more than a little concerned about Trapper's health. If all went according to plan, he was going to convince the old guy to stick it out here through the winter. He could be of help to Gwen, who only yesterday called to say they'd be home by the end of the week.

Leo did a bit of tidying up before he and Ollie headed back to the house. An unfamiliar red SUV sat beside his truck. Ollie ran over to give it a good sniff, then started barking like a maniac before he ran for the house.

"Ollie! Hold up!" What on earth had gotten into him now? Darn fool dog was as unpredictable as they came these days and, as Leo had learned last week, he'd also taught himself how to press his paw onto the latch and push open the screen door. At least he hadn't figured how to get out. Yet.

He followed, stomped his boots clean on the mat before he stepped inside. Ollie was whimpering something fierce as his nails clicked against the hardwood floor of the kitchen. "What's got you all worked…" Leo screeched to a halt in the doorway. "Skye." Her name felt like a prayer on his lips. He flicked off his hat, hung up his jacket as she huddled on the floor, petting and scrubbing Ollie's fur to within an inch of the dog's life.

"Hi." She turned that million-watt smile on him. The evening gown had been replaced with snug jeans and a T-shirt the color of ripe raspberries. She'd knotted her hair on the top of her head, and on her feet she wore the cowboy boots.

"What are you… Why are you…?" He couldn't seem to finish a sentence, not with the hope poised to burst in his chest. "Skye, are you…?"

"Can we go for a ride?"

"A—ride?" Had he heard her right?

"Yes. A ride." There was something akin to a challenge in her brown eyes, as if she was expecting him or maybe daring him to deny her the request.

"Okay. I'll go saddle Ginger—"

"I'll do it." She walked past him. In her wake, he caught the scent of her, the intoxicating combination of wildflowers and vanilla that had him following as if in a trance. "Stay, Ollie."

Ollie whimpered, sighed and lay down on the floor.

The questions that piled up in his mind remained unspoken as they walked to the barn. She moved in the area as if it were second nature, guiding Ginger out of her stall after saying a quick hello to the other horses. By the time they were saddled up, the silence had gone on for so long, he couldn't think of a thing to say to break it. He was terrified, right down to his bones, that she'd leave him again. That she rode alongside him as they galloped up the hill gave him the thinnest hope. Hope he wasn't going to relinquish until he had to.

She was almost leaping off before Ginger came to a complete stop, dropping to thick grass effortlessly. He watched, unable to take his eyes off her, as she loosened the girth and removed the bit from her mouth. Leo wanted nothing more than to reach out and catch those flyaway tendrils of fire-red hair blowing in the late-afternoon breeze.

She walked off, leaving Ginger to graze, and shot him a glance over her shoulder.

He remained where he was, in the saddle, Duke restless beneath him.

When she held out her hand, he could finally breathe. He dismounted, repeated her actions with Duke, and walked over and slipped his hand into hers.

He felt her tremble the moment they touched, saw her eyes fill before she turned to look out over the land that was as much a part of him as the blood that flowed through his veins.

"I missed this," she whispered. "So much."

He had no response other than to squeeze her hand. When she let go, he feared he'd done something wrong, but rather than moving away, she stepped closer and wrapped her arms around him. When she lay her cheek on his chest, he could feel her smiling. "I missed you, Skye." It was the only admission he could make at the moment. The only one that truly mattered.

"I missed you, too." She lifted her face, looked up at him as the sun caught the fire in her hair. "Even surrounded by all those people, even being back with my family, I wasn't me. I wasn't whole. I needed you, Leo." She reached up, brushed her fingers against his cheek. "I do need you. I love you."

He lowered his head, brushed his lips against hers and felt her breath catch. She stretched up on her toes, linked her arms around his neck and clung to him.

"You lied to me," she murmured against his lips.

He nodded and when he pulled away, he pressed his forehead against hers. "Yes." He pulled the clip from her hair and pushed his fingers into the silky strands. She leaned her face into his hand, into his touch, her lids flickering as her eyes filled with desire. And forgiveness.

"Don't ever do it again."

"I won't, darlin'. I promise."

"I'm going to hold you to that, cowboy." She reached up and pulled his mouth down to hers. "For the rest of our lives."

* * * * *

Don't miss the previous volumes in the
Coltons of Roaring Springs miniseries:

Colton Cowboy Standoff *by Marie Ferrarella*
Colton Under Fire *by Cindy Dees*
Colton's Convenient Bride *by Jennifer Morey*
Colton's Secret Bodyguard *by Jane Godman*
A Colton Target *by Beverly Long*
Colton's Mistaken Identity *by Geri Krotow*
Colton's Covert Baby *by Lara Lacombe*
The Colton Sheriff *by Addison Fox*

Available now from Harlequin Romantic Suspense.

And don't miss the next Coltons book,
Colton Family Showdown *by Regan Black,*
coming October 2019!

Get 4 FREE REWARDS!

We'll send you 2 FREE Books
<u>plus</u> 2 FREE Mystery Gifts.

Harlequin® Romantic Suspense books feature heart-racing sensuality and the promise of a sweeping romance set against the backdrop of suspense.

FREE
Value Over
$20

YES! Please send me 2 FREE Harlequin® Romantic Suspense novels and my 2 FREE gifts (gifts are worth about $10 retail). After receiving them, if I don't wish to receive any more books, I can return the shipping statement marked "cancel." If I don't cancel, I will receive 4 brand-new novels every month and be billed just $4.99 per book in the U.S. or $5.74 per book in Canada. That's a savings of at least 12% off the cover price! It's quite a bargain! Shipping and handling is just 50¢ per book in the U.S. and $1.25 per book in Canada.* I understand that accepting the 2 free books and gifts places me under no obligation to buy anything. I can always return a shipment and cancel at any time. The free books and gifts are mine to keep no matter what I decide.

240/340 HDN·GNMZ

Name (please print)

Address   Apt. #

City   State/Province   Zip/Postal Code

Mail to the Reader Service:
IN U.S.A.: P.O. Box 1341, Buffalo, NY 14240-8531
IN CANADA: P.O. Box 603, Fort Erie, Ontario L2A 5X3

Want to try 2 free books from another series! Call 1-800-873-8635 or visit www.ReaderService.com.

---

*Terms and prices subject to change without notice. Prices do not include sales taxes, which will be charged (if applicable) based on your state or country of residence. Canadian residents will be charged applicable taxes. Offer not valid in Quebec. This offer is limited to one order per household. Books received may not be as shown. Not valid for current subscribers to Harlequin® Romantic Suspense books. All orders subject to approval. Credit or debit balances in a customer's account(s) may be offset by any other outstanding balance owed by or to the customer. Please allow 4 to 6 weeks for delivery. Offer available while quantities last.

Your Privacy—The Reader Service is committed to protecting your privacy. Our Privacy Policy is available online at www.ReaderService.com or upon request from the Reader Service. We make a portion of our mailing list available to reputable third parties that offer products we believe may interest you. If you prefer that we not exchange your name with third parties, or if you wish to clarify or modify your communication preferences, please visit us at www.ReaderService.com/consumerschoice or write to us at Reader Service Preference Service, P.O. Box 9062, Buffalo, NY 14240-9062. Include your complete name and address.

HRS19R3

"I appreciate you coming," he said.

"You said it was important."

Paul nodded as he gestured for her to take a seat. Sitting down, Simone stole another quick glance toward the bar. The two strangers were both staring blatantly, not bothering to hide their interest in the two of them.

Simone rested an elbow on the tabletop, turning flirtatiously toward her friend. "Do you know Tom and Jerry over there at the bar?" she asked softly. She reached a hand out, trailing her fingers against his arm.

Her touch was just distracting enough that Paul didn't turn abruptly to stare back, drawing even more attention in their direction. His focus shifted slowly from her toward the duo at the bar. He eyed them briefly before turning his attention back to Simone. He shook his head. "Should I?"

"It might be nothing, but they seem very interested in you."

Paul's gaze danced back in their direction and he took a swift inhale of air. One of the men was on a cell phone and both were still eyeing him intently.

"We need to leave," he said, suddenly anxious. He began to gather his papers.

"What's going on, Paul?"

"I don't think we're safe, Simone."

"What do you mean we're not safe?" she snapped, her teeth clenched tightly. "Why are we not safe?"

"I'll explain, but I think we really need to leave."

Simone took a deep breath and held it, watching as he repacked his belongings into his briefcase.

"We're not going anywhere until you explain," she started, and then a commotion at the door pulled at her attention.

Don't miss
Reunited by the Badge *by Deborah Fletcher Mello*
available October 2019 wherever
Harlequin® Romantic Suspense
books and ebooks are sold.

www.Harlequin.com

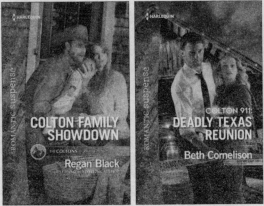